the R word

the R word

MARIANNE MODICA

MORNING JOY MEDIA
Spring City, Pennsylvania

To my family,
and to Janice

Published by Morning Joy Media.

Visit www.morningjoymedia.com for more information on bulk discounts and special promotions, or e-mail your questions to info@morningjoymedia.com.

Cover design: Staci Focht
Interior design: Debbie Capeci

Cataloging-In-Publication Data

Modica, Marianne.
  The R Word / by Marianne Modica.
    p. cm.
  Summary: A sheltered white girl becomes aware of subtle racism in her family and friends, and takes action to fight the injustice.
  ISBN 978-0-9826102-5-1 (pbk.)
  1. Racism—fiction. I. Title.

Printed in the United States of America

Contents

Foreword

What is the R word?

Michael O. Emerson, a scholar who studies race, asks an interesting question: What's the emotionally charged racial slur for white people? Is there an "N word" equivalent for whites? There is such a word, but it's not what we might think. It's not "honky," or "cracker," says Emerson. It's the R word, the word *racist*.[1]

While I'm not suggesting that whites can ever know the suffering that African Americans and other oppressed groups have experienced, it is true that the potential label, *racist*, has the power to make white people cringe. "A student called me racist," I once heard a white teacher say, "and it felt like someone kicked me in the stomach." Why such a strong reaction? Because this woman cared about racism. She considered herself to be a fair, non-prejudiced

---

1. Michael O. Emerson, "The Persistent Problem," *Christian Reflection: Racism* (Waco: Baylor University Press, 2010), 11–18.

person—colorblind, even. Calling her a racist, putting her in the same category as the ignorant people of this world, was devastating because it challenged her opinion of herself as someone who has risen above the racism of past generations. After all, in 2008 our country elected its first African-American president, proving that racism is a thing of the past, right?

Not so fast. While obvious racism may be harder to find, many people who study race believe that racism isn't gone, it's just gone underground. In other words, racism expresses itself in more subtle ways today, or in ways that are so much a part of our lives that we don't notice them any more. That's what this story is about. This is the story of what happens when one young, sheltered girl begins to think deeply about race for the first time, and about what it means to be white. This is the story of that girl's painful discovery and stubborn metamorphosis. I hope this is a story that many of us can relate to, directly or indirectly, and that perhaps reading this story will help us to see that the R word may not be as far away from where we live as we'd like to think.

the R word

Dear Dad,

Don't get upset when I tell you where I am. I'm speeding down the highway on a rickety old school bus that feels like it's falling apart. We're headed into the city—I'm not sure where. Between the pouring rain and the engine howling I can barely hear myself think. I hope you can read this—the bus is bumpy, but that's not the only reason my hand is shaking. I want to go home. What was I thinking? I just wanted to see what everyone in our family is so afraid of, but maybe this wasn't such a great idea after all. Maybe I should call Nana. One of the uncles could come and pick me up and that would be the end of my big adventure.

I can hardly see through the foggy windows, but it looks like we're getting off the highway now, driving on some winding road through a park, past a cemetery up on a hill. I could tell the driver to pull over and let me off here, but I don't think that would be safe.

Passing some fields, coming into a neighborhood—I've never seen houses like this before, Dad. Do people really live in them? And Dad, I'm not trying to be racist or anything, but I don't see any white people anywhere.

Keep an eye out for me, Dad. I might need your help today.

Rach

Chapter 1

The Web of Safety

A few weeks earlier...

Rachel stepped out to the back patio holding the kitchen scissors. She snipped the last remaining white rose from the vine that grew along Grampy's trellis and turned back toward the door, but something caught her eye. It was a black ant caught in a spider web, struggling to break free; the spider was nowhere in sight. Her first impulse was to brush the web away, but then she studied the ant more closely. "Poor thing," she said aloud, "you're stuck there, aren't you?" She plucked a leaf from the rose vine and used it to free the ant, which she placed gently in the grass at the patio's edge. Rachel knelt on the ground and watched the ant rub tiny bits of spider silk off its legs. "Now go," she said, "but stay out of Nana's kitchen—even I can't save you in there."

Back inside, Rachel took the dead rose from the vase on the windowsill and tossed it in the trash, replacing it with the fresh one she'd just cut. The aroma of tomato sauce simmering in a large stainless steel pot on the stove filled the room, as it did every Sunday morning. Rachel sat at the table, alternately flipping through the Sunday comics, scrolling through her friend list online, and texting her best friend, Antonella, while Nana stood over the pot, stirring with a wooden spoon.

"Mmm, doesn't that smell delicious?" Nana said. She walked from the stove to the table with a spoonful of sauce. "Taste," she commanded. "Blow on it first. It's hot."

"I know, Nana, we've done this before," Rachel said. Like the preparation of the sauce and the reading of the comics, this was part of their Sunday ritual. "Mmm," she said, "good. When are you going to give me the recipe?" Rachel had started collecting recipes in a composition notebook. So far she had three: white cake, copied from the back of a bag of flour; chocolate chip cookies, copied from the back of a package of chocolate chips; and cheesecake, copied from the back of a graham cracker crumb box. Rachel had only tried baking the chocolate chip cookies, but she could never get them to turn out as good as Nana's did.

"What recipe? There is no recipe." Nana gave a final stir and then tapped the excess sauce off the wooden spoon. "You put the ingredients together and you cook it. You've watched me enough times to know that."

"But how do you get it to come out the same every time?" Rachel persisted.

"It doesn't have to be the same. It just has to be good. Oops, I almost forgot the secret ingredient. Don't tell your grandfather." Nana added a teaspoon of sugar to the sauce and stirred, the loose skin of her underarms jiggling as she moved. Beads of perspiration popped up on her forehead, but her bright red hair, washed, teased and sprayed into a stiff helmet at the beauty parlor, remained perfectly in place.

"Your secret's safe with me," said Rachel. She pushed the comics aside and pulled a wad of papers out of her black and white checkerboard backpack.

"Secrets? Who's keeping secrets?" Grampy entered the kitchen through the back door. He'd been in the yard, tending to his tomato plants. "Here," he said, handing two large red beefsteaks to Nana. Then he turned to Rachel. "How's the baby today? You're not keeping secrets from your Grampy, are you?" Not expecting an answer, he took hold of Rachel's face with both hands.

"Grampy, stop! I'm not a baby. I'm fifteen years old."

"To me you'll always be the baby." Grampy bent forward as if to kiss Rachel, but instead rubbed his stubby, unshaven face across her smooth cheek.

"Ouch, Grampy!" Rachel squealed.

"Don't worry, I won't scratch up that beautiful face!" Now he did kiss Rachel on the cheek. "Bella," he said, calling her by the pet name he had used for her when she was a child.

Rachel squirmed away. "Of course you think I'm beautiful—I look just like you." She ran her fingers through her straight, wheat-colored hair, wishing it wasn't so fine. "Unfortunately for me, I'm short and chubby like you, and I'll probably be bald like you soon, too."

"What are you talking? You're a beautiful young girl. Nana, tell her she's beautiful."

"You're beautiful," answered Nana from a squatting position. She was halfway in the cabinet under the stove, digging out her pasta pot. She pulled out a stack of smaller pots and balanced them on her knee for a few seconds before they crashed to the floor.

"You people make enough noise to wake up the dead." Uncle Tommy appeared, shirt pressed, pants creased, clean-shaven, and every one of his dark, wavy hairs combed back in place. "Can't a hard working man sleep in on Sunday?" He winked at Rachel as he passed her on his way to the coffee pot. "Any good donuts left, or did you polish them all off again, Rach?"

"They're starting a new program at school," said Rachel, ignoring Uncle Tommy's comment. "Grampy, can you sign this form?" She handed a sheet of paper to Grampy, who was now sitting next to her at the table.

"It's time to get up anyway," Nana scolded Uncle Tommy. "You should have come to church with us this morning."

Uncle Tommy filled his mug with coffee, grabbed a cream donut and a napkin, and kissed his mother on the cheek. "I know Ma, but God will forgive me. I worked late last night."

"Don't tell me what you were doing. I don't want to know. Probably chasing criminals through dark alleys with a gun in your hand. Why you boys couldn't find safer jobs I'll never know. If Matty hadn't taken that job…"

"Ma, please, not again," Uncle Tommy interrupted. "And not in front of the baby."

When her father's name was mentioned Rachel felt a cold shadow pass over the otherwise warm, sunny kitchen. "I'm not a baby," she said half-heartedly, but she was too distracted now to argue. Although she didn't remember him, she knew that her father had been a cop, like her uncles, and that he'd been killed in the line of duty when Rachel really was a baby. She'd spent hours staring at his pictures, which Nana kept in a shrine-like display on a bookcase in the living room. In Rachel's favorite photo her father stood between his two older brothers, barely reaching their waists, holding a softball trophy. They all looked so proud, and so happy then. Nowhere on the shelf, or anywhere else in the house, had Rachel ever seen a picture of her mother. Rachel knew that her mother, too, was dead, and that she had left Rachel before she'd died, but she'd learned early on not to ask questions. There were more secrets in Nana's kitchen than the ingredients in her sauce.

Grampy had been studying the flyer from Rachel's school. He tossed it onto the table and removed his glasses in disgust. "What is this about?" he growled. "I thought you went to school to learn—what's with all these fancy programs?"

Uncle Tommy picked up the flyer and read out loud. "'Coventry Township High School is beginning a six-week program in multicultural education for juniors and seniors.'"

"What's wrong with that?" asked Nana. "I've always wanted to learn about different cultures. Did you know the Leones down the block are going to Florence next spring? We could use a little culture around here."

"Keep reading," ordered Grampy.

"'Special attention will be given to issues of racism and inequity faced by people of color...' seems they're starting a new program ... a pilot program, this says..." Uncle Tommy squinted at the page, reading silently. "Yeah, yeah, here we go," he sighed under his breath.

"I have half a mind not to sign it," grumbled Grampy.

"That won't do any good," said Uncle Tommy. "Listen to this—'Your signature indicates that you have been informed about this district-mandated program.' Sorry, Pop, 'district-mandated' means that nobody's asking your permission."

Grampy banged his right hand down on the table. "You see? What we think doesn't matter. After all we've been through, now this. When are those people gonna be satisfied?" He snatched the paper from Uncle Tommy.

"What people?" asked Rachel. Although it wasn't the first time she'd seen this reaction from Grampy, she hadn't expected it over a school permission slip. Grampy usually saved his anger for the news, and it almost always involved a protest or lawsuit or some other mention of someone's *rights*. "Rights!" he would rant, "What about my rights?" Rachel wished Grampy wouldn't go on that way. She fished around in her backpack until she found a pen and handed it to him. "It's just an eleventh-period program, Grampy. It's no big deal. Most of the kids will be doing their homework through it. Just sign the form, so I can get a bonus point."

"I know, I know, no big deal. Nothing is a big deal any more." Grampy continued to grumble as he signed. "This is what my hard-earned money goes to pay for—special programs for people who don't appreciate anything. Then they turn around and shoot you…"

"Eddy, that's enough!" Nana screeched. "I don't want to talk about this. Now stop it before you have a heart attack." She pulled a tissue from the pocket of her apron and blew her nose hard.

"Calm down, everybody," Uncle Tommy interceded. "It's not like Rachel's doing anything dangerous. It's just a school program—what harm could it do? Right, Rach?"

"Right." Rachel took the form from Grampy and put it in her backpack. She continued to sort through papers, hoping that the squall had passed, and glad that none of her friends had been there to witness Grampy's outburst.

Nana smoothed down her apron, took a deep breath, and picking up the bread knife, cut the end off a loaf of semolina bread and handed it to Rachel. "What else did you do at school this week, honey?" she asked, still trying to compose herself. She turned the loaf of bread around, cut the other end off, and bit into it.

"The usual, I guess. Let's see—we're reading Shakespeare in English, we had subs all week in chemistry and math—oh, I almost forgot! I need to interview someone—I have to write a report on 'an occupation or career that is vital to our community.'"

"That sounds like fun. You can interview me. Go ahead, shoot." Nana, back to her cheerful self, put the bread down and turned toward Rachel.

"No offense, Nana, but it has to be someone with a real job."

"Oh, and what I do is a fake job, right? All right, I'll go finish cooking our fake dinner. I have to make the fake salad. And after dinner I'll wash the fake dishes. Interview your uncle. He's real enough." Nana turned away, but Rachel saw she was trying hard not to smile.

"Thanks, Nana, I knew you'd understand. You're a *real* doll," Rachel said. "Okay, Uncle Tommy, ready?"

"Ready for what? Are we going somewhere?" Uncle Johnny appeared at the back door, as crumpled as his twin brother was crisp. He wore a Grateful Dead t-shirt that was so faded it was impossible to tell its original color. His gray gym shorts were frayed and his thick, black hair stood straight up like overgrown blades of grass.

"Don't come in here with those dirty shoes!" exclaimed Nana. "You're filthy! Where have you been?"

"I went running at the park, then I stopped at the car-wash on my way home."

"You should have washed yourself while you were at it," shot Uncle Tommy. "For a buck extra they let you lie on the hood while you go through the brushes. You come out clean, but I hear the wax is a b—"

"Tommy, please!" interrupted Nana. "Watch your language…"

"I know, I know…" Uncle Tommy nodded at Rachel and they finished the sentence in unison…"*not in front of the baby*. Sorry, Ma."

"So where're we going?" Uncle Johnny removed his muddy sneakers and stepped into the kitchen.

"Go wash!" Nana commanded.

"Okay, okay." Uncle Johnny backed away and disappeared down the hall.

"He'll never learn," Uncle Tommy muttered, shaking his head. "Go ahead, babe, ask your questions."

"Okay, first of all, what is your occupation?"

"You know my occupation. I'm a detective for the county. Ma, when are we eating? I'm starved."

Rachel sighed. "Uncle Tommy, pay attention. Okay, what would you say is your main responsibility?"

"I catch bad guys and put them in jail."

"Can you be a little more specific?"

"Officially, my mission is to 'prevent the flow of illegal narcotics into and out of the county.' To do that I have to catch bad guys and put them in jail. Simple."

Rachel typed Uncle Tommy's answers. "What do you like best about your job, and what do you find most challenging?" she asked.

Uncle Tommy thought for a moment. "I like the feeling that once in a while I make a difference. I find challenging that the rest of the time I'm never really sure if I'm making a difference. Does that make sense, kid?"

"Don't worry, it doesn't have to make sense. It's a school project. One more question—if you could do it over again, would you have chosen this career?"

Uncle Tommy frowned. He stared down at the table and began to stack the scattered newspapers together, as if his hands needed something to do. "I'd change lots of things, if I could," he said finally, and Rachel got the feeling he was thinking about her father again, but Nana was listening and she knew better than to ask. "But I guess when it comes right down to it, I'd still be a cop. I never wanted to be anything else." He stood and kissed Rachel on the top of her head. "Come on, let's clear the table. It's almost time to eat."

Dear Dad,

We talked about you today—almost. Grampy started to go into his thing, and Nana got all upset, but Uncle Tommy stopped them. What if you hadn't been a cop? Would you be here with me now? We'd live in our own house, that's for sure, and we wouldn't have any secrets. You would not call me a baby all the time. Maybe I'd even have a boyfriend by now, and he wouldn't be one of Antonella's rejects. It's not that I don't love them, Dad, but you know how they are, on me all the time, always worried about something. Will they ever let me grow up, or will I still be sitting around Nana's kitchen eating donuts when I'm 30 years old?

Speaking of Nella, this is her last week here. How will I survive without her next door? My life will be even more boring, if that's possible. I'm going to miss her so much.

Your slightly pathetic daughter,
Rachel

Chapter 2

Something New

Antonella Fatagati knocked gently at Rachel's front door.

"Rach, are you there? We're going to miss the bus!" she called in a whisper as loud as she could risk without waking Rachel's uncles. Nana scuffled to the door, wearing a pink and green floral housedress and blue dolphin slippers, a gift from Rachel last Mother's Day. She held a brown bag lunch with Rachel's name written on it; Antonella noticed a small heart drawn under the name and smirked.

"Come in, Antonella. She'll be right down." Nana held the screen door open wide enough for Antonella and her overstuffed backpack to fit through. "You girls are going to give yourselves hernias, carrying all those books around. Can't you leave some of them at school?"

"We need them for homework, Mrs. Matrone. Is Rachel ready? We're going to miss the bus." She heard a door close above and saw Rachel appear at the top of the stairs, standing lopsided from the weight of her backpack on one shoulder.

"I'm coming," said Rachel. She clumped down the stairs, holding on to the banister and stopping for a second to get her balance between each step.

"You sound like an elephant," said Nana. She helped Rachel tuck the lunch into her backpack, giving her a goodbye peck on the cheek. "Have a good day, girls," she said, locking the screen door behind them.

"Hurry up," said Antonella as they rushed down the block to the bus stop. Rachel, who was four inches shorter and twenty pounds heavier than her best friend, had to trot to keep up with Antonella's long strides. The bus chugged up to the curb just as the girls did, momentarily disturbing the suburban quiet of the late-summer morning. Rachel waved at Nana, who was still watching. Satisfied that Rachel was safe, Nana turned back toward the kitchen. Rachel followed Antonella to their usual spots in the back of the bus, Nella at the window and Rachel next to her in the aisle seat.

"This is the last Monday you'll ride the bus with me," said Rachel.

"It was almost the last Monday we missed the bus. What takes you so long in the morning?" Antonella had been waiting for Rachel every morning since they were in fourth grade, which was when Nana had finally agreed to let Rachel ride the bus to school.

"My hair, as usual. I wish I had your hair," said Rachel. "You always look perfect." From her thick, chestnut hair to her flawless olive complexion, Antonella's beauty leapt out at Rachel, who soaked it in like a thirsty sponge. Rachel figured that the next best thing to being pretty herself was having a beautiful best friend.

"I hate going back to school this early—it's still August!" Antonella complained. "And I hate riding this bus. Thank God my parents are buying me a car." She glanced at Rachel sympathetically. "Your hair looks fine," she added.

"It's so limp, I can't get it to do anything. An hour from now it'll be falling out of these clips, driving me crazy. Maybe I should cut it short again."

"I told you, guys like long hair." The bus gave a lurch and stopped, opening its doors for more arrivals. "Speaking of guys, there's Eric. Pretend you don't see him."

"Nella, don't. His heart is already broken. Don't make it any worse."

"I can't help that. I don't tell them to get attached so fast."

"But they always do. And then I get attached to them. And then you dump them and I have to unattach." Eric saw them and hesitated for a second before deciding to approach. At a lean, muscular height of six feet, he looked even taller stooping over in the cramped space of the bus.

"Oh, no, he's coming back here," said Antonella under her breath. Eric walked down the aisle.

"Hi, Eric!" Rachel called cheerfully.

"Hey," he said, choosing the seat across the aisle from Rachel. "What's up?" He tried in vain to make eye contact with Antonella, who was staring out the window. Instead, he settled for looking at Rachel.

"How was your weekend? Did you do anything special?" Rachel's chatter filled the awkward silence, but Eric grunted his responses, every now and then looking at Antonella, his crystal blue eyes pleading. She continued to ignore him. Rachel was relieved when the bus finally pulled up in front of school, and Eric walked away with his friends.

"That was awkward," she said. They trailed into to the school building like a double line of ants.

"You don't have to feel responsible for the happiness of my ex-boyfriends," replied Antonella, shaking her head so that her hair fell perfectly on her shoulders.

"I can't help it. It's not my fault that your parents won't let you hang out with boys alone." Rachel had received many a desperate phone call from Antonella, begging her to come over so that her latest love interest would be allowed entrance to their home. Rachel knew she should feel used by this arrangement, but she couldn't say no to Antonella, and anyway, how else would she ever meet boys that high up in the social order? Sometimes Mr. Hot Guy of the Moment, as Rachel thought of Antonella's boyfriends, even brought a friend along, and she allowed herself to fantasize that they were on a double date. Once in a while she let her fantasy flourish full bloom, and Hot Guy himself would abandon his quest for Antonella's affection and declare his love for Rachel, instead. "You're the one I really want," he would say in Rachel's imagination. "You have an inner beauty that I simply cannot resist." Back in the real world, though, her fantasy would wither, and

Rachel would find herself playing pool with Friend of Hot Guy (who usually turned out to be more lukewarm than hot), or watching a movie, trying to ignore Antonella and her boyfriend making out on the sofa across the expansive family room. Sometimes if they went further, Rachel pretended she was asleep. Not even the dragged-along friend had ever shown any romantic interest in Rachel, yet she still considered herself lucky to be Antonella's best friend.

Rachel plodded through her day and didn't see Antonella again until she got back on the school bus that afternoon.

"What a waste that was," Antonella complained. Rachel knew that her friend meant the multicultural program they'd just sat through during eleventh period. "That guy was such a jerk," Antonella continued. "All that stuff about language—what was he talking about? And that nun. Who ever heard of a black nun before?"

Rachel smiled and nodded in sympathy; she couldn't admit to Antonella that she'd found the session mildly interesting.

"We talked through the whole thing, anyway," said Antonella. Although she hadn't seen her, Rachel assumed that Antonella had been sitting in the back of the auditorium among the boys from the football team.

"Mrs. Morton would never let us get away with that," Rachel answered. Mrs. Morton, Rachel's least favorite teacher, had stood threateningly in the aisle, waiting to give out detentions at the first sign of trouble. Rachel had sat next to Tina Marie and Mark, brainiacs who'd spent the period doing their calculus homework. She'd listened politely during the presentation, especially when Sister Gloria took the stage. She, too, had been surprised that an African-American nun was in charge of the program, but there was something about Sister Gloria that Rachel liked. She was peaceful looking, with curly, cropped hair that added to her overall soft appearance. She wore a simple black skirt, white oxford shirt and black sweater, and the large silver cross around her neck glistened in the spotlight. Her clear, strong voice sparkled with an inviting quality that drew Rachel in. She was so different from what Rachel had expected.

When Rachel got home Nana was busy in the kitchen, as usual. She plopped down at the table, where a square of homemade apple cake and a glass of milk sat waiting for her.

"So what happened today?" Rachel asked.

"Not much," answered Nana. "No one knows who the father of Lila's baby is yet, and we still don't know who murdered Bill. That's about it, I think." She diced an onion into small cubes as she spoke. "How was your day?"

"It was okay. We started that new program this afternoon. I have to write a journal entry about language."

"That's nice. What language are you learning now? I thought you were taking French."

"No, Nana, not a foreign language. I have to write about the words we use when we talk about people from other races, or something like that."

Nana frowned as she chopped. "We don't use any of those words in this house."

"Huh? I don't think that's what they meant. It's more like when you call someone an Indian giver, it could be offensive to real Indians, I mean to Native Americans, or whatever. I don't know, I'm not explaining it very well."

"Everybody's offended these days. Why can't they leave well enough alone? So how's the cake? You got the first piece."

"Delicious. What's for dinner?"

"Chicken cacciatore, and we're eating early because your uncles have a meeting tonight. Why don't you go relax for a while? You work so hard at school. I'll call you when it's time to set the table."

Rachel went up to her room and turned on her computer and TV. She sat at her desk and flipped through the copy of *Romeo and Juliet* she was reading for English, but then decided to get her journal entry out of the way while the session with Sister Gloria was fresh in her mind. Let's see, she was supposed to write about … what was it? Rachel tried to remember the assignment—*write about the words we use when we talk about race, ethnicity, exceptionality, or sexual orientation.* Rachel wasn't sure what *exceptionality* meant, but she remembered that at the words *sexual orientation* a wave of snickering had crossed the auditorium. She sat at her desk and began to type.

> I'm not sure what to write, because we live in a regular neighborhood where everyone is pretty much the same. There are a few people of other races around, but no one's racist or anything, so they don't use any racist words that I've ever heard, anyway. My Uncle Johnny is friends with

this black guy down the block named Fred, and they go to ball games together sometimes. I even think my Uncle Johnny might have voted for Obama, but he won't admit it in front of my Uncle Tommy. (Not that Uncle Tommy is racist – he just likes to tease.) There's also an Indian family who lives across the street – I mean Indian Indian, not American Indian. They're pretty quiet, and I think the wife just had a baby. They always wave hello when they see me, but I can never remember their names.

Sometimes Uncle Tommy calls people fags, and I guess that's not very nice, even though he's only kidding. My grandfather gets upset when there's any kind of stuff about race on the news, like a protest or something. He doesn't use any bad language, though. Once when I went to the store with him I did hear some old guy he ran into use the N word, but that was a long time ago, and it only happened once, and my grandfather wasn't the one who said it.

Basically, I guess I can say that everybody's the same on the inside, and all people are good. I'm glad my family isn't racist.

Rachel thought about her family. Even though they were old-fashioned in some ways, and in spite of Grampy's occasional rants, they were good people; everybody said that. Nana was always baking something for somebody, and the uncles often helped raise money for one cause or another. Just last month Rachel had stood at a busy intersection with Uncle Tommy, jiggling a can of change when cars stopped at the red light. They'd been collecting for somebody's medical expenses—she wasn't exactly sure who it was, but she'd been glad to help. "You gotta give back," Uncle Tommy always said. Just like he'd said in his interview, he wanted to make a difference.

Rachel hadn't been paying attention to the TV, but now she glanced up and noticed that the screen was filled with laughing children jumping into a swimming pool. One African-American girl, dressed in a tie-dyed bathing suit, had long braids that flew over her head and hit the water a second after the rest of her body. She's so cute, Rachel thought. "You can make a difference for one child," the narrator was saying. "Give to the Fresh Air Fund."

Rachel typed,

> I'm glad we're having this multicultural program. We should all give something back. Someday I want to make a difference.

Chapter 3

Saying Goodbye

Nana spent two full days cooking for Antonella's going-away party, with Rachel helping sporadically.

"Does everything we eat have to be drenched in to-mato sauce?" Rachel asked the night before the party. Nana had poured a can of whole tomatoes over a tray of zucchini. "Can we eat something different for a change?"

"Tomatoes are good for you. They fight prostate cancer."

"Nana, we don't have prostates."

"I know that, but still. Go help Antonella get ready for the yard sale tomorrow."

Rachel walked next door and knocked. Antonella's mom greeted her, brushing her blond highlights away from her face.

"Hi Rachel. Nella's upstairs. Go ahead up," she said sweetly, then turned and shouted full volume, "Nella! Rachel's here!"

Rachel removed her shoes at the door and plodded up the thickly carpeted steps. In the hallway she passed Mr.

Fatagati, who was juggling several boxes that he had just retrieved from the attic.

"Hello there, Rachel. Come to help with the packing?"

"Sure, Mr. Fatagati," Rachel replied. Before she could say anything further, Mr. Fatagati turned away.

"Annette, we're going to need more boxes," he called down the stairs. "This is the last of them."

Rachel found Antonella standing on a chair in the doorway of her closet, reaching to the top shelf. "Rach, take this," she said. She hauled out a pink milk crate overflowing with long-forgotten items from her past.

"Are you going to get rid of all this stuff?" Rachel asked, sorting through a game of Boggle, an old leather purse, and a pink diary with a tiny lock.

"It's just junk," replied Antonella. "I'm going to sell some of it at the yard sale, and throw the rest away."

"It's not all junk." Rachel continued to dig through the crate, removing items and placing them on Antonella's blue eyelet bedspread. "Remember this?" She cradled a white bear wearing a soccer uniform and smoothed down its fur. "She's so soft. Remember, I got this for you at the mall? I wonder if she still talks." Rachel squeezed the bear's middle and a faint, high-pitched voice squeaked, "We'll always be best friends."

"I can't believe that was me!" Rachel exclaimed. "I sound so different!"

"Rachel, you were ten, of course you sound different. I can't believe it still works after my mother washed it six times. Anyway, it's been up there for years, and the rule is anything I haven't touched in a year or more goes."

"You can't sell this at a yard sale," said Rachel, frowning.

Antonella stopped rummaging for a moment. "You're right, Rach, of course I can't. Why don't you take it, to remember me? Okay?" She smiled down from her perch on the chair.

"Okay," said Rachel, stroking the bear's soft white fur.

"Come on, help me. We still need to do the price tags. Mom said to price everything between two and five dollars, but take off a dollar if they ask. That way people still feel like they're getting a bargain for all this junk." Antonella turned back to the shelf.

"It's not all junk," Rachel said, too quietly for Antonella to hear even if she had been listening. She put the bear aside, reached for the masking tape and spent the next few hours pricing items according to Antonella's directions.

That night before she went to bed, Rachel sat the bear on her dresser, next to the picture of Antonella and her from their trip to the shore last summer; she studied their windblown, radiant smiles. "That's a better place for you," she said to the bear. She squeezed its middle one more time before turning off the light.

Rachel's alarm blared at seven the next morning. She threw on some sweats and went next door to help Antonella cart stuff out to the front of the house. Nana followed Rachel over, wearing baking mitts and carrying a pan of coffee cake and a pile of napkins. "Watch," she said, "It's hot." She placed the pan and the napkins down on the end of the table.

The early birds began to flock to the sale before eight o'clock, and the girls sat at the table all morning like robins on a nest. Mrs. Fatagati bargained with the shoppers, nodding to Antonella to collect the money after they'd agreed on the price. Mr. Fatagati, Uncle Johnny, and Fred helped people load the larger items into their cars, vans or pickup trucks. Rachel smiled at him as he passed, carrying a swirly blue table lamp to an elderly woman's Ford Taurus.

"What a racket, huh girls?" said Mr. Fatagati, winking. "People pay you to haul off your old junk."

"It's not all junk," answered Rachel.

About midmorning a couple in an old brown station wagon pulled up to the curb; Rachel could hear them conversing in Spanish through the open car windows. They seemed to be arguing, but after a few minutes they got out of the car and approached the beige sofa that had once been in Antonella's living room. The woman pointed to the price tag of $100 and shook her head, continuing in rapid Spanish. Mrs. Fatagati's smile faded as she approached the couple.

"Can I help you?" she asked stiffly.

"Un momento, por favor," said the man. He returned to the argument with the woman.

"We speak English here," interrupted Mrs. Fatagati. She rolled her eyes and walked away, turning her back on the couple. The man's face went blank; he whispered something to the woman and they both got back into the car.

"They come here for our money, the least they can do is learn our language," grumbled Mrs. Fatagati as the car drove off.

Rachel shifted in her seat. She felt embarrassed for Antonella, who was pretending to be too caught up in counting money to have noticed the exchange.

"Have you written anything for that multicultural program yet?" She asked during a lull a few minutes later.

"That was random," replied Antonella. "Anyway, I'm moving, remember? I don't have to do that stupid program."

"Oh, that's right. I guess I'm trying to forget."

Antonella put her arm around Rachel. "You'll be okay, Rach," she said. "It's not like I'm going to the end of the universe. We can still see each other sometimes."

"And we'll still be college roommates, right?" asked Rachel.

"We'll see. Who knows what might happen by then? You'll probably make tons of new friends when I'm gone. Maybe you'll fall in love and forget all about me." Antonella laughed and Rachel laughed too, knowing that was the last thing either of them expected.

"That's if my grandparents ever let me leave the house again. You're the only person they trusted."

"If they only knew. But they've gotta set you free sometime, Rach, with or without me. Why are they so overprotective? I understood it when we were younger, but I thought they'd loosen up by now."

"I'm not sure. They're always afraid something bad will happen to me, as if rapists lurk at every corner. It has something to do with my father, but I'm not exactly sure what."

"Maybe you should put your foot down. I mean, you're almost sixteen. You can't be a baby forever." Although Rachel and Antonella were in the same grade, Rachel's late-summer birthday meant she was almost a whole year younger than Antonella and many of her friends. That, coupled with her smothering family, left Rachel feeling behind the crowd in more ways than one.

"I'm not a baby," she responded automatically.

"I know you're not," said Antonella, "but they do treat you like one." Rachel couldn't argue with that; she knew Antonella was right. She cut herself a second piece of coffee cake and chewed quietly while Antonella counted the cash.

Dear Dad,

Circle the correct answer—is it better to be:
pretty or smart
cool or nice
shy or popular
boring or fun
exciting or pathetic
loyal or hot
dangerous or safe

Tonight was Nella's going-away party—guess which of the above describes your daughter? Her cousins were here, but they hardly noticed me. Wonder why. Nella smuggled some beer downstairs to them, which made me nervous, but I got rid of the evidence before Nana noticed.

Is my only link with the real world of the American teenager leaving with Nella? I'm going to have to figure out some other way to get out of this house. Let me know if you come up with any ideas.

Love,
Rach

Chapter 4

Different

Moving day came and went and somehow Rachel managed to get to school on time without Antonella knocking at her door. The bus ride every morning was the most dismal part of her day. She stared out the window, sometimes pretending that Antonella was just absent that day and that she would be back tomorrow. When she really felt desperate she would text Antonella or call her cell, but usually there was no response, and knowing that Antonella was busy with her own life only made Rachel feel worse. She dragged through the school days and spent afternoons, evenings and weekends moping around the house, doing homework or watching TV. After a week or two even Nana noticed.

"Rachel," she said one day while washing out the inside of the refrigerator, "what's the matter with you? Nella only moved away, she's not dead, for goodness sakes. You've been in mourning long enough. Isn't there something you can do at school—a club, maybe? When I was a girl I was in the sewing club." The smell of ammonia from Nana's bucket made Rachel's eyes tear, but Nana seemed immune.

"Maybe I should get a job. Then I could save up for a car."

"I don't want you out late at night working at some burger joint—it's not safe. There's plenty of time for all that. Concentrate on your school work."

"You just said I should join a club."

"That's different. Don't be fresh." Nana turned and stooped back into the refrigerator, yellow rubber gloves flashing as she scrubbed with all of her might. Rachel knew that the conversation was over.

The next day, after the multicultural education session, Rachel was surprised when Sister Gloria approached her.

"Rachel, I wanted to thank you for your journal entries. I appreciate the way you really seem to be giving this program some thought."

"Oh," said Rachel. She didn't think she'd put any special effort into the journal, which meant that the other kids weren't trying at all. "You're welcome." She returned Sister Gloria's smile and, sensing that there was more to come, waited.

"I noticed you wrote about wanting to make a difference. Did you mean that?" Sister Gloria's eyes searched out Rachel's in quiet intensity. She'd seemed taller on stage, but now Rachel realized that they were almost the same height.

"Uh, sure," Rachel answered. She thought about the kids in the Fresh Air Fund commercial.

"That's great," said Sister Gloria. "As you know, I head up an organization called *The Tolerance Project*." Rachel didn't know—she guessed she hadn't been paying attention to that part of the session. "I wondered if you might consider joining an after-school club that we're sponsoring."

Could Nana have called Sister Gloria? No, that couldn't be possible. Yet it seemed incredible that Sister Gloria was repeating Nana's very words.

"Actually," she said, "I've been thinking of joining an after-school club. What kind of club would it be? Would I be working with underprivileged children?"

Sister Gloria raised her eyebrows and Rachel got the feeling she was trying to stifle a smile. "Er, no, not exactly, although we do have those kinds of opportunities in the summer, with our camp programs. This club involves making friends with students your own age from other schools, from different racial backgrounds than your own. Right now I'm thinking we would meet at my office in Strawberry Mansion."

"Oh," Rachel said again. Working with little kids was one thing—they were so cute—but meeting kids her own age at some office in the city just felt weird.

"How would that be making a difference?" she asked.

"I'm not quite sure, but I'd like to find out. Rachel, we'd be happy to have you help out with the younger children in the future—maybe next summer. But for now, I have something different I'd like to try. I'm sort of handpicking a small group of high school students from three schools—yours, and two from the city district—just to get to know each other and see what we can learn. Don't worry, we would provide transportation, if you don't mind an old blue school bus that my organization owns. Why don't you take a permission slip and think about it over the weekend?" As nervous as it made Rachel feel, the idea of doing something different was appealing. Antonella would be shocked to find out that she, too, was busy for a change, and busy doing something important. She pictured herself working in a summer program alongside new friends who didn't think of her as Antonella's dumpy sidekick. Maybe she could make up for some of Grampy's rants, and at the same time prove to her suffocating family that she was old enough to get out on her own. Rachel took the form from Sister Gloria and ran for the bus, all the while wondering how she would get permission to join this club she wasn't sure she wanted to join. Nana would not approve of her baby traveling into unknown territory to participate in unspecified activities with unidentified teenagers. And Nana would be the easy sell; Grampy would be even more difficult to manage. She remembered the fuss he'd made the last time she'd asked him to sign a permission slip, and this would be worse—meeting with kids of different racial backgrounds? How would she get that one past Grampy? She struggled with her dilemma all the way home, finally deciding to fall back on her usual strategy of getting Uncle Tommy in her corner first. Once he was on her side the battle was almost won.

That night at dinner when Nana asked the "how was school" question, Rachel chattered for several minutes about her multicultural class session, repeating some of what Sister Gloria had said. Maybe her family just needed to be educated. "Some people say food is a metaphor for race," she explained. "So which do you think we are— a melting pot, a salad, or a stew?" Nana, Grampy, Uncle Tommy and Uncle Johnny stopped chewing and stared.

"What's wrong?" asked Rachel.

"Look, kid," said Uncle Tommy, piercing a piece of roast beef with his fork. "You see this meat? It's perfect, just the way it is. It don't need nothing to spice it up, it's just a nice, juicy hunk of meat. Now, I love peanut butter, too, but if you put peanut butter on this meat, you're gonna ruin it. That's the way it is with people. Some things just don't mix. Not that they're bad, but they're just better off staying separate. Know what I mean?" He shoved the meat into his mouth and chewed, reaching for his water to wash it down, at the same time looking over at Grampy. "Right, Pop?" he said, smirking. Rachel wondered if he was kidding, saying all this for Grampy's sake. Sometimes it was hard to tell with Uncle Tommy. In any case, he wasn't going to be much help.

"Aw, come on, Tommy," Uncle Johnny said. "Stop giving her a hard time. He sounds tough, but he's all talk, Rach."

"When you mix, you get trouble," interjected Grampy. "Like when we lived in South Philly. Everything was fine, all those years. Then the block changed, and trouble."

"Who's talking about trouble?" asked Rachel. "Why is everyone getting so bent out of shape? Sister Gloria read this kids' book today, *Everybody Cooks Rice*…"

"Rice?" asked Nana. "If you wanted rice, I could have made rice. You should have told me. Eat your potatoes."

Rachel groaned. "That's not what I meant…"

"Give it a rest, babe," said Uncle Tommy, "before you get the old man all stirred up. Ma, more roast beef, please." He held out his plate.

"Who's an old man?" asked Grampy. "I can still do in a day what would take you a week."

"Rach, how about a movie tonight?" Uncle Johnny asked.

"I guess." Rachel looked down at her food and noticed that the tomato sauce from her string beans had seeped into the mashed potatoes. She mixed the two until the potatoes turned pink. "How about you, Uncle Tommy?" Maybe she could try again with Uncle Tommy later, when Grampy wasn't around.

"He's got a hot date," grinned Uncle Johnny. "Some woman named Joan."

"Yeah, and as a matter of fact, I'd better get going," said Uncle Tommy. "Thanks for dinner, Ma." He pushed himself away from the table and disappeared up the stairs.

"He'll be getting ready for hours," said Uncle Johnny, still smirking.

"It wouldn't hurt you to get out with someone your own age once in a while," chided Nana. She sliced more roast beef and piled it onto Uncle Johnny's plate. "You're never going to meet someone by taking your niece to the movies."

Uncle Johnny's smile faded. "Don't worry, Ma," he said. "I've got plenty of time."

Nana wasn't convinced. "You're almost forty years old," she said, shaking her head. "I just want to see you settled down and happy."

"Ma, I'm happy. Don't I look happy?" He forced a wide smile, displaying bits of string beans in his teeth. Rachel giggled. "Pop, tell her I'm happy."

"He's happy," Grampy said.

"You should be going out with people your own age, like Tommy does. How else are you going to meet a nice girl and get married?"

"That didn't work out so well for Tommy, did it? His marriage lasted what, two months? You don't want me to wind up divorced like him, do you?"

"Never mind Tommy. We're talking about you. And he's not divorced. His marriage was annulled."

"Same thing."

"It's not the same thing!" Nana said shrilly.

"Okay, okay," said Uncle Johnny. "Ma, calm down. I promise I'll get out more." Rachel had witnessed this exchange in various forms before, but this time it seemed to provide the perfect opening. She decided against the straightforward approach.

"Speaking of getting out more," she said cheerfully, "I've decided to take your advice and join an after-school club. I realized you were right, Nana, as usual. Thanks." Rachel took a bite as she spoke, wondering if Nana would see through the flattery that oozed out of her like the juice from the meat on her plate.

"That's wonderful, honey. What kind of a club?" Nana asked.

"Oh, it's just kids getting together to make friends, you know, hanging out together."

"Aren't you going to be doing something? Like cooking, or chess, or something?" asked Uncle Johnny innocently.

43

"A cooking club would be nice. I could come and help sometimes," Nana suggested.

"Thanks, Nana. I'll let you know if we decide to cook anything. So Uncle Johnny, what movie do you want to see?"

Rachel waited until she was about to leave the house on Monday morning before presenting the permission slip to Nana. They stood at the door, juggling her backpack, lunch, the form and a pen.

"You should have asked me to sign this earlier, Rachel," said Nana, annoyed. "I don't even have my glasses on."

"Just sign on the line at the bottom of the paper. I'll fill in the rest. Hurry up, the bus is coming!" Nana obediently scrawled her signature, leaning on Rachel's backpack for support. When she was finished Rachel snatched the paper out of her hands and ran out the door to the bus.

Mission accomplished—she had gotten her way. The permission slip was signed and she'd managed to keep the location of the club under Nana's usually keen radar. She should feel satisfied, even proud of her skill in manipulation; Antonella had done the same many times. Of course, Antonella would never have gone through all this trouble for an after-school club; her master plans usually involved boys and breaking some kind of parental rule, most likely involving curfew, cars, or both. I'm not actually doing anything wrong, Rachel told herself. They never actually *said* I couldn't join this club. Then again, she'd never actually asked. Why couldn't I just come out and tell the truth? she wondered. What's so wrong about meeting some new people? Because Nana and Grampy would not approve, that's why. They'd start to worry about me and I'd never stop hearing about it. What are they so afraid of? Rachel continued to argue with herself through most of the school day. Was it worth all this subterfuge? Did she really want to join this club? When she finally handed the permission slip to Mrs. Morton that afternoon she felt as if the single sheet of paper had gained weight while lying in her backpack all day. Unfortunately, getting rid of it didn't lighten her load one bit.

Chapter 5

Second, Third, and Fourth Thoughts

Dear Dad,

So I'm thinking of joining this club at school, but it's not actually at school. I'd have to take a bus to Philly, to someplace called Strawberry Mansion. I've never heard of it before, but it sounds nice. Anyway, Nana doesn't know about it. And the worst part is I'm the only kid going from my school. Apparently I'm the only idiot that Sister Gloria could hook—they're sending some broken down old school bus just for me. I'm not sure what to do—maybe I should cancel. I could really use some advice right now—I think I'll call Antonella. No offense, Dad, but I need to talk to someone who hasn't been dead for 15 years.

Rach

Rachel put her pen down and got into bed with her cell phone. She surrounded herself with her stuffed animals, the light from her desk casting a forest of shadows on the wall next to her. She called Antonella and described her dilemma in detail, stroking the soft fur of Antonella's old white bear as she spoke. When Rachel finished, there was a long silence on the other end.

"Nella, are you still there?"

"Yeah, I'm here."

"So what should I do?" asked Rachel.

"Rach, to be honest, I'm not sure what you're talking about. Why would you want to join this club in the first place? It sounds stupid."

"I don't know. I guess I just wanted to make some new friends—you know, give something back, try something different."

"What happened to all your old friends? Why don't you call Tina Marie, or Lindsey, or Katie? God, Rachel, why do you need new friends! Forget about this stupid club."

"I guess you're right," Rachel mumbled.

"Listen, I gotta go. Someone's picking me up in two minutes. Talk to you later, okay?" Rachel heard the click before she could even say goodbye. She turned and looked at her alarm clock. Nine-thirty on a Friday night, and here she was in bed already while Antonella was just going out. She knew that Nella was right; there were plenty of girls she could call. But Antonella had been the social organizer, and for all of the years of their friendship Rachel had been content to let her take the lead. Slumping down into her pillows, she turned toward the shadows on her wall and moved her stuffed animals around until they covered her own dark form completely. Downstairs Nana and Grampy were watching TV; Rachel listened to their husky laughter.

"Talk about being in a rut," Rachel said to the white bear. "Even Nana's not in bed yet." Antonella was right; she needed to start getting out with her old friends—what did she need new friends for? And there'd be plenty of time to make a difference later, when she was older. She grabbed her cell phone and texted Tina Marie, Katie, and Lindsey, but after several minutes no one had responded. No matter, she thought, tomorrow she would call them and make plans for the rest of the weekend, and then she would call Sister Gloria and tell her to cancel the bus. Rachel was glad she wouldn't have to talk with Sister Gloria in person—the office was sure to be closed on the weekend. She felt a burden lift as she turned off the light and snuggled with Antonella's bear.

The next morning she lazed around the house, doing some homework, cleaning up her room, and checking out her friends' posts online to see if anything interesting had happened while she'd slept. When she finally got around to calling Tina Marie, she learned that all of the girls were busy working on the homecoming committee. Rachel hinted that maybe she'd be available to help, but Tina Marie did not take her up on her offer. "You should have signed up a month ago, Rach," she said apologetically. "All of the positions are taken, and they're really strict about who's allowed to attend the meetings. You know, they want to keep the theme a secret and all. Sorry—we'll get together when homecoming is over, okay?"

Rachel tried to cover up her disappointment as best she could. Homecoming was still weeks away. Well, she'd just have to find some other way to occupy her time for now. Maybe she could join a *real* club, one that really did meet at school. She dug through her backpack for Sister Gloria's business card, planning to leave her message to cancel the bus, but she was surprised to hear a quiet "Hello?" on the other end of the line. Panicked, she hung up instantly. Was it a sin to hang up on a nun?

Nana passed by Rachel's open door and noticed her staring into her cell phone. "Everything all right, honey?" she asked. "You look upset. You didn't have a fight with one of your friends, did you?"

"No, Nana, everything's fine," Rachel murmured.

"Any plans for the weekend?"

"Guess not."

"I have to return a few things at the mall. Why don't you come with me? Maybe we can get a bite to eat while we're there."

"Sure," said Rachel, placing her cell phone down on her desk. Hanging out at the mall with my Nana, she thought. And Sunday we'll make sauce again—a nice, quiet, and above all, *safe* weekend. She began to think that her only escape from all this safety would be the blue school bus that hadn't been cancelled.

Chapter 6

Thursday Afternoon with Henry

Sitting on that school bus all alone, except for the driver, Rachel couldn't shake the feeling that she was making a huge mistake. What was she doing here, anyway? Why hadn't she had the nerve to cancel with Sister Gloria? Now she was stuck on this bus on a cold, wet Thursday afternoon, and there was nothing she could do about it except wait for it to be over. Someone had carved the words, "I hate this bus" on the back of the seat in front of her. She shivered and pulled her jacket tight around her.

Outside it was so gray and rainy that Rachel could barely see where they were going. Of course, she knew they were on the expressway, but she couldn't read any of the road signs through the rain and the dirty, clouded windows, and even if she'd been able to, she hadn't been to the city often enough to know where they were headed. She wished now she'd paid more attention on the bus last spring when her class visited the art museum, instead of sitting in the back with Antonella, guessing at Mrs. Morton's weight—maybe something would look familiar now. She thought of doing homework, but she was too nervous to concentrate, so she wrote in her journal instead.

After several minutes Rachel's whole body leaned as the bus pulled to the left and exited the highway, circling around a huge curve. They rambled along a narrow, winding road, through a wooded area, past a playing field where boys in football uniforms battled each other head on. *This doesn't look too bad*, Rachel thought. But a block or two later the scenery changed and Rachel inwardly squirmed. She'd never seen houses like these before. They were row houses, she knew that much, set among small, overgrown lots, and once they might have been pretty, like the houses she'd stayed in during weekends at the shore. Now they were so run-down that they were almost like ghosts, Rachel thought, faded versions of themselves in various stages of decay. She wondered for a second if anyone really lived here, but yes, of course they did—there was an elderly man sitting on a porch with broken railings, and two little girls drawing on the sidewalk with chalk under a graffiti-laced stop sign. Rachel jolted as the bus stopped short when a football escaped into the street; the bus driver waited patiently for a boy to retrieve the ball. She noticed peeling paint, decaying roofs, and splintered or missing trim, but what shocked Rachel most was that a few houses had empty dark spaces where second-story windows belonged. The bus swerved around a police van with lights flashing, and they passed a square two-story house that was literally chopped in half—surely no one could live inside that, Rachel thought. On the next block she saw a mural painted on the side of a building. A *Tribute to Urban Horsemen*, it said, and as they passed it she studied the spectacle of men in cowboy hats tending horses while kids played in the street. Rachel thought grimly that even counting the people in the mural, hers was the only white face around. She suppressed an impulse to call Nana, confess everything, and beg to be picked up. Finally, the bus pulled up beside the parked cars in front of a small, lonely brick building standing self-consciously between two empty lots and stopped, opening its doors. Rachel sat like a stone.

"This is it," the bus driver called back to her. "I'll pick you up here in an hour."

Rachel gathered up her belongings and walked to the front of the bus. "I'm not sure where I'm supposed to go."

"That's the building, right there," said the driver. "You have to get off now. I'm blocking traffic." As Rachel looked out of the open bus doors, she saw Sister Gloria coming toward her.

"You made it!" Sister Gloria said, standing between the parked cars under a red umbrella. "Welcome!" She offered a hand to help Rachel down the steps, and they walked to the curb, crowded under the umbrella. "Thank you," Sister Gloria said to the bus driver. "See you in an hour, Joe."

An hour, Rachel thought as she heard the bus pull away. Only an hour. A whole hour! She followed Sister Gloria into the building, down a dreary cinder block hallway, past closed doors studded with locks and peeling paint, to a door with the words *The Tolerance Project* printed on the outside. When Rachel stepped into the small suite of offices, she felt like Dorothy looking into the Land of Oz. The room was painted in pastel colors, and right smack in front of her was a large bouquet of daisies sitting at the edge of a polished wooden desk. She breathed in a ripple of something familiar—freshly baked chocolate chip cookies. For the first time that afternoon, she smiled.

"This is really nice," she said.

"Thank you. It's amazing what a few cans of paint will do. The kids from our summer program picked out the colors. Come into the conference room and meet the others." This room, with an orange ceiling, was the source of the lovely smell; on a long table pushed over to the side, the chocolate chip cookies sat invitingly in a white plastic platter which was just like the one that Nana had bought at the supermarket with a coupon for two dollars off. Across the room, five kids were sunken into two red faux-leather sofas. They looked about Rachel's age, but that was where the similarity ended. For the first time in her life, Rachel was in the minority. She glanced down at her watch—fifty-six minutes to go.

Sister Gloria pointed toward the sofa nearest Rachel. "Rachel, have a seat next to Damara and we'll get started." The tall, thin African-American girl sitting on the end slid over without looking up and Rachel sat down next to her. "Let's start by sharing your name, the name of your school, and your reason for joining this club. Who wants to go first?" All six teenagers looked off in different directions; no one moved a centimeter. Rachel felt her insides fall into a slow collapse.

"I know this is awkward," said Sister Gloria. "How about if I start? As you know, I'm Sister Gloria, and I'm a member of the Franciscan order. I'm also one of the founders of *The Tolerance Project*, a community organization that sponsors various programs for young people. We're completely nonprofit, which means we depend on grants and donations to function."

"So you mean you're poor," said one of the two African-American boys on the sofa across from Rachel. He was slouched into the sofa with his hood up and he looked down so that Rachel couldn't see his eyes. She sensed Damara, sitting next to her, tense.

Sister Gloria chuckled. "Yes, Darrin, you could say that. We depend on the kindness of others, which is not necessarily a bad thing. One of our most recent donations allowed us to buy the school bus that got Rachel here. We'll use it to take our kids on field trips and to summer camp, too. Now, who would like to be next?" Still no one moved or spoke, until the girl diagonally across from Rachel giggled.

"I don't know about everybody else, but I'm hungry. Sister Gloria, can we get some of those cookies?" she asked, pushing off from the sofa. Rachel watched her stride over to the table, tugging at her tight jean skirt as she walked. She was about the same width as Rachel, but taller and much fuller in front, and she moved with an air of total confidence. As she reached for a cookie she looked down at her own chest and adjusted her black V-neck top so that not quite so much cleavage showed.

"Sister Gloria, did you bake these?" the girl asked. "Oh

my God, they're delicious!" She took a bite and closed her eyes. "Mmm, I was starving all afternoon at school." She shoved another cookie into her mouth, talking as she chewed. "These are just like the ones my grandmother makes."

"Thanks, Sandra, I'm glad you like them," said Sister Gloria. The phone rang out in the reception area. "I have to take this call—make yourselves comfortable." She rushed out of the room, leaving the door open behind her.

Rachel walked over to Sandra and took a cookie. "My grandmother makes these cookies, too. She even has the same platter." Her voice sounded tinny to her own ears, and for a minute she worried Sandra hadn't heard her. Or maybe I sound as stupid as I feel and she's ignoring me, Rachel thought.

"I know it's just the recipe on the back of the chocolate chip bag," Sandra answered, "but I've tried to make them a hundred times and they never come out as good as my Buela's."

"I know—mine always burn." Rachel felt a little braver. "Did you say Bella?" she asked. "That's what my grandfather calls me."

"No, Buela, short for Abuela—grandma in Spanish. I live with my mom and my grandmother."

"I live with my grandparents, too, and my uncles. You're Sandra, right? I'm Rachel."

"Hi Rachel. Let's go sit down. Wait, we need more cookies first." She grabbed a handful. "Take some."

"Well, okay—like I need cookies, right?"

"What are you talking about?" asked Sandra, surveying Rachel up and down. "You're fine and full, like me." As they approached the sofa Rachel hung back for a second, letting Sandra squeeze in next to Darrin, the boy who had spoken earlier. Sandra leaned toward him. "What do you think?" she asked. "Don't you think women should have curves?"

"Sounds good to me," he answered, looking down at Sandra's curves in appreciation.

"Okay, that's enough, back up to the eyes," said Sandra, and nervous as she was, Rachel had to laugh. The boy on the other couch laughed, too.

"I'm Henry," he said, "and you already heard this is Darrin. He's Damara's little brother."

"Little?" asked Darrin. "Only little compared to you, and only around the middle." Both boys were nearly six feet tall, but Henry was much huskier than Darrin.

"Yeah, yeah," answered Henry, and Rachel got the feeling they'd bantered this way before. Do they all already know each other? she wondered. Am I the only outsider?

Henry confirmed her suspicions. "The three of us go to Jefferson," he said.

"I'm Sandra, and this is Rachel. And that's Leah, over there—we both go to Northside." An Asian-American girl sitting next to Damara on the other couch waved. When she smiled, Rachel noticed that she was wearing braces.

"Where do you go to school, Rachel?" Henry asked. His voice was so friendly that Rachel almost forgot about being an outsider for a minute.

"I go to Coventry Township High."

"Where's that?" Darrin asked. His tone was skeptical, as if Rachel had claimed to attend school in Alaska.

"It's ... in Coventry Township," she answered, turning pink.

Henry burst out laughing. "Don't mind him, he doesn't get out much. It's out in the suburbs, Darrin." He continued to laugh, but Darrin was clearly unhappy.

"Shut up, fat boy," he scowled. "How was I supposed to know she was from all the way out there?" He turned to Rachel sullenly. "Why the ef did you come all this way?" Rachel's heart pounded in time to the rain on the windows.

"Don't act like you're all ghetto, Darrin," Damara said before Rachel could answer. "She's probably here for the same reason we all are—it counts as community service, and it looks good on the college application." Rachel hadn't even considered listing this club on a college application. Her grades were good, and she'd assumed she'd have no trouble getting into college.

Darrin sounded more annoyed every time he spoke. "I'm not worried about any college application. I'm here because I was forced to come," he said to his sister.

"Do you really want to talk about that here?" Damara asked.

"Yeah, Darrin," said Henry, "tell us what your parents found in your backpack, and why they won't leave you home alone anymore!"

"What's in your backpack?" Darrin shot back. "Pictures of naked men?"

"Hey, relax you two!" said Sandra. "We're supposed to be getting to know each other, not starting a brawl. I joined because Sister Gloria comes to my parish sometimes, and she helped my family out once when we were in trouble. Leah, what about you?"

"To tell you the truth," Leah answered, "I joined to get out of taking care of my little sister while my parents are at the store. They think this is a study group."

"Study! This gets worse every minute," Darrin said.

"No one is gonna make you open a book, Darrin," said Henry. Darrin shifted his weight and continued to scowl, and for the moment all was quiet. Rachel stared down at her feet, but she sensed someone looking at her. When she glanced up Henry caught her gaze.

"What about you?" he asked. "You sure came a long way. Why did you join?" It was the second time Rachel had been asked the question, but this time her heart, which had stopped pounding, fluttered a little. She had no idea how to answer.

"Well, I ... I guess I wanted to do something different. You know, make new friends, meet different people, make a difference."

"Are we *different* enough for you?" Darrin laughed. "I guess they don't have any black people where you live, huh?"

"Leave her alone, Darrin," Henry said. "She didn't mean it that way." Again Rachel had needed to be rescued from Darrin. She clamped her mouth shut. "Don't mind him," Henry said softly, smiling again, but this time he didn't release his gaze until Rachel smiled back.

Sandra jumped up from her seat. "Let's play a game," she said, walking to the shelf on the other side of the room. "Let's see what we have—UNO, Catch Phrase, or Scrabble?"

"This is pathetic," said Darrin.

"Maybe we better stick to UNO," Henry suggested. He grabbed the deck from Sandra. "But let me tell you about the house rules." He launched into a set of instructions that Rachel tried to follow, but all she could remember when he finished was "reverse if you throw down a two."

"Okay, everybody ready?" asked Henry, dealing the cards. Darrin groaned and pulled his hood lower over his eyes, but picked up the cards in front of him.

Rachel stared at the cards in her hand. She always had trouble thinking clearly when she was nervous. "I'm not sure I can remember all these rules," she said.

"Don't worry, just play," said Leah. "We'll get it as we go along." When Rachel thought back on the afternoon she wasn't sure if she ever did get it, but it hadn't really mattered. They'd followed Henry's lead, reversing and trading hands when he told them to. Darrin got heated when it looked like his sister might beat him for the second round in a row. His only hope at stopping her from going out was to reverse the hand away from her; he threw down a yellow two with such gusto that his whole body bounced on the couch, creaking the plastic upholstery in just the right way to create the sound of escaping air.

"'Scuse you," said Sandra.

"I didn't do nothing," Darrin answered.

"That's Darrin's way of playing," said Henry. "He farts instead of saying 'Uno.' He calls it, '*Funo*.'" Rachel tried not to laugh because she didn't want to get Darrin mad at her again, but she couldn't help herself.

"Kiss it. I'm going out now anyway," Darrin said, gripping his last remaining card with both hands. On his next turn he threw down the card in victory. Sister Gloria returned just in time to hear him say, "Schooled! Can we get out of here now?"

Winning must have put Darrin in a better mood, because on their way out he brushed next to Rachel. "Hey," he said, "you know I was just playin' with you before, right?" He slumped so that he didn't tower over Rachel quite as much. It was the first friendly thing Rachel had heard him say. She thought he almost smiled.

"Sure," she answered, surprised.

The rain had stopped and the air had turned brisk when Rachel stepped out of the building and onto the bus. She leaned back into her seat and relaxed, letting her mind wander through the highways and the traffic. As the bus pulled into the school parking lot, they passed Grampy waiting in his pick-up, engine running. What if he sees me get off the bus? Rachel worried. I'm supposed to be in the school building. "Can you let me off around back?" she asked the driver. Grampy was looking down, reading something; he didn't notice the bus drive by, and he didn't look up until Rachel opened the passenger side door of the truck. He greeted Rachel with his usual, "How's the baby today?" Rachel responded with her usual, "Fine. And I'm not a baby," and, as usual, that was the end of the conversation until they reached home. Rachel kicked off her shoes at the back door, dumped her backpack on the floor and kissed Nana on the cheek.

"How was the club?" asked Nana.

"It was fun. I made some new friends. What's for dinner?"

"Spaghetti and broccoli. Wash your hands."

"You look happy tonight, Rach" said Uncle Tommy at the dinner table. Rachel had been smiling; with a start she realized she'd been thinking about Henry.

"She joined a club at school, that's why," said Nana. "She made some new friends, just like I said she should."

"So who are these new friends?" asked Uncle Tommy. This would be a good time to tell them, Rachel thought. What could they say—I'm almost sixteen, I can be friends with whoever I want. It's not like I did anything wrong. I'll just tell them the truth. She took a huge bite of spaghetti.

"Just some kids," she said through chews. "Nana, this is delicious. What's your secret ingredient?"

"No secrets this time," said Nana. "Just spaghetti and broccoli."

Rachel felt a rush of satisfaction. For once, she was the one keeping the secret.

Dear Dad,

I feel a little better now than the last time I talked to you. The club turned out okay.

The neighborhood was scary, but I met some kids, and they weren't what I expected. Actually, I wasn't sure what to expect, but I liked them, mostly. There was this one guy I wasn't so sure about. But it felt good to do something different for a change.

Dad, the club was run by a nun, Sister Gloria—did I tell you about her? Anyway, I snuck around as if I were smoking pot or meeting boys in a dark alley or something. Why am I so afraid to tell Nana or Grampy, or even Uncle Johnny? There must be something wrong with them—or maybe with me.

One more thing. As you know, the big day is coming up. Thank God I'm not having a party—I wouldn't know who to invite anyway. Nana always tries to look happy, but she can't help being sad. I know it's not your fault, but I wish you hadn't died on my birthday.

Love always,
Rach
XXXOOO

Chapter 7

Colores

The next week went more quickly for Rachel than any since Antonella had left. Everything felt different, somehow. For one thing, the weather was turning cool; soon the remnants of summer would be gone for good. Rachel dragged her box of fall clothes out from the back of her closet and greeted her sweaters as if they were old friends. Her birthday was largely uneventful (Uncle Tommy had insisted they go out for dinner, and although Nana did not approve of restaurant food, she gave in for the special occasion), but Rachel savored the idea of being sixteen, letting it melt in her mouth all week like a never-ending morsel of chocolate. Was that why she felt so different, or did it have more to do with her secret? Big secret, she berated herself—other kids her age were partying or sleeping with their boyfriends, and here she was, worried she'd get caught attending a meeting run by a nun. She had to admit, though, that the days flew by until Thursday afternoon when she found herself headed for the city again. This time the sun glared so brightly through the windows of the bus that she could barely see the words on the pages of the open book in her lap. She managed to get most of her math homework done by the time she spotted Sister Gloria's building.

"Finally!" Henry said when Rachel walked into the conference room. "What took you so long to get here?"

"Rachel has the farthest to travel," explained Sister Gloria. Rachel looked around the room and noticed that someone was missing.

"Okay, we're all here," said Sister Gloria. "Leah couldn't make it today."

"Maybe her parents caught on," said Darrin. "Shoot. I was hoping she'd bring some Chinese food sometime."

"She's Vietnamese," said Sandra. Henry laughed and Darrin glowered, but Sister Gloria spoke before a fight could erupt.

"She may be back next week," she said. "It's important that her parents are fully aware of where she is and what she's doing." Rachel's face froze—she hoped Sister Gloria wasn't looking at her. "So, how would you like to spend our time together today?" Sister Gloria continued.

The refreshments had been set out on a coffee table in front of the sofas, and the stacks of games from last week were piled on the floor nearby. Rachel grabbed a handful of pretzels.

"I'm not playing UNO again, that's for sure," said Darrin. "Damara cheats."

"I do not cheat, Darrin. You just hate to lose." Rachel liked the way Damara spoke in a quiet, steady hum. She allowed herself to notice the similarities in the siblings' appearance; both Darrin and Damara were tall and thin with copper complexions and high cheekbones. Both had dark round eyes and the same arch to their eyebrows, and Rachel noticed that although both had long eyelashes, Darrin's were even longer than Damara's. She realized that she was staring and turned her eyes away.

"I thought you might want to begin by coming up with a name for the club," said Sister Gloria, "and then maybe we could talk about the idea of taking on some kind of a project. It might be fun to work toward a common goal."

"Work!" exclaimed Darrin to Damara. "You didn't say anything about work!"

"Hush, Darrin." Damara said.

"Don't worry, I'm not going to put you to work, Darrin," said Sister Gloria. "I just meant that the group might want to take on some kind of a project, maybe to raise money for a worthy cause. I'll let you talk about it while I go take care of a few things." She turned and walked out into the reception area.

If Damara's voice was a hum, Sandra's was a crash. "Do you notice how she always leaves? Like she knows we can't really be ourselves in front of her."

"Yeah, but she always keeps the door open," said Henry.

"Maybe she thinks something else might go on in here if she closes it," Darrin laughed.

"Shh," whispered Damara. "She'll hear you."

"Anyway, I have some ideas for a name," said Sandra. "How about *Amigos?* That means friends in Spanish."

"We know what amigos means," said Henry.

"Not that I care, but how about *The Black Mob?*" asked Darrin. Rachel tried to picture herself telling Nana that she had joined a club called *The Black Mob.*

"In case you hadn't noticed, we're not all black," scoffed Sandra.

"How about *Homies in the Hood,* Darrin?" said Henry. "Or maybe, *Dawgs in the Dizzle?*"

"*Fags in the Field?*" Darrin suggested, smirking at Henry.

"Don't you two start," warned Damara.

"Okay, okay, forget it," said Henry. "Rachel, what do you think?"

"I don't know," said Rachel. "I can't really think of anything."

"How about *Colores?*" Sandra suggested. "That's colors in Spanish—you know, for the colors in this room. It's a Spanish song, too." Rachel looked around. Did Sandra mean the colors of the wall or the colors of her new friends? Either way, it fit.

"I like it," she said.

Henry rolled his eyes. "Okay Sandra, you win," he said. "We'll go with the Spanish name—*Colores.*"

"Now what?" asked Damara.

"I think we should try to get to know each other better," said Sandra, reaching for the UNO deck.

Darrin protested loudly. "We're gonna sit here and play games again like little kids? Can't we just listen to music and chill?"

66

"This is different from regular UNO—we're going to play my house rules this time." Sandra's expression was filled with mysterious possibility. She flipped through the deck quickly, removing all the draw two and draw four cards. "Here's how you play—if you draw a red card you're bold, so you tell something brave or bold about yourself. Green stands for growth, that's happy—tell something that makes you happy. Blue is sad—tell what makes you sad, and yellow, that means you're afraid, so tell something that scares you. If you draw a wild card you have to tell something wild about yourself, but it doesn't have to be true, and we have to guess if it's the truth or a lie. Other than that, you just play the regular way. Okay?"

The other members of the group stared at Sandra as if she had just splashed a cold bucket of water in their faces.

"Whoa, slow down, girl," said Henry. "You want to run that by us again?"

"It's easy, you'll see." Sandra dealt the cards as quickly as she had spoken. "You go," she said to Darrin, who was sitting on her left.

"Why do I have to go first?"

"It's clockwise. Go!" Rachel was sitting on Sandra's right, which meant she'd go next to last. At least she'd get to hear what some others said before her turn.

"Ha!" Darrin threw down a red card to match the one showing in the discard pile. "Your turn," he said to Damara. Damara threw down a red card as well. Rachel surveyed her hand—no reds. Maybe Henry would change the color.

Henry discarded a red. "You go, Rachel."

"Oh. I guess I have to draw a card." She reached down to the pile and drew a blue three.

"You have to tell something that makes you sad," instructed Sandra.

Rachel hesitated. She could think of plenty of things that made her feel sad, but nothing she wanted to say out loud. "My best friend moved away," she said finally. "That made me really sad."

"That is sad," said Sandra. "I go."

"Wait a minute, doesn't Rachel have to keep picking until she gets a red?" Darrin asked.

"Not in this version," Sandra replied. "You just pick one. I don't have any red either." She chose a green five. "Okay, green—happy. Easy—I passed my math test today. You go, Darrin." Darrin and Damara each threw down red cards and the play passed to Henry, who drew a yellow from the deck.

"Tell something that scares you," Sandra said.

"You mean other than Darrin's face?" Henry asked. Damara laughed behind her cards.

"You won't be laughing when you lose this game," Darrin said, glaring at his sister.

"Come on, Henry, tell us something that scares you," Sandra said.

"Something that scares me … I guess I'm scared that my car will break down and I won't have the money to fix it."

"I'd be scared, too, if I drove that piece of crap," said Darrin.

"No comments allowed," said Sandra.

"At least I have a car," said Henry.

"Are you two fighting for the alpha male position or something?" asked Sandra. "Rachel, you go." This time Rachel drew a wild card. "Tell something wild about yourself, and then we have to guess if it's true or not," instructed Sandra.

Something wild. Something sad was easy, but thinking of something wild presented Rachel with a challenge. "I guess joining this club is probably the wildest thing I've ever done," she said finally. Sandra coughed, nearly choking on her cookie, and Darrin spit a sip of juice from his mouth back into his cup.

"Lie!" said Sandra. "That's got to be a lie!"

"Definitely a lie!" said Darrin.

"I'm not so sure," said Henry, looking at Rachel closely. "I say it's the truth."

"Damara, what do you think?" asked Sandra.

"I guess I'll say it's a lie."

"No, it's the truth," said Rachel. She lowered her voice, so as not to be overheard by Sister Gloria. "My grandparents think I'm still at school right now. They would never have let me come this far by myself."

"*This* is the wildest thing you've ever done?" Darrin was incredulous. "Sitting here, eating junk food and playing UNO with a bunch of losers?"

Rachel flushed. "My family is overprotective, I guess."

"There's only one loser here, Rachel, and it ain't you," said Henry.

"UNO again," said Sister Gloria, entering the room. She pulled a chair over to the group. "So, have you come up with a name for the club?"

"It's *Colores*, after the colors of the room," Sandra announced.

"Good choice," said Sister Gloria.

"I still think *The Black Mob* was better," said Darrin.

Sister Gloria looked puzzled, but didn't ask for an explanation. "Any thoughts about my other suggestion? About undertaking a service project?"

"I guess we forgot about that," said Sandra.

"My church is having a fall fair on Saturday to raise money for the day care center. I know they still need workers," offered Damara.

"That sounds good—I don't work till six," said Sandra.

"I guess I can get Saturday off," said Henry, looking at Rachel.

"I have to be there anyway," said Darrin.

"What about you, Rachel?" asked Henry.

Rachel tried to think of a quick excuse. "You mean *this* Saturday—that's only two days away. Um, I'm not sure. I don't know where it is, and even if I did I'd have no way to get there."

"I can pick you up," said Henry. Rachel tried to keep her face neutral. How could she admit to this group that the idea of being picked up by a boy that her family had never met, and a black boy at that, was unthinkable? She knew they would be offended no matter how she tried to explain.

"Well, okay, but maybe we can meet at the mall. I have to do a few errands there in the morning." Henry's smile faded a little, but he agreed; Rachel wondered if he saw through her weak attempt at a cover-up.

Cell phone numbers were exchanged, and Rachel spent the bus ride home trying to figure out what she would tell Nana about Saturday. She could say she was involved in a school project to help underprivileged kids. Nana couldn't argue with that, she thought, and it would be the truth, sort of.

Tina Maria caught up with Rachel at school the first thing the next morning. "Great news!" she said. "One of the girls on the homecoming committee had to drop out because her grades were so low. There's an opening, so you can join now! We have an all day work session tomorrow. I'll pick you up at nine, okay?"

"Oh … I'm busy tomorrow," said Rachel.

"Can't you change your plans?"

"I guess I'm kind of committed." Rachel surprised herself—this was the chance she'd been waiting for. Why didn't she just cancel with Henry and the others?

"Rach, do you want to be on the committee or not?" asked Tina Marie.

"Of course I do, but it's just that I can't make this one meeting. Can't I come next time?"

"If you don't take this spot right away, somebody else will," answered Tina Marie. "But no problem, it's your choice," she said, shaking her head. "Promise you'll think about it, and call me if you change your mind." They went their separate ways, both hurrying to class. Rachel did think about it—in fact, she thought about little else all day, until her head felt like the ping pong ball they had smacked across the table during gym that afternoon.

Chapter 8

The Fair

Rachel thought about canceling with Henry at least a thousand times, but somehow she couldn't bring herself to disappoint him. She abandoned the underprivileged kids story for Nana, figuring a total lie (a day at the mall with her friends) would be less complicated. Getting a ride to the mall on Saturday morning was easy—Uncle Johnny was glad to drop her off there on his way to work. The temperature had suddenly dropped overnight, but Rachel had escaped the house before Nana could insist she wear a jacket.

"So what's the plan, Rach?" he asked as he drove. "Shop until you drop, or what?"

"That's about right," replied Rachel. "Just shop and hang out, that's all. We might catch a movie or something this afternoon." Rachel stared out the window. She had never lied to Uncle Johnny before.

"Do you have enough money on you?" Uncle Johnny reached for his wallet, which lay on the seat next to him.

"I mean for lunch and all. How 'bout I treat for the movie? How much do you need?"

"I'm fine, Uncle Johnny. I have all my birthday money, remember? I'm rich beyond my wildest dreams." Uncle Johnny laughed, and Rachel turned toward him. As always, Uncle Johnny looked like he had just fallen out of bed, but not just because he was rumpled; he had a dream-like quality to him, as if he existed in that first waking moment before awareness fully dawns. When she was growing up, Nana and Uncle Tommy took care of the important stuff—feeding her, checking her homework, talking to teachers and making arrangements with other parents. But it was Uncle Johnny who played with her, spending hours at the kitchen table drawing pictures or playing a board game. Sometimes she even convinced him to play Barbie—Uncle Johnny would be Ken, the perfect boyfriend, escorting Rachel's Barbie from place to place in a romantic night out on the town. If Uncle Tommy happened in on one of these sessions he would shake his head in disgust, but that never stopped them. Uncle Tommy spent time with Rachel, too, but when they'd play cards Rachel noticed he kept one eye on his hand and the other on his watch. Uncle Johnny was different—he never seemed to tire of playing with Rachel. As she got older the time they spent together settled into an occasional movie or trip out for ice cream, but Rachel always knew that Uncle Johnny was there, waiting in the background if she needed him.

"You should be a dad," she said.

"Huh? You mean right now, today? Jeez, I don't know if I can fit that into my schedule, Rach."

"No, I mean Nana is right—you should get married and have kids. You'd be a great dad."

"I'm not sure what brought that on, but thanks. I don't know, though—maybe I make a better uncle than a dad."

They pulled into the mall parking lot, which was beginning to fill up with cars. Rachel saw a beat-up white Dodge Neon sitting close to the entrance. The engine was running, and she made out Henry's figure in the driver's seat. Uncle Johnny saw him, too.

"Watch yourself, Rachel," he said. "Where are you meeting your friends? Do you want me to come in with you?"

"No, Uncle Johnny, I'll be fine. Just drop me off right here. I'll call you later if I need a ride home." She jumped out of the car and hurried to the entrance of the mall, hoping Henry hadn't seen her. Uncle Johnny pulled away slowly, hesitating in front of the white Neon on his way out of the parking lot. When she was sure Uncle Johnny was gone, Rachel came out and walked to Henry's car.

"Hi," she said, sliding into the front seat next to him. She kicked over a cascade of wires hanging down from the console to make room for her feet. "Been waiting long?" Had Henry witnessed her little game with Uncle Johnny? If he had, he didn't let on.

"Just a couple of minutes. All set?" he asked, waiting for her to buckle her seat belt. The car sputtered and lurched a few times before sliding into gear, but once it began to pick up speed, it settled into a steady wail.

"How long will it take to get there?" asked Rachel. She turned and glanced out the back window, expecting to see

Uncle Johnny following, but his car was nowhere in sight.

"Always depends on traffic. We have to pick up Sandra on the way." Henry looked over at Rachel. "Hey, relax," he said. "I know the car sounds bad, but I'll get you there in one piece, I promise." Good, thought Rachel, he thinks I'm nervous about his car. "Here, put this in, it'll cover up the noise." Henry handed Rachel a CD—Smokey Robinson, one of Uncle Tommy's favorites. Seeing Smokey staring up at her all curly hair and smiles took Rachel's anxiety down a notch. She slid the CD in, turned up the volume, and sat back in her seat.

"So, what exactly are we going to be doing today?" she asked.

"Haven't you ever been to a church fair? You know, food, games, stuff for the kids to do. There'll be a couple of tables where people sell stuff, too. Some of the money goes to the church."

"Damara said it was to raise money for the day care center."

"Whatever. Churches are always raising money for something. I should know—my grandpa's a minister." Rachel let this bit of news settle in. She thought of Grampy, who rarely went to church.

"Are we going to be outside?" She rubbed at her arms and shivered, realizing that Henry's car, which should have been toasty warm by now, was blowing cold air into her lap.

"Nah, don't worry. Not much room outside, anyway. Are you cold?"

"A little. Do you have the air conditioning on?"

Henry laughed. "Sorry," he said. "I think the heater is broken. I'll turn it off. Here—use this if you need it." He reached behind him, pulled an orange and blue striped afghan off the back seat and handed it to her, never taking his eyes off the road. Rachel covered her lap with the afghan, admiring its intricate rows of stitches.

"Who knitted this?"

"My grandmother. She's always worried I'm going to freeze or something. I've got three more in the trunk if we need them."

Rachel laughed. "I know exactly what you mean. My grandmother is the same way. She's always worried about something—'Are you warm enough?' 'You look tired, are you getting enough sleep?' And of course, 'You look hungry, eat.' She never stops feeding me—that's why I'm so fat." Rachel hadn't exactly meant to say that; it popped out from sheer habit. Years of comparing herself with Antonella had conditioned her to point out her own physical flaws before anyone else had the chance. It was less painful that way. Her friends would then offer sympathy and advice on diet, make-up, hair style or clothing, which Rachel would agree to try, but never did. It was a well-established and comfortable pattern of interaction. The only difference today was that until now Rachel had only had this type of conversation with her girlfriends—never with a boy.

"What?" Henry practically yelled. "Are you crazy? You're not fat! You think you're fat? If you're fat, what am I?"

"That's different. You're a guy."

"So what? How is it different? Look, you have a little

meat on your bones—nothing wrong with that. You're definitely not fat."

"You sound like my Nana."

"Then your Nana is a smart woman; you should listen to her. And I'll tell her that if I ever meet her."

At the thought of Henry meeting Nana, Rachel changed the subject. "So where are we?" They had exited the highway and were driving through crowded streets. The sidewalks bustled with pedestrians of all ages—parents pushing strollers or holding on to kids, teenagers traveling in packs, and people pushing shopping carts in and out of the small stores and bodegas. Henry made a few turns and they passed several blocks of compact brick row houses.

"This is the Northeast. We'll be at Sandra's building in a minute. Then the church is over west, closer to my neighborhood."

"How come you know your way around so well?"

"It's not really that hard. Besides, I worked summers with my dad, delivering furniture. You get to know all the neighborhoods pretty well."

"So your dad works at a furniture store?"

"He used to. Now he drives a truck across state. He's not home as much, but it pays better. I still work at the store after school sometimes. There's Sandra now." Rachel turned to see Sandra waving at them. Henry eased into a space in front of a fire hydrant several feet ahead, and Sandra jogged to the car, with a purse the size of a suitcase in tow. Instead of getting in the back seat as Rachel expected, she opened the door next to Rachel.

"Hi. Shove over," she said, sliding in. Her first attempt to shut the car door failed when her purse got in the way, but she managed to close them in on the second try. Rachel found herself squeezed alongside Henry so that their thighs could not help but touch.

"This is cozy," laughed Henry.

"I can't sit in the back. I get carsick," said Sandra.

"At least you're not claustrophobic. Better lock that door before we pop out," Henry instructed.

"I could sit in the back," volunteered Rachel.

"It's not that far," said Henry. "I guess we'll make it okay." They drove for several minutes with Sandra chattering away and, again by habit, Rachel receded into the background. She took in the sights of the neighborhoods, trying to figure out what she was feeling. The rows of brick houses they passed, the small blotches of grass here and there, the trees surrounded by cement, the car lots, auto repair shops, burger places, ragged curbs and broken sidewalks left her with a yearning feeling, but for what, she didn't know. She almost said something, but she was afraid she would sound stupid to Sandra and Henry, who were arguing over the music. After all, she wasn't that far from home, and some of the kids from school took the train into the city every weekend to shop or see a show, although Rachel didn't think this was the part of the city they'd come to. Until this moment she hadn't fully realized how sheltered she had been. Now Rachel felt like an alien in her own backyard.

"What do you think, Rachel?" Henry was asking.

"Huh?"

"Were you off on another planet somewhere?" asked Sandra. "The music! Tell Henry to change this music!"

"Oh—I like Smokey Robinson, but I don't care if you change it."

"That's a big help," said Sandra. "Can't you make a decision?"

"Hey, leave Rachel alone," said Henry. "She's just too nice to say your taste in music sucks. Anyway, we're here." They turned down a long, thin driveway beside a large brick church. Rachel noticed the name on the marquee— FIRST BAPTIST CHURCH. She had never been inside a Baptist church before. Under the church name it said, PUT GOD IN THE DRIVER'S SEAT. Rachel glanced over at Henry. The driveway led to a small parking lot, which was full.

"Looks like we'll have to park on the street," Sandra said.

"Hold on," answered Henry, "I see a spot." He drove around the parked cars to a space directly in front of a large green dumpster, and they spilled out into the brisk air. Rachel felt like an Italian sausage that had escaped from its casing.

"I have to leave early with my brother, so I guess you can have Rachel all to yourself on the way home," Sandra announced. Rachel looked at her sharply, but Henry pretended he didn't hear. He walked ahead a few steps and entered the church first.

"I guess I'll go find Darrin," he said over his shoulder.

"I think Henry likes you," Sandra said as soon as Henry was out of hearing range. "Can't you tell?"

Rachel was speechless. This was a new experience for her. Suddenly she was the girl in the spotlight being liked by a boy and Sandra was the friend on the sidelines. "Oh," she said finally. "What do you mean?"

"It's the way he's always sticking up for you, and making sure you sit next to him. And if he says something funny he checks to see if you're laughing. Take my word for it—the signs are all there. That's why I squeezed into the front seat. I wanted to give you two a chance to get a little closer. You can thank me later. You're blushing—what's wrong? Do you only date white guys or something?"

"No, it's not that—it's just … well, to be honest, I haven't really dated any guys before."

"How come? Oh, I know—your family is overprotective, right? You said that. Well, I know how that is. I've had to come up with some lame excuse plenty of times to get out. My brother, on the other hand, gets to do whatever he wants. But still—you're telling me you've never been out with a guy? Not even once?"

"It's not exactly like they've been banging down the door. Mostly they were interested in my best friend, Antonella—the one who moved away. Sometimes we'd go out with groups of kids—you know, a bunch of guys and girls together. But that's not the same as a date."

They walked into a large lobby bristling with kids and adults, all milling around a maze of tables, which were filled with little wooden necklaces, homemade Christmas ornaments, used mugs, picture frames, silk flowers, cupcakes, cotton candy, and a wide variety of other goods, all for sale. Rachel spotted Damara in the far corner, sitting at a small table next to long line of children waiting to have their faces painted.

"There's Damara," said Sandra. "Let's go help her."

Damara smiled, relieved to see them. "Grab a brush," she said. "I've been doing this all morning." Sandra took the only other seat at the table while Rachel squatted next to her.

"I've never actually done this before," said Rachel.

"You've never done a lot of things before. Relax—it's a breeze. I'll give you the easy ones. So what would you like painted?" Sandra asked a girl of about five who was next in line. They painted hearts, rainbows, and a ninja sword or two until Rachel's legs ached. She stood and rubbed her knees.

"There's more chairs in the kitchen," said Damara. "You can get one if you want."

Rachel wove her way around groups of kids making beaded necklaces at one table and painting pumpkins at another. She walked past several crafters' tables and glanced casually at the holiday wreaths, wondering which ones Nana might like. When she reached the kitchen she was surprised to see Henry standing inside the doorway.

"Hey," he said. "What are you doing in here?"

"I came to find a chair. Are you helping with the cooking?"

"No, I'm hiding from Darrin. He's begging me to play basketball with the boys."

"What's wrong with that?"

"I hate basketball. Shh, I think he's coming—quick, hide in here!" He grabbed Rachel and led her through the kitchen.

"Henry!" Darrin called. Henry panicked and ducked into the pantry, dragging Rachel with him. Luckily, none of the church ladies noticed.

Rachel stood in the dark with Henry, trying not to laugh. Darrin's voice trailed off as he continued his search in another direction. "Henry, where are you, you blob! Come on, we need one more person! Henry…"

"I guess you must *really* hate basketball," Rachel giggled.

"Shh, if those ladies find us in here I'm sunk. They all know my grandfather."

"Is this his church, too?"

"Nah, we're AME, but these ladies know everybody."

"What's AME?"

"African Methodist Episcopal. Listen, we've gotta sneak out of here. Let me see if they're watching." He tried to turn the door handle but nothing happened. "Shoot. I think it's locked."

"What? How can it be locked from the inside? Are they afraid the canned corn might escape?"

"Maybe it's not locked, but the door knob is loose or something. It's not catching. You know, these old churches are falling apart. Nothing works anymore. Maybe I can open it with a credit card—do you have one?"

Rachel wondered how much experience Henry had opening locked doors with credit cards. "I left my purse in the lobby. Is there a light in here?" She groped the wall looking for a switch, but instead knocked something off the shelf with a loud clatter. They froze, waiting for someone to come to the pantry to investigate, but apparently the noise was drowned out by the four sizzling frying pans on the stove.

Henry reached over his head and found a small chain hanging from the ceiling, which he pulled gingerly. A dim light appeared in the pantry. Rachel saw that they were surrounded by platters, pots, cooking utensils, and enough canned food to fill a small store. She wondered if her church had a pantry like this, although she could not remember ever eating a meal there—Communion didn't count.

"Check this out," said Henry. He read a tattered note posted on the inside of the door. "'Doorknob is broken. To open use pliers on shelf.' They took the trouble to write a note and leave the pliers, but not to fix the doorknob." He picked up the pliers, carefully squeezed the exposed innards of the doorknob and turned. Rachel heard a click.

"Thank God," she said, "let's get out of here. I'm suffocating."

"Not so fast—I don't want one of these ladies telling my grandma they caught me coming out of the closet with a white girl. Hold on."

Rachel knew there was no chance of Nana ever meeting any of these ladies, but she understood Henry's dilemma. He opened the door a crack and peeked out. "Okay, they're all busy cooking. I think we can sneak out now." He continued to open the door slowly and motioned for Rachel to follow him, pressing his finger to his lips.

They had just cleared the doorway when Rachel heard a loud voice say, "Rachel, where have you been? How long does it take to find a chair? I should have known I would find you two together." Sandra stood facing them, hand on her hip.

"What are you kids doing in here?" asked a tall woman with her hair tied up in a purple scarf. "It's not time to eat yet—Henry, is that you? Why is that pantry door open? I might have guessed you'd be in here looking for food. Go on out and help set up the tables. We'll be eating in a little bit."

"Sure, Miss Johnson, no problem," said Henry.

"Are your grandparents coming by later?" Miss Johnson asked.

"Uhh, I think so."

"You be sure to tell them I say hello if I don't see them."

"I will, Miss Johnson," Henry turned away from her and glared at Rachel and Sandra. "Let's go," he said under his breath, heading for the doorway and not looking back. Once they were safely out of the kitchen he turned toward the girls.

"I told you. Sandra, you almost blew it for us!"

"Blew what? What were you two doing, anyway?"

"We went in the pantry to hide from Darrin and then we got stuck in there," explained Rachel, "and Henry was afraid to come out."

Sandra eyed them up and down with a knowing little smile. "Sure you did," she said. "Um-hum." She sashayed to the far end of the fellowship hall, where tables were being opened.

"No, really, that's what happened," said Rachel, following her. "The doorknob was broken and we got stuck…"

"You don't have to explain to me, I understand perfectly," said Sandra.

"No, we really were stuck…"

"Forget it, Rachel," Henry interrupted. "Let her think what she wants. Come on, grab the end of this table. I'd rather do this than play basketball any day." Several men and women were getting the room ready for lunch. One of the men walked over to Henry and smiled.

"Henry, why don't you introduce me to your friends?"

"Sure, Mr. Thomas—this is Rachel and Sandra. They're from our after-school club." He turned to the girls. "This is Mr. Thomas—Darrin and Damara's father." Mr. Thomas shook hands with both girls.

"Welcome. We appreciate your help today. Why don't you girls set the tables—you'll find everything you need in the kitchen pantry."

Sandra laughed out loud. "Some of us found what we needed in there already," she said. Mr. Thomas frowned.

"Don't mind her," Henry said. "She's a little strange."

For the next several minutes they worked steadily under the direction of the adults. Throughout the process Rachel watched people stream into the hall, carrying one plate of food after another and placing them on the tables in the front of the room. Try as she might, Rachel could not spot a drop of tomato sauce anywhere. She found that she was starving.

"Here you are!" Darrin burst into the room holding a basketball. "Ha! You had to set up tables while we played!"

"Yeah, tough break, huh?" replied Henry.

"Darrin, don't you bring that basketball in here!" Mr. Thomas boomed from across the room. "And go wash up before you come in here to eat." Darrin scowled but did as he was told, and within another minute the hall filled up with people. Lunch was officially served. Damara got in line behind Rachel, Henry, and Sandra.

"I hope I never have to paint another rainbow," she said. "Where did you all run off to?"

"Long story," said Henry, "but we ended up here. Hey, there's Sister Gloria." Rachel turned to see Sister Gloria enter the room with two women dressed much the same as she.

"Those must be some of her nun friends," Sandra speculated. She waved and Sister Gloria waved back. As they filled their plates an elderly man cleared his throat loudly from behind the serving table.

"Let me take this opportunity to welcome everyone to First Baptist, and thank you for participating in our fall fundraiser. All proceeds will go to benefit our childcare center, run by Mrs. Bethany Thomas."

"That's my mom," Damara whispered over the polite applause that followed.

"Now, let's take a moment to ask the blessing on this wonderful meal. I'd like to ask one of our neighboring ministers, Reverend Henry Sayers, to do us the honor."

"That's my grandpa," said Henry. Rachel felt as if she were the only person in the room who wasn't related to someone. Henry's grandpa prayed in a deep, resonating voice, ending with a loud "Amen."

"Amen," repeated the crowd.

"That's your grandpa?" Rachel asked Henry.

"Yeah, why are you so surprised?"

Rachel thought of Grampy. She had never heard him pray once, although she had heard him say God's name many times. "He's just so different from my grandfather, that's all."

Henry's grandparents, who had been circulating through the crowd greeting people and shaking hands, made their way to the table. Henry stood as they approached and introduced them to Sandra and Rachel.

"Nice to meet you," said Henry's grandmother. "Thank you for helping out today. Henry, can I assume you'll be home on time for dinner tonight?"

"Yes ma'am. I just have to run Rachel home when this is over."

"And where do you live, Rachel?"

"In Coventry Township," Rachel answered. "But actually, Henry only has to take me as far as the mall. I'm meeting someone there." If Henry was surprised, he didn't show it, but Rachel thought she saw a look pass between his grandparents.

"You be careful, Henry," said his grandfather. "Watch your speed."

"I doubt his car goes over forty," mumbled Darrin.

"Well, you enjoy your lunch," said Henry's grandmother, and the elderly couple moved on to the next table.

"It looks like they know everybody," said Rachel.

"They do know everybody. My grandpa's been a pastor for forty years. I think he kind of expects me to follow in his footsteps." Rachel wasn't sure what to say to this. Sandra, though, was never at a loss for words.

"That sucks," she said. "You should be able to decide for yourself what you want to do with your life. Take my brother, Raphael ... oh, there he is now. I guess it's time for me to go." She shoveled up one last forkful of macaroni and cheese, at the same waving furiously at her brother. Raphael spotted them and walked over to their table. When he came into focus, Rachel saw that he was smiling a shy, half-smile; the dimple on his left cheek made him seem like a little kid, although the stubble of his beard told her that he was probably older than Sandra. He was thin, slightly built, from what Rachel could tell underneath his jacket. His complexion was a dark tan, like Sandra's, but while she wore her black hair pulled back, his was curled in ringlets that fell just to the tips of his long eyelashes. His eyes were the darkest blue that she had ever seen—almost purple. Rachel didn't know eyes came in that color. She thought that she hadn't seen anyone so beautiful since Antonella moved away.

"This is my brother, Raphael," Sandra was saying. "I'd introduce you all but he won't remember your names, anyway. I gotta go. See you Thursday, okay?" Sandra leapt up from the table and took her brother's arm.

"Bye," he said, allowing Sandra, who was chatting away in Spanish, to pull him across the room. Raphael smiled just long enough over his shoulder for Rachel to see his dimple one last time before they walked through the door. Was Rachel imagining it, or did Raphael make eye contact with her when he smiled? She tried to keep the image of his face in her mind so that she'd remember what he looked like when she thought about him later at home.

"You can relax now," Henry whispered. "He's gone."

"Huh?"

"You started purring when he walked into the room. Guys like him do that to women without even trying. But he's gone now, so you can come back to reality."

"Was it that obvious?" asked Rachel.

"It was to me, but I don't think anyone else noticed. Don't worry, your secret's safe with me." Rachel had never had this kind of conversation with a guy before. She looked into Henry's round, honest face.

"Okay," she said, "and I won't tell anyone your secret, either."

"What secret is that?" asked Henry, surprised.

"That you hate basketball, of course," Rachel answered. "What other secrets do you have?"

"I guess that'll do for now. Come on, let's clean up these tables, and then I'll take you home."

A few minutes later they pulled out of the church driveway. "Are you sure you don't want me to take you all the way?" Henry asked.

"No, it's fine. I have some stuff to do at the mall. I'll get a ride from there."

"You had stuff to do there this morning, too. But suit yourself." They drove in silence for a while, which wasn't very silent because of the rattling of the car engine and the roar of the exhaust system. Rachel spread the afghan over her lap and settled into her seat as if she had ridden in this car a hundred times before.

"I had fun today," said she finally. "I'm glad I went."

"Me, too." Henry reached over and opened the glove compartment, pulling out a new CD. "Put this in, okay?"

He handed the CD to Rachel—it was someone named Sam Cooke. Rachel had never heard of him, but she was too embarrassed to say so. Henry sang along in a low voice, glancing at Rachel every few seconds: "*...it's been a long time coming, but I know change gonna come, oh yes it will...*" Sandra is right, thought Rachel, he does give me a lot of attention. Yet he didn't seem at all upset about the Raphael thing before—if he liked me, wouldn't he be jealous? She couldn't quite figure Henry out.

When they arrived at the mall she hesitated for a moment before getting out of the car. "See you Thursday, right?" Was that an okay goodbye? Should she give him a hug or something? Before she could decide what to do, Henry leaned over and kissed her on the cheek.

"Talk to you later," he said. "I'm blocking the entrance—I'd better get out of here before mall security gets on my case." Rachel jumped out and watched the car clang away into the darkening early evening. When it was out of sight she took out her cell phone and speed-dialed home.

"Uncle Johnny? Can you come and pick me up at the mall? I'm ready to come home." She hung up and waited in a kind of floating limbo, hovering between two worlds.

Chapter 9

Stealth

Three club meetings and countless text messages later, Sandra sat on the edge of the red sofa holding two plates in one hand and a cup of punch in the other. For once she was whispering. "So you'll come, right? My mom loves Sister Gloria, and she's all excited about this surprise party."

"Do nuns have birthdays?" Darrin asked.

"No, they descend full grown from the heavens," said Henry. "Of course they have birthdays, fool. Anybody who's born has a birthday."

"I know that. I mean, do they celebrate their birthdays? Isn't that against their religion or something?"

"Darrin, please stop," said Damara. "Yes, we can come, for a little while, anyway. Can we get a ride with you, Henry?"

Darrin clung stubbornly to his line of reasoning. "What I meant was, don't they take a vow of poverty? Aren't birthdays materialistic, with presents and all?"

"That's a good point—should we buy her a present?" Rachel asked.

"Maybe we could chip in and get her something—but what?" said Sandra.

"Don't ask me," Darrin said. "Only present I want is a new Xbox 360." Henry rolled his eyes, but when Rachel pictured Sister Gloria sequestered in the convent playing the latest version of Halo, she laughed.

"I saw her take out her wallet to pay for lunch that day at the fair," Damara said. "It was all tattered and frayed. Maybe we could get her a new one."

"That's a great idea," said Henry. "How about if I pick everyone up early and we'll stop at the mall near Rachel's to get the wallet first?" Was Henry making it easy for her to meet him at the mall, knowing that was what she would suggest anyway? Rachel looked at him, wondering, but his smile revealed nothing.

So it was decided and plans for Saturday were set. Now, thought Rachel, all I have to do is figure out what I'm going to tell Nana. When she arrived home, the smell of sautéing onions greeted her at the door. She disposed of her coat and backpack, washed up in the bathroom and greeted Nana in the kitchen.

"Mmm, that smells good," she said as she began to set the table.

"How was your club?" asked Nana.

"Good. Oh, before I forget, one of the kids is having a birthday party this weekend, so I'll be gone most of Saturday."

"But isn't this weekend homecoming?" asked Nana. "Who would have a birthday party during homecoming?"

Rachel could have kicked herself. She'd been so busy lately that she'd forgotten all about homecoming, which wasn't something she'd ever really enjoyed, anyway, since in past years she mostly tagged around after Antonella and watched her flirt. Hanging out with Henry and the others at Sandra's house seemed much more appealing to her now, and besides, Raphael would probably be there, too. Although Rachel knew she stood no real chance with a boy like Raphael, fantasy dating was a habit hard to break.

Homecoming would have provided the perfect excuse to get her out of the house on Saturday, but it was too late now—she'd told her story and she'd have to stick with it. She needed to think quickly. "Not everyone goes to homecoming, Nana," she said. "Besides, it's a party for somebody's cousin, who doesn't go to our school."

"Well, excuse me," said Nana. "So who's having the party, and will there be parents there?"

"Of course. It's my friend, Sandra, and her grandmother will be cooking for us."

"Hmm, Sandra. I've never heard of Sandra before."

"She's new at school."

"Oh, that's nice. So what is this grandmother cooking? Are they Italian?"

Rachel hesitated for a moment, knowing she needed to be careful not to give herself away. "It won't be as good as your cooking," she said, resorting again to flattery to throw Nana off track. "I don't know, I think they're Irish, or German or something," she lied.

"German, huh? You'd better eat something before you go. I once had sauerbraten at a restaurant—don't even ask what it tasted like, because I couldn't describe it if I tried…" Nana continued to relate story after story about the hazards of non-Italian food as Rachel finished setting the table. Another stealth mission accomplished, at least for now, she thought.

Chapter 10

The Truth If You Dare

This time Rachel made sure that Uncle Johnny dropped her off at the mall early to avoid any possible problems. Henry had picked up Darrin and Damara first, and when they arrived Rachel stood waiting for them at the usual entrance.

"Sandra says we need to buy a card, too," said Damara. "Then she wants us at her house early so we can help decorate."

"She's bossy," said Darrin.

"Where should we look for the wallet?" asked Henry.

Rachel led them to one of the large department stores, but as they walked through the crowded mall she realized that she was taking a chance—what if she ran into some of her old friends? How would she explain who she was with? What if one of them told her parents, and word got back to Nana or the uncles? Luckily, everyone would be busy getting ready for homecoming tonight. This would have to be a quick trip, and she would have to be careful to avoid the nail and hair salons.

They walked through the store, making their way through juniors and jewelry before finding the scarves, belts and wallets. Rachel walked ahead with Damara, stopping briefly at the make-up counter. When she turned toward Henry and Darrin she saw that Henry's easy smile had been replaced by a self-conscious grimace, and Darrin had given up his usual smirk in exchange for total blankness.

"Oh," she said, "sorry. I guess guys don't like to hang out at the make-up counter."

"It's not that," Henry whispered. He barely moved his lips as he spoke. "It's him," he said, nodding toward a man dressed in khakis and a brown flannel shirt. "He's been watching us since we got here." Rachel noticed that both boys stood straight with their hands at their sides.

"What do you mean? Do you know him?" asked Rachel.

"He's waiting for us to steal something," murmured Darrin. For a second Rachel thought they were joking, but their expressions told her they were not.

"Maybe we'd better go," said Damara.

"That's ridiculous. We're not doing anything wrong." Rachel marched over to a round table filled with black faux-leather wallets in rectangular boxes. Henry, Darrin and Damara followed her and, sure enough, the man in khakis followed them.

"These look nice," she said, picking up a wallet and taking it out of the box. "Feel how soft." She held the wallet out to Henry, who touched it lightly with one finger. Khaki Man leaned in to watch.

Rachel turned and faced him squarely. "What do you think? Do you think a nun would like this wallet?" She tried to imitate Antonella's bold tone. The man seemed taken aback.

"Er, I wouldn't know."

"Maybe this one would be better," said Rachel, picking up a larger version of the wallet. "No, maybe not. Nuns don't usually carry big purses." The man looked them over one last time, attempted a weak smile, and moved away. Rachel glared after him for a few seconds before turning to the others.

"What nerve," she said, shaking her head. She expected them to agree and to congratulate her on her audacity, as Antonella would have.

"What was that about?" asked Henry. "I told you he was watching us. Were you trying to get us in trouble or something?"

"We weren't doing anything wrong. How could we have gotten into trouble?"

"It doesn't matter what we were doing. He could have dragged us in and searched us and held us for an hour or two," said Darrin. Both boys were agitated.

"Take it easy," Damara said. "She didn't know. Come on, let's go pay for the wallet and get out of here."

"He wasn't even a real cop," Rachel said as they headed through the parking lot toward Henry's car. "My uncles call them wannabes."

"Your uncles?" asked Darrin.

"Yeah, they're detectives. They'd be furious if I told them some rent-a-cop followed me around the store."

"Your uncles are detectives? How come this is the first we're hearing it?" asked Henry.

"I don't know—I guess it hasn't come up before. Anyway, real cops have better things to do with their time than follow innocent teenagers around the mall."

"Don't be so sure," said Darrin.

"What do you mean?" Rachel asked, but no one seemed in the mood to answer and they drove away in silence, out of the suburbs and toward the city, Henry's car sounding like a hospital ward of whooping cough patients. Rachel sat in the front seat next to Henry, his grandma's afghan on her lap, and tried to ignore the melancholy that threatened to descend. She felt confused by what had happened—she had done something wrong, but she wasn't sure what. Why was Henry so quiet all of a sudden? As Rachel watched the browns and oranges of autumn give way to the one season-fits-all gray concrete landscape, she felt lonely. Henry glanced at her and turned up the radio, which was playing classic rock.

"Oh my God," groaned Darrin from the back seat, "The only thing worse than the noise this car makes is this music. Can't you find something better?"

"It's his car," said Damara.

"It's the Beatles, you cretin," said Henry. "Only the greatest rock band in the history of the universe."

"Don't call me no cretin!" Darrin exclaimed. He turned to Damara. "What's a cretin?" They laughed and the mood lightened. Henry sang along to the music, making up his own words where the lyrics were unintelligible.

Rachel shifted sideways against the door, turning so that she could see everyone in the car.

"See," Darrin complained, "that's what I'm talking about. What the heck kind of song is this about some chick coming in through the bathroom window? Put on some music that means something."

"That shows what you know. This song is an indictment of the white ruling class," said Henry, winking at Rachel. "It's just too deep for a kid like you to understand."

"Deep? The only thing deep in this car is the bullcrap you're shoveling out." Henry laughed again, pleased at the reaction he was getting from Darrin, who, for all his complaining, seemed to be enjoying himself, too. "I'll tell you what's deep—your stomach is deep," Darrin muttered, launching into a string of fat jokes directed at Henry, who laughed them off lightly. Damara smiled and shook her head. The more Rachel got to know Damara, the more she liked her, maybe because Damara reminded her of herself. Rachel was thankful that the tension had dissipated. Finally, Darrin ran out of wisecracks, reached into the pocket of his hoodie and pulled out an iPod.

"Lucky I carry my own music with me," he said, putting on the earphones and relaxing back into his seat.

"Lucky for us," said Henry.

"Don't forget we have to stop for the card," Damara reminded after a few minutes.

"Right." Henry pulled into a spot next to a fire hydrant. "You jump out and get it, Damara. If I have to move I'll drive around the block." While they sat there Henry saw a parking spot open up a few cars down.

"I'm taking this spot," he said. "We're not that far from Sandra's—we can walk the rest of the way." He backed into the empty spot in one smooth maneuver. As they lingered on the sidewalk, waiting for Damara, Henry surveyed his car proudly. "How was that for a perfect parallel park?"

"Amazing," said Rachel. "I want to get my license soon."

"Maybe when you do I'll let you drive my car sometime."

Darrin, who had just taken his headphones off, doubled over in a loud guffaw. "Man, I thought you liked the girl. Now it turns out you're trying to kill her."

"Real funny. You can laugh while you're walking home tonight. Come on, Rachel, here's Damara." He took Rachel's arm and led her away as if Darrin were contagious. Darrin followed, still smirking when they trudged up the stairs to Sandra's third-floor apartment.

"Come on in," Sandra said, opening the door. "Mommy, they're here!" she shouted. Rachel smelled the familiar aroma of onions and garlic frying. "Take off your shoes—my grandmother's a fanatic about keeping the carpet clean." Rachel had already begun to kick off her low-cut suede boots before Sandra finished speaking.

"Bossy," said Darrin, the last to comply.

"He's just worried his feet smell," said Henry.

"Don't start, you two," said Sandra. "We have work to do. Henry and Darrin, I need you to hang these streamers—you're tall enough not to need a ladder. Rachel and Damara, you can help me finish the banner. Did you get the gift?"

"Oh, we got the gift all right," Darrin said. "And we almost got busted, too."

"Huh?"

"Aren't you going to introduce me to your friends?" A petite women, dressed in a pink cowl-neck sweater and a straight brown skirt, swept into the room.

"Everybody, this is my mom," Sandra said. "Mom, meet Rachel, Henry, Damara and Darrin. Damara and Darrin are brother and sister, and Rachel and Henry are not related, at least, not yet." Rachel felt her face flush.

"Sandra, why do you embarrass your friends?" said Sandra's mother, brushing her daughter aside. "Ignore her, please. How about something to eat?"

"Relax, Mom, I'm just kidding. And no food until we get this work done. Let's get going." Sandra handed the boys a roll of crepe paper streamers and some masking tape, then continued giving them directions while they looked more and more annoyed. She ended with "And don't use too much tape, we just painted."

"We get it, Sandra," Henry said flatly. "Why don't you go wrap the gift or something?"

"And make sure you twist the streamers before you tape them," Sandra replied.

Darrin stopped what he was doing. "Let me put it another way," he said calmly, "Get the freak out of my face."

"Okay, okay, I know I'm hyper. I just want it to be perfect for Sister Gloria." Sandra walked across the room to an oak desk and fished around in a bottom drawer until she found a sheet of wrapping paper. Then she joined Rachel and Damara at the coffee table in front of the sofa, where they were coloring in the letters on a banner made from several brown grocery bags cut open and taped together. Rachel looked down the hallway to her right, wondering if Raphael would pop out from behind one of the closed doors she assumed were the bedrooms, but all remained quiet in that part of the apartment.

"So what happened with the gift?" Sandra asked in a low voice. "What was Darrin talking about?"

Rachel and Damara exchanged an uncomfortable look before Damara answered. "We didn't almost get busted, but we were being watched at the store."

"And I guess I made it worse by being rude to the guy, sort of," Rachel explained.

"Anyway, he left us alone and nothing bad happened," said Damara.

"I still say that real cops would never follow kids around a store for no reason," Rachel said. This time Damara and Sandra exchanged a look.

"Rachel, you are naïve, even for white girl," teased Sandra. She put the finishing touches on wrapping the present and read the card silently. "Very nice. How should we sign it?"

"How 'bout, 'Thanks for bringing us together'?" Damara suggested.

"Sounds good to me," said Rachel. "How old do you think Sister Gloria is?"

"I don't know. It's hard to tell a nun's age, since they don't wear make-up and they always wear the same clothes. I'd say in her forties somewhere," Sandra said, just as Henry and Darrin, finished with their assignment, joined them at the table.

"Forty years old and never had a man," said Darrin.

"Hey!" exclaimed Sandra, "That's disrespectful. You don't talk about nuns that way."

"Stop showing off, Darrin," warned Damara.

"Besides, you don't really even know that's true. She wasn't born a nun," said Sandra.

"Can we change the subject?" Henry asked. "This is grossing me out."

"All done?" An older woman entered the room carrying bowls of chips and salsa. She looked very much like Sandra's mother, except that she was a little shorter and a lot wider. Both women wore the same short hairstyle, but while Sandra's mother had dark brown hair like Sandra, this woman's hair was frosted blond.

"Thanks, Buela," said Sandra. "This is my grandma, everyone. Buela, meet Henry, Rachel, Damara and Darrin."

"Pleased to meet you. Here's a little snack to keep you until dinner," she said, putting the chips down. Henry and Darrin dove in as if they hadn't eaten in weeks.

"Now let's see," said Sandra, "we'll need to hide when she gets here. Where can we all fit? The closet?"

"Are you crazy? You want all of us to squeeze into a closet with that?" Darrin pointed at Henry's stomach. "Do you want us to suffocate?"

"No more closets for me," said Henry, winking at Rachel.

"Okay, okay. If we pull out the couch we can hide behind it. Come on, guys, give me a hand."

"Are you sure about this?" asked Damara when they had positioned themselves crouching behind the sofa.

"We don't want her to have a heart attack or anything."

"Yeah, that'd be great—'Surprise! ... Oh my God, call 911!'" quipped Henry. Rachel giggled, lost her balance and tipped over, taking Sandra down with her.

"I can see tomorrow's headlines—'Nun Dead, Teens Arrested.' Get off me, girl," Darrin said, giving Sandra a push.

"Just another black-on-black crime statistic," followed Henry.

"Will you two shut up?" said Sandra in a frantic whisper. "I hear something." They listened intently to the sound of footsteps approaching the door. A woman's voice echoed down the hall. "Olivia, get your butt down here!"

"That don't sound like no nun to me," said Darrin.

"That's my neighbor." The sound faded as the woman passed. "Wait—here comes somebody else. This must be her." Again they waited in silence. This time the footsteps stopped in front of the apartment.

"Get ready," whispered Sandra.

"My foot is falling asleep," said Darrin.

They heard a jingling sound outside the door.

"Does Sister Gloria have a key?" asked Henry. The doorknob turned and in walked Raphael. A groan rose from behind the couch.

"What's going on?" Raphael asked.

"It's Sister Gloria's party, remember?" Sandra answered. "Close the door." No sooner had Raphael pushed the door shut when, once again, they heard footsteps approach.

"This has got to be her," said Sandra. Sure enough, a few seconds later there was a knock at the door.

Raphael stood uncertainly. "What should I do?"

"Not too much going on upstairs, huh?" sighed Darrin.

"Answer it!" said Sandra in a stage whisper.

Raphael slowly opened the door. "Surprise!" Sandra shouted and popped up from her hiding place. She rushed at a startled Sister Gloria and ushered her into the room. The others followed weakly.

"Happy birthday!" Sandra exclaimed. "Mommy, she's here!"

"Well, thank you. What a nice surprise!" said Sister Gloria. "And how wonderful to see all of you."

"Are you feeling okay?" asked Darrin. "You don't feel faint or anything, right?"

"I'm fine, Darrin," said Sister Gloria. "Although I'm not exactly sure why you're asking."

"Welcome, welcome!" Sandra's mother and grandmother rushed at Sister Gloria and the crowd parted like the Red Sea. Each of the women took one of Sister Gloria's arms and led her into the dining room, where the table had been set with their best china. Sandra had, of course, seated Rachel next to Henry. On her other side was Raphael, as quietly beautiful as Rachel had remembered. The idea of talking with him made Rachel quiver inside, but fortunately for her Henry kept her occupied with a torrent of topics ranging from what movie he wanted to see next weekend to how he might get his car to last through college. Rachel was thankful to be rescued from her own awkwardness. As the plates were being cleared Rachel heard her cell phone ring in the next room. It was Nana.

"I'm fine," she said. "No, we didn't have sauerbraten—I found out they're not exactly German. I'll tell you when I get home. I'll get a ride. I'm not sure what time. Don't worry, Nana, I'll be fine. Bye."

"Everything okay with your Nana?" asked Henry, who had followed Rachel into the living room.

"The usual. She's worried about how I'll get home later."

"So am I driving you home, or do you want to be dropped off at the mall again? I doubt it will be open, but maybe you can do some midnight window shopping." Rachel thought she heard an unusual edge in Henry's voice. Her mall diversion hadn't fooled him one bit. She tried to read his face. Was Henry hurt, or irritated, or both?

"Maybe we should talk for a minute." She sat down on the sofa and motioned for Henry to join her. Sounds of dishes clanging and lighthearted conversation came from the kitchen. How could she make sense of her family for Henry when she hadn't even figured them out herself? "It's not about you," she began, "it's just that my family is really overprotective." Rachel felt as if she'd used that word at least a hundred times in the last few weeks. "I mean, picture a mother bear protecting her cubs on one of those nature programs, then times it by about two hundred. That's my Nana. And my uncles are worse."

"Is it because I'm a guy, or because I'm black?"

Rachel hesitated, but she knew she had to answer Henry honestly; he deserved that much, at least. "Both, I guess. They don't mean any harm, but they're just really old fashioned. It's like being raised by Rocky Balboa."

"Rocky Balboa wasn't racist."

The word took Rachel's breath away. She tried to inhale, but she felt as if her airway had closed. She stared down at the orange pumpkins on her socks, trying to think of an answer. Finally, a feeble "They're not racist," was all that she could manage.

Henry softened a little. "Look, I'm not trying to insult your family, but what else would you call it? They don't want you hanging around with a black guy, it's as simple as that."

"But you don't know them! They're really good people."

"You're right, I don't know them, and it doesn't look like I'll ever get the chance to, does it?" Henry spoke with calm resignation. He shifted his gaze away and fiddled with the initial ring he wore on his right hand.

Again, Rachel searched unsuccessfully for words. She felt like she was on the witness stand, wanting to defend her family, but deep down knowing that Henry was right—they would not have understood her friendship with him. Sitting there, the next room bursting with noise and her loving family a phone call away, Rachel felt absolutely alone. For weeks she'd been lying to people, but she saw now that she'd mainly been lying to herself. She'd told herself that race didn't matter to her family, but she knew that it did. Rachel could hardly picture how they would react if they saw her get out of Henry's car, but she knew it wouldn't be pretty, and it wasn't just because he was a guy. Without a doubt if Henry and the others had been white she would have invited them over by now and Nana would have stuffed them full of pasta and meatballs, overjoyed to have new mouths to feed. But *racist* was such an ugly word. *Racist* meant slurs and horrible jokes and hate crimes on the TV news. She could hardly bring herself to think the word, no less say it out loud.

"Before I met you all I never thought about race," Rachel said. "I guess I just thought of my family as old fashioned. It was easier that way. But I see what you mean, Henry. I'm sorry." She was certain that she had lost Henry's friendship—how could she expect him to be friends with her after she'd hurt him this way? Rachel's throat tightened and her nose began to run, a sure sign that she was about to cry. She searched around the room for a tissue to stave off the oncoming flood.

"Hey," said Henry, handing her the box of tissues from the end table next to him, "take it easy. It's not your fault." He slid his foot over to hers and nudged her gently.

Why did Henry have to be so nice all the time? The look on his face only made Rachel want to cry more. She blew her nose and tried to regain her composure. "So does that mean you're okay with it?"

Henry thought for a moment. "No," he said, "I'll never be okay with it, but it's not the first time and it won't be the last. Anyway, we all have crazy stuff to deal with. I guess I just needed you to be straight with me, that's all." He looked like he might have reached over and touched her if they hadn't been interrupted by a loud crash coming from the kitchen, followed by Buela's even louder voice. "Ay, Sandra, you're lucky that wasn't my china. You're like an elephant bumping around my kitchen."

Rachel giggled through her tears.

"I guess we'd better get in there before Sandra thinks we're having a lovers' quarrel," Henry said.

"So you've noticed her subtle attempts to push us together?"

"Sandra is as subtle as a brick flying through a window." He stood and Rachel followed, gathering up the wad of tissues she had accumulated on her lap.

"Henry, thanks," she said.

"For what? All I did was make you cry."

"For not hating me. And for helping me face the truth."

"Yeah, well, that's something we've all got to do from time to time." Rachel thought she saw a flicker of sadness in Henry's eyes, but when she looked more closely it was gone.

When they came back into the dining room Sandra was too busy ordering people around to notice that Rachel had been crying, but Damara looked at her long and hard. She said nothing, but brushed Rachel's hand with her own as she went to take her seat. Along with a store-bought chocolate cake, Buela served something called *flan* for dessert, which reminded Rachel of vanilla pudding.

"Thank you for the delicious meal," Sister Gloria said, finishing her last sip of coffee. "And thank you," she continued, turning to Rachel and the others, "for the great surprise. It was so wonderful of you. Will I see you all again on Thursday?"

"We'll be there," said Henry.

"You don't all have to leave yet, do you?" asked Sandra after Sister Gloria was gone. "Come on, let's play a game." Rachel glanced at her watch—it was only 8 p.m. I guess nuns go to bed early, she thought. She figured she had a good couple of hours before Nana sent the uncles out to look for her.

"We'll play in my room," Sandra said.

"Keep the door open," her mother called after them.

"What is it with adults and doors?" asked Darrin. "Do they think we tear our clothes off and break out the crack every time a door closes behind us?"

"They think you do," said Henry. "The rest of us are guilty by association."

"Okay, let's play," said Sandra once they were seated on the floor in her room. She reached under her bed and pulled out a Jenga game. Rachel felt a layer of self-consciousness wrap itself around her like a second skin when Raphael sat down next to her, close enough so that her knee touched his. Henry, who had found a paperclip in the thick ivory carpet, tossed it at Rachel; it missed her face and went down the front of her shirt, landing in her bra. No one but Henry noticed Rachel fish it out.

"That's a handy place to keep your stationary products," he said, laughing.

"Pay attention, Henry," Sandra interrupted. "This is Jenga Truth or Dare. There's a store-bought version, but we made up our own." Sandra built a tower with the small wooden blocks as she spoke. "You play it just like regular Jenga, except you have to either answer the question or do the dare printed on the block. If you pick a blank block you don't have to do anything."

"So you sat there and wrote on all those blocks?" Darrin asked.

"Yeah, me and Raphael did. What's so amazing about that?"

"It's only amazing to a person who doesn't know how to write," said Henry.

"I meant because the letters are so tiny, so why don't you go check out the drive-thru, fat boy?"

"That's original."

"Please!" Sandra begged. "Stop the fighting and let's play. Rachel, you go first."

"Okay." Rachel selected a block with no writing, pulled gently, and squealed when the stack came crashing down.

"Maybe I forgot to mention that the object of the game is to avoid toppling the pile over," said Sandra, stacking the blocks again.

"I was trying to get a blank one," said Rachel.

"Try again, and this time don't knock the whole thing down."

Rachel surveyed the tower, looking for a block she could remove without a crash. She chose one from the top. "'When was your first kiss?' I knew this would be embarrassing. First kiss—what exactly does that mean?" Rachel knew very well what it meant, but she hoped that if she hemmed and hawed long enough the question would go away.

"It doesn't mean a peck on the cheek," said Sandra. "You know, a real kiss, like maybe when you're hiding in the closet with someone."

Rachel tried to ignore Sandra's remark. "Okay, you're not going to believe this, but I guess I'm still waiting for it."

Everyone in the room had a different response. Sandra, skeptical, smirked and nodded. "Sure," she said. Darrin hooted as if he had just won the lottery. Damara met Rachel's eyes kindly, but was quickly distracted by Darrin's hooting and glared at him, covering her ears. Henry, too, looked sympathetic, but also, somehow, relieved. But it was Raphael's reply that Rachel noticed.

"I think that's sweet," he said in a soft voice. That was it, but, coupled with his dimpled half-smile, it was enough to make Rachel's heart race.

"Somebody else go," she said.

"I guess it's my turn," said Henry. "'Imitate a pop star,'" he read from a block. "That's easy. Do I have to stand up?"

"Please don't," said Darrin.

"Okay, here goes." He cleared his throat, closed his eyes, and burst into falsetto. "'*Oh, I wanna dance with somebody, I wanna feel the heat with somebody. Oh-oh, I wanna dance with somebody, with somebody who loves me...*'"

Now it was Darrin who covered his ears. "Ugh, please. You would imitate a girl, too."

"Damara, you go," said Sandra. Damara studied the tower intently, checking it out from every angle. Rachel knew that she was looking for a blank block so that she would not have to answer a question. In Damara, Rachel had finally met someone more reticent than she was. Apparently, Darrin had received all the noisy genes in the family.

"Go, slow-poke!" he shouted.

"Okay, I see one. 'What's your biggest fantasy?'"

"That's easy," said Henry. "It's gotta be that you're an only child."

"Yeah, that's it," Damara laughed. She put the block down as if her turn were over.

"Not so fast," said Sandra. "You have to answer for yourself. Come on, Damara—we all have fantasies."

"All right—I guess my biggest fantasy is that I'll get into a top music college, like Julliard."

"That's not a fantasy," said Henry. "With your voice you will get in."

Damara brushed over the compliment. "You go, Darrin." With very little effort, Darrin chose a blank block and the play passed to Sandra.

"This one is a dare," she said. "'Trade an article of clothes with someone.'"

"Okay," said Darrin, "now we're talking."

"Rachel, hand over a sock."

"That's it?" Darrin asked, disappointed. "Don't you have to trade shirts or something?"

"In your dreams. Go, Rafe."

"'What's your deepest, darkest secret?'" Raphael read. "For real? Do I have to answer this?"

"It's okay if you don't want to," said Sandra.

"What? How come Damara had to answer but he doesn't?" Darrin's voice rose as he spoke. "That's not fair! Either he's playing, or he's not."

"It's only a game, Darrin," said Damara. "It doesn't matter."

"No, he's right," said Raphael. "I'll answer." He stared at the block for a second. "I guess my deepest, darkest secret is that I was almost a dad." Even Darrin was quiet now. "My girlfriend got pregnant, but she decided not to go through with it." Raphael shrugged and Rachel felt torn between her desire to comfort him and her shock at what he had revealed. She realized that her fantasy about Raphael was about to fall to pieces as certainly as the Jenga stack.

"I was almost an aunt." Sandra looked off into space, looking sad for the first time since Rachel had met her. The others waited awkwardly. Finally, Henry spoke.

"Well, this is a fun game."

Sandra laughed. "Oh well, it is what it is, right? Your turn, Rachel."

"'What is your biggest *dissapointment?*'"

"More stupid questions," Darrin complained. "When is someone going to get a good dare?"

"Shut up, Darrin," said Sandra without even looking at him. "Go ahead, Rachel."

"You spelled disappointment wrong. It's one s and two p's."

"So you can spell. Stop avoiding the question and answer. And don't tell us it's that your best friend moved away," said Sandra. "We already know that. Find something else."

"Why don't you just answer for everybody, Sandra?" asked Henry. "Think of the time we could save."

"Shut up, Henry. Go ahead, Rachel."

"Bossy," mumbled Darrin.

"Let's see … my biggest disappointment … okay, I guess really my biggest disappointment is that I never got to know my mom or my dad."

This was something Sandra could sink her teeth into. "What happened to them?"

"My dad got shot—he was a cop. I'm not really sure what happened after that. I guess my mom freaked out or something and left me with my grandparents. Now she's dead, too. I don't remember either one of them."

"Did you ever try to find your mom?" asked Sandra.

"Nope. My Nana removed every trace of her when she left and I learned pretty early not to ask about her. I always pictured her in my head, though, as this beautiful woman, but then I realized one day that I was picturing the woman from the Jello commercial." Rachel had been looking down as she spoke; she glanced up at Henry and noticed that, as usual, his eyes were locked on her face. She looked away again.

"I guess that's it," Rachel said. "For a long time I day-dreamed that my mother would come back for me some-day. Finally, my Uncle Johnny told me that she died, too, but I'm not sure how."

"Don't you want to find out? What if she had some horrible disease that's hereditary?" asked Sandra.

"Sandra, stop," said Damara.

"What's the difference? My dad couldn't help it, but she had a choice and she left me on purpose. That's all I need to know." Rachel felt that she might cry for the second time that evening.

"People don't always have as many choices as you think," said Henry.

"I guess. Anyway, you go."

Henry, Damara, and Darrin pulled blank blocks and it was Sandra's turn again.

"'What is your dream come true?'" she read.

"God, Sandra, all these questions are the same!" exclaimed Darrin.

"Next time you write them. This is an easy one—it's that we find a house we can afford."

"You're moving?" asked Rachel. She was just getting to know Sandra—would she be moving away now, too?

"Yeah, but not far," said Sandra. "When my grandpa passed away he left us all some money. So we're using it for a down payment and we've been looking around for a house. That's why I had to leave the fair early that day."

"The house next door from me is for sale. Maybe you could buy it," Rachel said eagerly. The idea of Sandra filling Antonella's empty house fit like a missing puzzle piece sliding into place. It would be perfect. She was surprised at Sandra's hesitation.

"I don't know … I think my mom wants to be closer to Center City. But I'll tell her—thanks, Rachel."

"And besides, isn't your neighborhood too white for them?" Darrin blurted out.

"My neighborhood isn't all white," said Rachel weakly. "There's Fred."

"Wow, lucky Fred," said Darrin.

"It's okay, Rachel, you meant well," said Raphael. He chose a block and smiled as he read, "'Kiss another player on the lips.' Hmm, this is a tough choice." He looked around the circle, eyes sparkling.

"Now why couldn't I get that one?" asked Darrin.

"Okay, Darrin, if you insist…" Raphael motioned toward Darrin as if he were going to hand him the block, but grabbed his hand, pulled him across Sandra's lap and bent down to fake a kiss instead. Darrin jumped away with the force of a tsunami. "Hey, get off me, man!" he yelled, and although Raphael had not actually touched his lips, Darrin wiped away at them furiously. "Are you crazy?" he spat. Rachel laughed, but didn't stop wondering if Raphael would choose her.

"Come on, Rafe, you have to kiss someone for real," said Sandra.

"Yeah, *Rafe*, and stay the freak away from me," warned Darrin.

"Sorry, man, it was just a joke. Okay, well, I guess I have two choices, and they're both so beautiful it's hard to decide." Raphael looked back and forth from Rachel to Damara, and Rachel couldn't stop herself from staring at the curl of his hair and the color of his eyes. It would be so easy for him to lean over to kiss her—he would hardly have to move at all. Maybe tonight would be her first real kiss, and with the most beautiful boy she had ever laid eyes on. Raphael made his decision; he crawled across the circle on his knees to Damara, kissed her gently on the lips, and crawled back to his own place again.

"Somebody open a window," said Henry. "It's getting hot in here." He picked up a TV listing that had been lying on the floor nearby and fanned himself, sending some of the breeze over to Rachel for good measure.

"Rachel's turn," Sandra said. Too disappointed to care, Rachel chose a block at random, pulled it out, and the remainder of the tower fell into a heap.

"Thank God," said Darrin. Enough of this weak game."

"We'd better go," said Damara.

Twenty minutes later Rachel sat alone in the car with Henry; since Darrin had a strict curfew, he and Damara had been dropped off at home first. "So where to?" he asked casually.

Rachel glanced at her watch—10:15. Too late to call home for a ride from the mall. "Would you mind driving me all the way?"

"You're sure it's okay?"

"I'm sure," she said, although she didn't feel sure at all. But by the time they reached Rachel's house Grampy was in bed, Nana was sleeping in front of the TV, and the uncles weren't home. No one saw her get out of Henry's car. She felt as if she had lived through a year in the hours since Uncle Johnny had dropped her off at the mall that morning. Maybe she still hadn't been kissed, but she'd grown up in another way. She got ready for bed, but made a quick entry in her journal before turning out the light.

Dear Dad,

Sixteen and still never been kissed, although I came close tonight. You're probably happy.

I have to ask you something, Dad. Here goes—are Nana and Grampy racist? What about Uncle Tommy and Uncle Johnny? Were you racist, Dad? Am I?

Your speedy reply would be greatly appreciated.

Love,
Rachel

Chapter 11

Visits

Time, which had passed so slowly at the beginning of the school year, now hurtled toward Thanksgiving. Rachel managed to meet up with Henry almost every weekend, sometimes joined by the others, but often it was just the two of them walking around the city. Although Henry still picked her up at the mall, he drove her straight home at night. He stopped far enough away from the house, though, so that no one could see who was driving.

"Did Tina Marie drive you home?" Nana asked one Saturday evening when Rachel came in.

"Yeah. Her car died so she's driving her brother's for now. He's away at college."

"It doesn't sound so good," Nana commented absentmindedly. She was too involved in her TV show to notice the guilty look on Rachel's face.

The night before Thanksgiving, Rachel helped Nana in the kitchen.

"Why do we have lasagna on Thanksgiving?" she asked. "I'm always so stuffed by the time we get to the turkey that I can't even enjoy it."

"Your grandfather likes lasagna, that's why. Here—cut up these apples." Nana passed a stainless steel bowl filled with peeled apples over to Rachel, and then rolled out the first of several pie crusts on the counter.

"Will you be putting tomato sauce in the apple pie?" Rachel asked.

"Very funny." Nana placed the wooden rolling pin in the center of the flattened crust and pushed out in quick, even movements, which reminded Rachel of rays jutting out from the sun. "So how's your friend Sandra? You never did tell me about the party at her house."

After her talk with Henry that night Rachel knew that she would need to be honest with Nana, but she preferred to do it in her own time. In a way she was glad that Nana brought up the subject now; they were alone in the house, and baking never failed to brighten Nana's mood.

"Oh yeah, I forgot all about it," she answered, careful to keep her tone casual, and trying desperately to remember what she had told Nana before the party so as not to contradict her story now. "I thought the party was for Sandra's cousin, but it was actually a surprise party for Sister Gloria, the nun that works at the school." Nana could hardly object to a party for a nun.

"That sounds nice. And where does Sandra live?"

"She actually lives a ways from here, but she's moving. Her family is looking for a house."

"How could she go to your school if she lives 'a ways from here'?"

"Did I say she goes to my school? I meant that I met her through a program at school—you know, that after-school club that I joined."

"Oh." So far so good. Nana still didn't know where the club met, but that piece of information would be better saved for another time. "And where exactly is 'a ways from here'?"

"Somewhere closer to the city."

"And how did you get to this 'somewhere'?"

"Nana, stop repeating what I say. My friend drove us—there were a bunch of us from the club that went."

"What friend?" Rachel would have to think quickly before this conversation spiked out of control.

"Just this kid that you never met." Rachel hated herself for describing Henry as 'this kid,' but her immediate goal was to introduce Nana to the idea of Sandra, and she needed to deal with one new friend at a time. "Anyway, remember I said I thought Sandra was German or something? I don't know why I thought that, because she's actually Puerto Rican! Isn't that hysterical?"

"I don't see what's so hysterical." Suspicion was dawning in Nana. "Slice those apples thinner or they'll never cook. So what kind of a neighborhood does Sandra live in?"

"Oh, just a regular neighborhood with stores and everything. You should see Sandra's apartment—she lives with her grandmother, too—isn't that amazing? And their apartment is really nice—her grandma cooks and cleans like crazy, just like you. She made this delicious meal—have you ever heard of flan? It's sort of like vanilla pudding, but better." Rachel chattered on and on, sprinkling compliments at Nana now and then. "We chipped in and gave Sister Gloria a wallet for her birthday. She really liked it."

"That's nice."

"I thought I might invite Sandra over sometime soon. You wouldn't mind, would you?"

"Why would I mind? Your friends are always welcome here."

Rachel took a chance. "I mean, because she's Puerto Rican."

Nana stopped rolling and looked up. "I have nothing against the Spanish," she said. "You know, Spanish is very close to Italian."

"What about Grampy?"

"Don't worry about Grampy. I'll take care of him. Rachel, I knew something was bothering you over the past few months—is this what it was? Were you afraid to tell me about your new friend?"

"Well, sort of." Rachel hadn't counted on Nana being so receptive. Should she continue with a full confession, or quit while she was ahead?

Nana continued. "There's good and bad in all kinds, that's what I always say." Although Rachel had never heard Nana say that, she didn't interrupt. "I've met some Italians that I wouldn't give a nickel for. You invite Sandra over any time you want."

Rachel felt a burst of relief. This was too good to be true; Nana was practically shining with tolerance and goodwill. Why had she been so worried all these months?

"Thanks, Nana, you're the best. Oh, remember I said Sandra's family wants to buy a house, right? Well, I told them about Antonella's house being up for sale. They don't know if they want to move this far away from the city, but wouldn't that be cool? It would be so great to have a friend next door again, and then we really could go to the same school. I gave her the address and her mom's going to check it out."

Nana's face underwent a total eclipse. She frowned, positioned the next ball of dough on the counter top, and struck it in the middle with her rolling pin. "Rachel," she said, "that's not such a good idea. You have to understand about property values. If the neighborhood changes, the value of our home goes down. It's all well and good to be friendly, but what about us and our neighbors?"

"What do you mean?"

"People work all their lives to afford a house in a nice neighborhood. Like Grampy did."

Rachel stopped slicing apples. "I don't see what that has to do with Sandra. She's not going to do anything to your house."

"I'm sure Sandra is a very nice girl. But we've been through this already, Rachel. We saw our block change right in front of us—other people moved in and everything went down. We barely managed to sell in time."

"That was a long time ago, Nana. Things are different now. What about Fred? He's lived down the block for years, you never seemed to mind that."

"Rachel, I have nothing against Fred, and I have nothing against your friend Sandra. But we have to be careful, that's all. One or two people don't make a difference, but if you get too many, it could be a problem."

"But it's not fair. Why shouldn't Sandra's family get to live anywhere they want?"

"What about what's fair to us? Look, we don't have much, Rachel, but we have this house. It's our only real investment. You can't blame us for wanting to protect it."

I can blame you for being racist, Rachel thought, but then hated herself for thinking it. She tried to erase the ugly word from her mind. After all, this was Nana, the woman who had painted her toenails and braided her hair and peeled the cloud decals off the ceiling of her room when Rachel had grown tired of them. She was just old, that's all, and old people are stuck in old ways. Then she remembered her talk with Henry and she wasn't so sure. She tried to imagine what he would think, but she didn't have to try very hard. He would have no trouble seeing through Nana's excuses.

"Are you finished with those apples?" Nana asked. "The crust is ready."

Uncle Tommy had invited a guest for Thanksgiving dinner—Joan, the woman he'd been dating. There was a time, remembered Rachel, when female guests of the uncles, infrequent though they were, excited her. She'd size them up as potential aunts, figuring that even though an aunt wasn't as good as a mother, she was better than nothing. She knew that before she was born Uncle Tommy had been married briefly, and sometimes she'd pictured his wife as a nameless, faceless figure, like an outline in a sticker book waiting to be filled with a paper face and body.

Rachel ate quietly, listening to Nana grill Joan on her knowledge of cooking. When Joan claimed that lasagna was one of her favorite dishes to make, Nana pounced.

"What kind of sauce do you use? Probably from a jar, right?"

"No, actually I make my own sauce."

"Really. A young girl like you knows how to make sauce from scratch? That surprises me."

Joan, who didn't look all that young to Rachel, laughed. "I'll take that as a compliment."

"So, how do you make your sauce?"

"Excuse me?"

"I always like to learn from other cooks." That would be like the Pope learning how to say Mass from a church mouse, thought Rachel. She helped herself to another sliver of lasagna and waited for Joan's response. Uncle Johnny caught her eye and smiled.

"Well, I start by sautéing an onion in some oil."

"What kind of oil?"

"Olive oil. Then I guess I add the tomato puree…"

"What about the garlic?"

"Ma, for God's sake!" interrupted Uncle Tommy. "Can we change the subject? Joan can e-mail me her recipe tomorrow if it's that important to you."

"Don't be rude," said Nana. "I was only making conversation."

"Actually, Tom loves my sauce, don't you, Tom?" Uh-oh. The mouse had roared, but was about to be trapped. Poor mouse. Poor Uncle Tommy. He was in a no-win situation and he knew it.

"Mmm. Pop, what time is the game on?" he asked.

"Six," answered Grampy. It was the first word he had spoken since they sat down to eat.

Joan continued. "In fact, he said it was the best he'd ever had."

Nana took a second to compose herself. "He's always been such a polite boy," she answered with a benevolent smile. Conversation over, go in peace, Joan, and thanks be to God. Rachel could barely contain a giggle.

"Rachel, did I tell you that the Fatagatis are stopping by tomorrow? Or maybe Antonella told you herself."

"I haven't talked to Nella for a while."

"They were our neighbors for years," Nana explained to Joan as if the previous tête-à-tête had not taken place. "Antonella is Rachel's best friend."

"Was," corrected Rachel, but no one paid attention.

The next day Rachel tried to feel excited about seeing Nella again, but the only feeling she could muster was anxiety. Had Nella changed in the months they'd been apart? Would she look the same? Would she notice that Rachel had gained a few pounds this fall? Rachel remembered Antonella's frequent pep talks about keeping in shape, and how she'd dragged Rachel out of bed for early morning jogs around the neighborhood. Eager to please, Rachel had readily acquiesced to these bouts of fitness, even though she hated panting to keep up while Antonella glided effortlessly through the quiet streets. Now the memory of it left her feeling slightly humiliated, as if she'd been tethered to Nella like an overgrown dog on a leash. She found herself calling Sandra.

"Remember the friend I told you about that moved away? She's coming for a visit today."

"Cool. How was Thanksgiving?"

"It was good. Anyway, it's been so long since we've seen each other. I'm a little nervous."

"Nervous? I thought she was your best friend."

"She was. It's just that she's so perfect, and I think I've gained weight since she left."

"Are you saying that hanging around with me made you fat?" Sandra laughed.

"My Nana took care of that a long time ago. I wish I'd gone on that diet I saw online—the one with the grapefruit."

"Rachel, what is this, a freaking beauty contest? She's your friend, isn't she? What does she care what you look like?"

"I know, you're right. I'm being stupid. It's just Nella is so perfect…"

"You said that already. I don't get it—there must be some reason you were friends with her all those years."

After they'd hung up Rachel thought about Sandra's words. Of course, there were a million reasons Antonella had been her best friend. Unfortunately, at that moment she couldn't think of one of them.

Rachel changed out of sweatpants into her best jeans, laying flat on her bed and sucking in her stomach as she inched the zipper up. When the Fatagatis arrived, Nana greeted them as if they were lost sheep returning to the fold, but to her disappointment Antonella's parents refused any offer of food.

"We're just stopping by for a few minutes. We have dinner reservations after the show later," said Mrs. Fatagati.

"A little snack then, to tide you over," said Nana.

"No, really," said Mrs. Fatagati, "we just ate. If we eat another thing we'll explode."

Nana agreed, but placed a tray of cookies on the table anyway, which Mr. and Mrs. Fatagati reached for immediately.

"Let's go upstairs," said Nella, "before they detonate."

"So how've you been, Rach," she asked once they'd settled in. "We haven't talked for a while—sorry, I've been so busy. You're not still pining away, are you?"

"I'm fine. Actually, I'm great. I've been busy, too."

"Good for you. What's up at school? Any new hookups?"

"I'm not sure. I haven't been hanging out with kids from school much."

"So what have you been doing? Not sitting home studying all the time or going to the movies with your uncle, I hope."

"No. Remember that club I told you about? I ended up joining, and I've been hanging out with the friends I made there."

"Club? What club?"

"The one that Sister Gloria runs—remember her, the nun from the multicultural program?"

"Oh yeah, I forgot about that stupid program. Thank God they don't have it at my school. I do remember—you called me about the club one night, right? I remember I told you to forget about it—so you decided to go anyway?"

Antonella seemed shocked that Rachel had not followed the advice that she hardly remembered giving.

"Yeah. I've been hanging out with the kids I met there."

"Oh."

"Don't say anything to your parents, though, because I haven't exactly told my family the whole story yet."

"Why not?" Antonella grinned. "What could you be doing, Rachel, that you're afraid to tell them about?"

"I'm not doing anything wrong, but you know how they are. I'm afraid they'd freak out if they heard I was hanging out with black kids, well, not all black—Sandra's Puerto Rican—and you know, going to the city and everything."

"Oh," Antonella said again. "Rachel, I don't get it. Are you okay? I feel like after I left you kind of went off the deep end. I'm sorry I didn't call you—it's just that I got so busy."

Here she was, on the witness stand again, trying to explain one world to another, just like in her conversation with Henry. This time, though, Antonella was the prosecutor, judge and jury all rolled into one.

"All I've done is make some new friends. What's wrong with that?"

"I don't know—it just seems weird, that's all."

"Nella, let's go!" Mrs. Fatagati called up the stairs.

Antonella stood. "Listen, call me. I promise I'll answer from now on." She gave Rachel a quick hug and was gone. Rachel unbuttoned her jeans the minute Antonella left the room.

Dear Dad,

Nella was here today. I know she thought I was weird, but to me she seemed like the weird one. Being with her made me feel bad—fat and ugly, to be exact. Have I changed, or has she? Or maybe I just never noticed it before. Sandra eats what she wants and she never thinks about weight—neither does Henry. You'd like them, Dad. I know you would.

Love,
Rach

Chapter 12

No Home for the Holidays

Rachel never found out if Antonella meant to keep her promise, because she didn't call her. Their brief visit had left her feeling depleted, and she had no desire to repeat the experience.

Rachel had chosen Henry's name for the club holiday gift exchange. She wandered through the mall with Uncle Johnny one Friday night, trying to decide on a gift for Henry and drifting aimlessly from store to store while waves of people pushed past them.

"Hey Rach, want to go see Santa?" Uncle Johnny asked.

"Aren't I a little too old for that?"

"Come on, you're never too old for Santa. This isn't the real Santa, of course," said Uncle Johnny. "The real one is much too busy in his workshop this time of year to be at the mall."

Rachel laughed. "I remember when you used to tell me that."

"So what are you asking Santa for this year?"

"I don't know … let's see. I kind of have everything I need." When she was little Rachel used sit at the kitchen table with Uncle Johnny and write her list of toys for Santa, knowing that she would receive every last one of them on Christmas morning. She always made a second list, though, which she kept in her head and didn't share with anyone. That list contained just two items—a mom and dad. As she got older she continued to write a Christmas list, although the items on it changed every year, but the second list faded from her memory. Rachel didn't know why she'd thought of it now.

"You'd better think of something!" said Uncle Johnny. "Christmas is almost here."

"How about peace on earth? Or even better, racial equality for all?" Rachel didn't know why she'd thought of this, either; she certainly hadn't planned on saying it.

"Huh?"

"Never mind. Let's go. I have shopping to do." She grabbed Uncle Johnny's arm and dragged him from Santa, back into the crushing current of the mall.

The following Thursday Rachel and her friends sprawled on the familiar red sofas and exchanged gifts. Michael Jackson sang "Santa Claus is Coming to Town" in the background, and the usual chocolate chip cookies were replaced by candy canes and star-shaped sugar cookies.

"Hello everyone—Merry Christmas," said Sister Gloria, entering the room. She sat down on the sofa next to Sandra. "Sandra, tell us about your search for a house. Have you found anything yet?"

"Not yet. My mom says it's a bad time of year—people are busy with the holidays. A lot of people wait till spring to put their houses on the market. We might have better luck then." Rachel remembered her conversation with Nana. She looked away, hoping someone would change the subject.

"We've made a lot of calls," Sandra continued. "We even called about the house next door to Rachel—imagine that! They said it sold already, though. I wonder who your new neighbors will be, Rachel."

"Oh … I didn't know it sold."

"That's what the man said, anyway."

"I'm sure things will pick up after Christmas," said Sister Gloria. "Does anyone have any special plans for the break?"

"Our Christmas program is coming up at church," said Damara. "You're all invited—it's next Sunday night."

"Damara's too shy to tell you, but she leads the whole kids' musical," said Henry. "It's really good—you should come. Maybe you could come to my house for dinner first." The invitation was for everyone, but Henry looked at Rachel as he spoke.

Rachel sensed the familiar inward squirm that came when the group made plans. She would need to construct a story for Nana.

When she got home later the first thing she did was check the realtor's sign in front of Antonella's house. There was no change, no SOLD in big bragging letters pasted over the original sign. She questioned Nana about it as they cleaned up after dinner.

"Did Antonella's house sell?"

"Not yet. It's a bad time of year—people are busy with the holidays."

"Yeah, I heard that," said Rachel.

"Pass me that pot." Rachel took the pot from the stove and placed it on the counter next to the sink with a little more bang than usual.

"What's wrong with you?" asked Nana.

"Nothing. I've got homework." She brushed past Grampy on her way out of the kitchen, shaking off his hand as he reached to pat her head.

"What's wrong with her?" Rachel heard Grampy ask on her way up the stairs.

"Hormones, I guess," replied Nana. Rachel closed her door and put the TV on loudly enough to drown out the sounds of her family below her.

Chapter 13

Stories

Henry lived in a three-story Victorian with a rounded tower at the side and a wraparound porch trimmed with wooden spindles in front. Painted in an elaborate pattern of dark red, yellow and muddy brown, it stood out imposingly from its neighbors. While the other houses on the block were marked by peeling paint and overgrown shrubs, Henry's house had an air of majestic dignity. As Rachel walked up the steps, she noticed a small porch on the second story as well.

"I love this house," she said to Henry. "It reminds me of a castle."

"A castle? It's just an old parsonage that's falling apart. When my dad is home he spends most of his time fixing stuff."

"I love the colors."

"You wouldn't love it if you had to help paint it."

When they entered the hallway, Henry hung Rachel's jacket on a coat stand positioned in the corner like a sentry. Rachel could see Darrin and Damara already sitting in the living room, chatting with someone whom she took to be Henry's father. He looked very much like Henry (or Henry looked like him)—tall and large enough around the middle to make the buttons of his white shirt strain when he laughed, as he was doing now.

"Oh, Henry, here you are," he said. "Introduce me to your friend."

Mr. Sayers shook hands with Rachel and invited her to sit down. The room seemed small to Rachel, but she couldn't stop herself from looking at the high ceiling edged by carved wood molding.

She heard footsteps coming down the creaking staircase. Henry's grandparents joined them, dressed in their Sunday best. They sat next to Damara, asking about the musical—how many numbers was she leading? Who'd be playing piano? Would she be singing a solo tonight? Rachel listened quietly, trying not to feel like an outsider.

Sandra arrived just as they were sitting down for dinner. Henry's mom lit red and green taper candles in crystal candle holders, while his dad served them soda in ruby glass goblets. Rachel placed her gold cloth napkin in her lap.

"So, Reverend and Mrs. Sayers," Sandra blurted out, looking toward Henry's grandparents, "how did you two meet?" It was such a random question, and asked with such conviction, that everyone burst out laughing.

"Tell us your story," Sandra persisted. "I love romantic stories."

"You are a funny one, Sandra. But okay, here goes." Henry's grandma told of a hot summer day fifty years ago, when she and Rev. Sayers met. She described every detail completely, from the blue gingham cotton dress she was wearing to the sheets she was hanging out to dry when a young man with slicked-back hair and a suitcase full of Bibles knocked on her door. Rev. Sayers joined in now and then, adding or changing some detail that his wife had forgotten, the two of them sharing the spotlight like partners in an intricate dance. Rachel listened intently. Henry's grandparents must be about the same age as her own, she thought, but she had never heard Nana and Grampy talk like this. They never reminisced about anything, their conversations usually consisting of questions, instructions, or commands. She realized that she'd never tried to picture them young, and that she didn't even know how they'd met—she'd assumed that they'd always been as they were now—old and cranky.

"Wow," said Sandra when Mrs. Sayers had finished, "that was great."

"Oh well," she answered, waving her hand in dismissal, "everybody's got a story." Do they? wondered Rachel. Do Nana and Grampy have a story? Do I?

She was still thinking about it on the way to the church later, sitting next to Henry in the front seat of his car.

"Isn't it funny that we all live with our grandparents?" asked Rachel.

"I don't," said Darrin.

"I mean Henry, Sandra and me. I just think it's kind of weird."

"You mean like fate drew us together?" asked Henry.

"Yeah. Something like that."

Rachel had been sorting through a mental list of her old friends, and she couldn't think of a single one who lived with her grandparents. In fact, living with Nana and Grampy had always made her feel different, like she wasn't exactly normal. Henry's family was different too, she realized, and so was Sandra's. Maybe she wasn't so abnormal after all.

The church was packed with people who looked to Rachel like they were dressed for a wedding. Since Henry had warned Rachel to dress up, she had worn one of the few skirts she owned. Unfortunately, he had forgotten to tell Sandra, who was dressed in jeans and a pink Penn State hoodie. Sandra didn't seem to notice, though. She led them to an empty pew in the back of the sanctuary with the confidence of a long-time church member.

"Wow," Rachel whispered, "it's so crowded." She saw Henry's family walk up the center aisle to the second pew, where an usher dressed in a black suit and white gloves greeted them.

"Welcome, Reverend Sayers," said the usher. "Please be seated." He removed a RESERVED sign from the pew and Henry's family took their seats, smiling and nodding to those seated around them.

"It looks like they got the place of honor," said Sandra.

"Black churches always make a big deal over visiting ministers," explained Henry. "It's just a thing."

Rachel watched the children's choir take the platform, led by Damara. About thirty kids dressed as angels, shepherds, sheep, and wise men filed in, followed by Mary (holding a baby doll wrapped in a blanket) and Joseph. In the middle of the third song Mary tripped and almost dropped the baby Jesus, but fortunately Joseph made a last minute save before Jesus hit the floor, grabbing the infant Savior by the foot and flinging him back up to the Blessed Mother. A little girl dressed as an angel stood at the very front. She was under the watchful frown of an older girl, but that didn't stop her from jumping straight up and down to the beat of the music, holding on to her silver garland halo with one hand and her aluminum foil wings with the other, and pausing periodically to yank at her tights from under her angelic robe. Rachel, Henry, and Sandra were overtaken with an uncontrollable fit of giggling. They laughed as quietly as they could at first, heads down and hands over their mouths, but the more they tried to hold back, the giddier they became. People around them turned and stared at Sandra, who was snorting like a pig. Rachel's neck ached from the tension of trying to stop from giggling through the rest of the musical program, but then the preacher approached the pulpit, and when he started his sermon Rachel sobered up. She'd heard plenty of sermons before, but never one like this. He was so loud and fiery, pacing back and forth in a half speaking, half singing voice. She wasn't sure what he was saying, but she knew it wasn't funny. Henry paid rapt attention, smiling at her once in a while. Finally, the preacher finished, the benediction was pronounced, and they found their way to Henry's family, standing in the church foyer.

"I'll be back in awhile, after I drive the girls home," Henry said.

"Be careful," said Mr. Sayers. "Remember what we talked about."

"What did your father mean?" Rachel asked once they were outside.

"The usual warnings."

Rachel wasn't sure what the usual warnings were, but she didn't ask. She settled in for the ride, taking for granted that Henry would drive Sandra home first. Henry's car sounded louder than ever, sputtering and coughing through the silent winter streets.

"Thanks for the ride, Henry," Sandra said when they'd pulled up to her building. "Now, you two don't get in any trouble on the way home." Keys in hand, she slammed the car door, ran across the sidewalk and disappeared into the building.

"She never gives up, does she?" Henry said, driving away.

"I guess she can't figure us out."

"We should pretend to be together, just to drive her crazy."

Rachel decided to take a risk. "That's what we'd be doing—pretending, right?"

"What do you mean?"

"It's just that I can't really figure us out, either. I've never been friends with a guy like this before. That's what we are, good friends, right?"

Henry's voice turned serious. "Yeah, we're friends. What else would we be?"

Rachel shifted in her seat. "Well, I can see how Sandra might think we're together. You do pay a lot of attention to me. I mean, you can see how she might get the wrong idea." Henry was quiet. "This is embarrassing," Rachel continued. "I shouldn't have said anything."

"Sandra can think what she wants," Henry said after a few seconds, "but you know we're just friends, right? But good friends—really good friends." He glanced at Rachel with concern.

"Yeah, I guess, but it did take me awhile to get used to it. When we first met I did wonder if you liked me."

"I do like you."

"You know what I mean—I thought maybe you *liked me* liked me. Forget I brought it up. It doesn't really matter now, anyway."

"Okay. But I didn't hurt your feelings or anything, right?"

"No."

"I mean, it's not that you're not hot."

"Come on, Henry, I know I'm not hot. Antonella was hot."

"Who cares about Antonella? You've been ruined for life by one skinny white chick. I think you're really pretty."

"It doesn't matter. Let's forget it."

"It does matter. You're pretty. Lots of guys would want to go out with you."

"You just said you didn't."

"That's different. There're things you don't know about me."

Rachel laughed. "Like what? Don't tell me—you're married and you have three kids, right?"

Henry did not join in her laughter. "No. Like maybe I'm not sure about myself yet…I don't know…I might be…questioning." It was Rachel's turn to be surprised. They were on the expressway now, and Henry started to pick up speed. "It's not like I've ever done anything. I just feel confused sometimes, like maybe I'm different." He stared straight ahead as he spoke, his words accelerating with the car. "I've never told anyone before. You met my family—can you imagine what they'd say? Can you imagine what guys like Darrin would say?" Henry sounded so sad. She had no idea how to respond, so she nodded.

"I guess you're shocked, huh?"

"A little." Rachel was shocked, but she tried not to show it. She thought back to their conversation at Sister Gloria's birthday party. "We all have crazy stuff, remember?" she said. "You told me that yourself."

"Well, now you know how crazy my stuff is."

"Yeah. I guess it is pretty crazy."

Henry laughed. "Thanks. I feel much better."

"Sorry—not crazy, just different. Let's not worry about it right now, okay?"

"Okay."

When Rachel tiptoed through the back door she was glad that Nana was asleep in front of the TV, since she was in no mood to talk. She got ready for bed and thought of writing in her journal before turning off the light, but decided she was too tired. So many new experiences in a few short hours—and now this weird conversation with Henry. She needed time to sort it all out. She slid under her comforter and drifted off to sleep.

Chapter 14

Caught

How did you and Grampy meet?" Rachel asked Nana the next morning. She sat at the island counter, watching Nana move between a pan of scrambled eggs and a bowl of sugar cookie batter.

"What? We never actually met."

"So you've been married for all these years to someone you've never met? Come on, Nana. Think back."

"Our parents were old friends. I guess we grew up together. Here—eat your eggs."

"Thanks. So when did you fall in love?"

"Why are you asking all these questions?"

"I just want to hear your story."

"What story? We got married. We had children. You came along and here we are."

"But why did you get married? There must have been some reason you chose Grampy. Why did you fall in love with him?"

The back door swung open and Grampy stood in the doorway, holding a bag of groceries. A gust of frosty morning air invaded the kitchen. "No graham cracker crumbs," he growled.

"What do you mean, 'no graham cracker crumbs'?" Nana took the bag and placed it on the counter. "How could that be? Where did you look?"

Grampy threw his coat over a chair and took off his work boots. "I looked up and down the cracker aisle three times. They didn't have any."

"The cracker aisle? Did you look in the baking aisle?"

"They're cracker crumbs. It stands to reason they'd be in the cracker aisle."

"They're used for baking. Now how am I supposed to make the cheesecake?"

"Make something else."

"I don't want to make something else."

"Then go yourself." Grampy sat down, ready for breakfast.

"Go wash your hands," said Nana.

"My hands are clean."

"You just came in, how could they be clean?"

"I had my gloves on the whole time."

The conversation continued this way for several minutes until Grampy gave in and headed off to the bathroom. Nana filled a plate with bacon and eggs and set it down on the table in Grampy's spot. She took his mug from the cabinet, filled it with coffee, cream, and two teaspoons of sugar, and heated it up in the microwave for exactly twenty-six seconds. Grampy returned to the kitchen, sat down to his breakfast, and opened the newspaper, ignoring Nana's mutterings about people, common sense, and donkeys. Rachel abandoned her quest for story and finished eating in silence.

"So what's your plan for the day?" Nana asked.

"I don't know. I'm kind of tired." Rachel walked her plate over to the sink. "I guess I'll just hang out today." She stretched her arms over her head and yawned.

"Poor kid," Rachel heard Nana say as she dragged herself up the stairs. "They work them too hard at school."

It was only 9 a.m. and the long, boring day stretched before Rachel. Tomorrow was Christmas Eve. She had a few gifts to wrap, some reading to do for school, and she supposed she could always wander into the kitchen to help Nana with her Christmas baking. She knew that someone would soon be going out to buy graham cracker crumbs; maybe she should ask for a ride to the store, where she could stock up on DVDs for the break. Rachel got back into bed and tried not to think about her conversation with Henry last night. She lay there for a while, staring up at the ceiling, when she heard the muffled ring of her cell phone from her coat pocket downstairs. She jumped out of bed and ran down the stairs, missing the bottom step and stumbling through the living room on her way to the closet. She grabbed at the end table and knocked over the Nativity scene that sat on top of a mass of sterile cotton, next to Santa and his reindeer. Rachel had never been able to convince Nana that the baby Jesus had not been born at the North Pole.

"Slow down!" Nana called from the kitchen. "You're going to kill yourself."

"I thought she was tired," Grampy grumbled from behind the newspaper.

By the time Rachel got to her phone it had stopped ringing. She ran back up the stairs and was careful to close her bedroom door before she called Henry back.

"Are you doing anything today?" Henry asked.

"Absolutely nothing. I'm bored out of my mind. What's up?"

"We're putting up our Christmas tree—want to come and help?"

"Really?"

"Yeah—I always invite a couple of friends over, 'cause my Dad won't yell at me in front of them."

"Why would he yell at you?"

"You know—'Hold it straight, son. Straight, I said! Don't you know what straight means?' The tree is usually so big that we have to bolt it to the wall so it doesn't tip over."

"You get a real tree? Ours is fake, and we put it up the day after Thanksgiving."

"We always wait till my dad gets home from his last run before Christmas. Anyway, want to come? I invited Sandra, but she's busy this afternoon. She can meet us for a movie later."

"Sounds good. Can you pick me up?" Rachel didn't bother asking what movie, because the truth was she didn't care. Anything was better than doing nothing at home all day.

"Yeah—the usual spot?"

Rachel hesitated. Although she had let Henry drive her home under the cover of darkness, she wasn't quite ready to be picked up by him in broad daylight. After the holidays, she told herself.

"Are you okay with that?" she asked Henry.

"Fine. See you around one."

Several hours later Rachel sat in the front of Grampy's truck, trying to be patient as he inched his way through the congestion of cars and pedestrians that engulfed the mall.

"They must be giving something away," Grampy said.

"It's Christmas, Grampy. People shop. I'll just get out here."

"Okay, baby. What time should I pick you up?"

"I'm going to a movie later, remember? I'll get a ride home with Tina Marie."

"Be careful." Grampy leaned over and kissed Rachel on the top of the head.

"I will," Rachel answered. She ran between the stopped cars toward the mall entrance, hands in her pockets because she had forgotten her gloves. Knowing that Grampy would watch until he thought she was safe, she turned and waved at him as soon as she reached the curb. Satisfied, Grampy rejoined the slow procession of cars trying to leave the site. Rachel waited nervously. She thought she'd given herself enough time between being dropped off by Grampy and picked up by Henry, but she hadn't counted on all this traffic. It was already after one o'clock, and if Henry got there on time there was a chance Grampy would look into his rear view mirror and see his old white car pull up in front of Rachel. Would he be able to see who was driving? What if Henry got out of the car?

Henry, though, was not on time. Rachel stood in the cold, trying to stay out of the way of the people rushing in and out of the mall. She held the door open for a woman pushing a stroller piled so high with packages that the baby was nowhere in sight. A full fifteen minutes later, Henry arrived.

"It took forever to get here," he said as he leaned over to open the door for Rachel from the inside. "Come on, we have to hurry—my dad doesn't like being kept waiting."

"Good luck with that," answered Rachel. "Traffic has been crawling since I've been here. I guess it's the last minute Christmas rush."

Henry forced his way into the flow of cars leaving the parking lot. His car chugged and sputtered as if every move might be its last. Henry ignored it and turned up the radio. There was no humming or singing along, however; Henry was too tense for that. After a few minutes they made it to the boulevard that encircled the mall and merged with yet another line of cars moving in slow motion.

Henry's cell phone rang.

"It's my dad," he said. "Hello? I'm on my way—there's traffic. Okay. I will." He hung up, flicked his turn signal down, and turned to wave at the driver of a minivan on his left, looking for an opening to change lanes. The driver frowned, but let him in the lane. "He didn't sound too happy," Henry said. "He wanted to get the tree done by early afternoon." More horns honked from behind, this time in small clipped toots.

"I'm sorry I made us late. Your dad's not going to be mad, is he?"

"He'll get over it. And it's not your fault there's so much traffic."

"I should have known the mall would be crazy today. I shouldn't have made you pick me up here." Rachel shivered.

Henry tossed her the afghan that was balled up on the seat between them. "It's okay. We're moving along now. We should be there in another six or seven hours at the most." He glanced sideways at Rachel and smiled.

Snow fell in big, wet flakes. Within ten seconds Rachel's cell phone rang. She rolled her eyes. "Hi, Nana. Yes, I see the snow. Yes, I'll be careful. Yes, she's a very good driver. Okay. Okay. I will. I have to go now, Nana. Bye. Love you, too. Bye."

"*She's* a good driver? Who's *she?*"

"They think I'm with my girlfriends." Rachel shifted under the afghan and stared out into the snow. "I'm sorry, Henry. I'm going to tell them about you after the holidays. I promise."

"I get it—you don't want to ruin Christmas, right?"

"I didn't say that. I just need a little more time, that's all."

Henry didn't answer and they drove around to the entrance of the expressway, headed toward the city. After a few minutes traffic subsided a bit and Henry accelerated, moving into the left lane. The back tires skidded on the slippery road, but Henry steadied the car without losing control.

"Be careful!" Rachel said again.

"Sorry. I'm getting new tires for Christmas." He eased up on the accelerator and moved back into the right lane. Rachel watched Henry, and Henry watched the road, concentrating on driving in the thickening snow—or maybe he was pretending to concentrate to avoid talking to her. Rachel wondered why this friendship was getting so complicated. Had she hurt Henry's feelings this time? She'd detected that sad look in his eyes again, but she had no idea what to do about it—should she say something more, or leave it alone? This was all so new to her. With her old friends, she'd been a minor player—a piccolo fluttering in the background of Antonella's fully resonating flute. They hadn't cared enough about what she thought to be affected by it one way or the other. Now she felt powerful and powerless at the same time. They drove along without talking, Rachel feeling guiltier by the minute. Finally, she had to speak.

"Henry," she began, "listen..."

"What could you want?"

Rachel was stunned. "Huh?"

"Not you, him. Turn around."

There, through the clouded, dripping windshield, Rachel saw a police car following them closely, lights flashing. Its siren gave two quick yelps.

"Shoot," said Henry. "What did I do?"

"He's probably just trying to get out of this traffic," said Rachel. "My uncles do that all the time. Pull over to the shoulder and he'll pass you."

Henry obeyed, careful to put on his right turn signal first. The police car pulled over behind him. "I don't think he wants to pass me," he said.

"Don't worry, cops stop people all the time during the holiday season. You didn't do anything wrong."

Henry put the car in park and rolled down his window. "Of course, he'd be white," he muttered under his breath. Rachel looked at him in surprise. What did that have to do with anything?

The officer stooped down and peered at them through the window. He looked familiar to Rachel, but she couldn't quite remember where she'd seen him before. She knew, though, that he had to be somehow connected with her uncles. "License and registration," he said. His voice was very distinct and Rachel searched her memory, trying to place it. For some reason she thought of Frank Sinatra, although this cop looked nothing like him, and didn't sound like him, either. Henry took his wallet out of his back pocket and handed his license to the officer. Then he reached past Rachel's knees into the glove compartment, the officer watching his every move. His first attempt at opening the glove compartment door failed.

"The latch gets stuck," he explained weakly. "I have to bang it." The officer nodded and Henry gave the door a solid blow with the side of his fist. Several CDs spilled out onto Rachel's legs. The cop watched Rachel gather them up, and even though it was broad daylight, he shined his flashlight in on the wires hanging from the dashboard. Henry fished around until he found a small folder containing his car registration. He handed it to the officer.

The officer glanced back and forth from Henry, sitting still as stone, to the picture on the license, comparing them until he seemed satisfied. Then he looked over at Rachel, now holding the CDs in a pile on her lap. Rachel thought she saw a flicker of recognition in the officer's eyes, followed by a trace of puzzlement. He'd realized that he knew her from somewhere too, but it had probably been several years since he'd seen her, maybe when she was much younger. She hoped he wouldn't remember her enough to realize who she was. He started to say something to her, but then thought better of it and turned back to Henry.

"Have you been celebrating the holidays early today?" he asked.

"No, sir," Henry replied without making eye contact. Rachel, too, looked away, still hoping to avoid detection. She knew she needed to keep quiet and let the officer do his job as quickly as possible so that they could move on to their afternoon plans. She still felt sure this was just a routine traffic stop.

"I saw some erratic driving back there. How do you explain that?"

"I guess I skidded in the snow." Rachel heard the anxiety in Henry's voice; she wished there was some way she could calm him down.

"You did more than skid," said the officer. His voice grew more determined, and again, Rachel heard Frank Sinatra in her head. Suddenly she remembered the officer's off-key karaoke version of "My Way" at a party her uncles had dragged her to the Christmas before last. He'd gotten so carried away with the emotional finish of the song that he'd stood on a chair, eyes closed under a lopsided Santa hat. She remembered Uncle Tommy next to her, hooting with laughter. If Henry hadn't been so nervous Rachel might have giggled.

The officer, however, couldn't have been more serious. "Do you know you could have caused a major accident back there?" he asked. What was he talking about? Henry had changed lanes twice, both times using his turn signal and checking his blind spot. Was this cop trying to provoke Henry into an argument?

Henry didn't answer. He reminded Rachel of a kid who'd been sent to the principal's office. She felt herself wanting to defend him.

"Where are you headed in such a hurry?" the cop asked. Rachel was sure they hadn't driven over thirty miles an hour the whole time she'd been in the car.

"Just going home from the mall." Only Henry's lips moved; he didn't turn his head or change his facial expression in any way. His fists were closed tightly around the steering wheel. Rachel felt herself getting annoyed. She looked into the officer's face and frowned. He noticed.

"And what about you, young lady? Are you going home, too? Do your parents know where you are?" Rachel knew she looked young for her age, but surely not too young to be out with a friend in the middle of the afternoon. What was this cop's problem?

"We haven't done anything wrong," she said flatly. Henry shot her a pleading glance, which she ignored. Didn't this cop have better things to do? Why didn't he go chase some real criminals, like her uncles did every day of their lives?

"Is that right?" the cop answered. "I guess, since I'm wearing the badge, I'll be the judge of that." He stared at Rachel, trying to remember her. Rachel smoldered right back at him, mouth set in a firm line. "How about some identification?" he asked finally.

Rachel opened her purse and fished for her school ID. She knew there was a strong likelihood this cop would recognize her last name, but now she was too annoyed to care. In fact, part of her hoped he would. She knew Uncle Tommy was farther up on the pecking order than this guy, and she wanted to see him embarrassed that he had hassled them for no good reason. Sure enough, as soon as he read her license Rachel saw recognition register on his face.

"Matrone, huh? Are you related to Tom Matrone?"

"He's my uncle."

"Your uncle, huh?"

"That's right."

"And does your uncle know where you are right now?" The cop looked over at Henry.

"I can't see how that's any of your business," Rachel replied. She heard Henry gulp for air, but she continued to meet the officer's steady gaze.

"We'll see about that." He shifted his eyes back to Henry. "I'm going to give you a warning this time, but if I see you on the road again without fixing this muffler you'll get a citation for disturbing the peace. Do you understand?"

"Yes, sir," said Henry, visibly relieved. "Thank you."

The officer scribbled on a pad, ripped off the top page and handed it to Henry. "Now get this hunk of junk off the road before I change my mind."

"Thank you," Henry said again. The officer gave Rachel one last stern look, and again, Rachel looked steadily back at him, not trying to hide her displeasure. Finally, he turned and walked to his car, stepping on the balls of his feet; Rachel sensed he was still listening, waiting for a reason to turn back. Henry stared into the rear view mirror until the police cruiser pulled off the shoulder and disappeared into the traffic. The snow had stopped by this time and the sun glimmered along the edge of a cloud, trying to grant some light to the dreary afternoon. Henry said nothing. He eased the car back onto the highway and drove slowly in the right lane.

"I knew that guy," Rachel said as she shoved the CDs back into the glove compartment. "I remember him from a Christmas party. He's probably going to tell my uncle he saw me."

Henry stared at her in disbelief. "You're worried about your uncle?" he spat.

Henry was obviously still upset about their previous conversation. "Well, yeah. But I was about to say, before that cop pulled us over, I'm through lying to my family. It's terrible. You must think I'm embarrassed by you, or something, and I'm not, really. I mean, come on, this is the twenty-first century. I can't help it if they're still living in the past. I'm going to tell them all about you, all of you, over the break, and I don't care if they like it or not. They can't stop me from hanging out with you. I'm not doing anything wrong. Once they get to know you, I know everything's going to be okay." Rachel felt pleased with herself, proud of her decisiveness. She slouched back into the seat and smiled at Henry expectantly. She'd prove to him that she was a friend worth having, no matter how difficult things got at home. She knew that when her family saw how important this was to her they'd eventually come around. She didn't care how long it took, she'd make them change.

Henry's expression was cold. "Are you done?" he asked.

"Yeah, I guess. What's wrong? Come on, Henry, don't stay mad. I said I'm sorry. Things are going to change, I promise."

Henry only became more rigid. Rachel began to feel afraid in the pit of her stomach. Was it too late? Had that phone call from Nana been the last straw? Maybe she'd hurt him too deeply to be forgiven. "I'm sorry about what I said to Nana," she added.

"What are you talking about?" Henry asked, accentuating each word as he spoke. "You think I'm mad about your Nana?"

Rachel blinked. "Aren't you?"

"Do you have any idea what happened back there?"

"You mean the cop? I told you, it's okay. I don't care if he tells my uncle. I'm kind of glad, in a way."

"Your uncle? Your uncle! Who cares about your uncle? You could have gotten me into serious trouble back there!" Henry hardly ever raised his voice, but he was getting louder with every word. Rachel tried to understand.

"What are you talking about? You didn't do anything wrong."

"You just don't get it, do you? You don't have to do anything wrong to get in trouble. It's called DWB—driving while black."

"What?"

"You heard me. When a black kid, especially a guy, gets pulled over by a white cop, there's a certain way to act to avoid trouble. You gotta be respectful, and quiet. You don't give the cop any excuse to go off on you, and the last thing you want to do is smart-mouth him and try to stare him down. Are you crazy?"

Rachel thought back to the incident at the mall while shopping for Sister Gloria's wallet. "Oh," she said. "I'm sorry. I guess I forgot."

Henry sighed, and Rachel felt some of his anger dissolve. "Rachel, there're certain rules you can't forget when you're with me."

"But you act like every cop is out to get you." She thought about her uncles. "They're not all racist, you know."

"I know that, and I'm not saying they are. But you never know, and you don't want to take a chance. Why do you think my family's always warning me to be careful, especially when I'm driving in a white area? Did you think they're afraid I'll trip and skin my knee?"

"Are you saying your family doesn't trust white people?" Rachel felt herself getting defensive. "Isn't that racist, too?"

"Call it whatever you want. There's reasons. It's reality."

The prospect of an afternoon of tree decorating didn't look as inviting as it had earlier in the day, but Rachel knew there was no turning back. Neither one of them was in the mood for more conversation, so Henry turned up the radio broadcast of twenty-four hour Christmas music. Rachel tried to sort out her feelings. How could Henry be so sure that the cop's behavior was about race? What if it had nothing to do with that? Maybe he was just tired, or in a bad mood. After all, Henry's car was loud—she was sure he was breaking some law by driving it around in that condition. The cop could have given him a citation, but didn't. That had to count for something.

By the time they got to Henry's house it had stopped snowing and the sun had won the day, but Rachel still felt like she was under a cloud. Even the sight of the old Victorian didn't cheer her up much. Henry's dad, tired of waiting, had managed to get the seven-foot tree into the stand on his own.

"Well, it's about time," he said when they entered the room. "Hello, Rachel. Henry, hand me those lights." Henry obeyed, and for the next few hours they were taken up with the mechanics of tree decorating and cookie eating. Rachel welcomed the distraction from her thoughts. Henry's mother and grandmother helped, reminiscing over ornaments much in the same way Nana did when they decorated their tree at home, but minus the edge of sadness she'd always sensed in Nana.

"Will you two be eating here tonight?" Henry's mom asked.

"We promised to meet Sandra at the movies. We'll grab something there." Thank goodness they were meeting Sandra—she was just the person to make them forget what had happened that afternoon. There was no need to try to make conversation when Sandra was around, since she talked enough for all of them.

The ride to the theater was quick, and Henry seemed in better spirits. He sang along to "Grandma Got Run Over by a Reindeer" in full falsetto, glancing at Rachel now and then to see her reaction. She laughed and rolled her eyes on cue, relieved that things between them seemed to be almost back to normal. When she saw Sandra and Raphael waiting for them outside of the theater, she relaxed even more.

Before the movie started Rachel and Sandra got in a long line in the ladies' room while the guys made their way to the concession stand. Rachel looked around her—she was not the only white person in the theater, but she was certainly in the minority. She surprised herself at how comfortable she felt.

"So how was tree decorating?" Sandra asked over the sounds of flushing, running water and hand dryers.

"It was fun. Getting there was a little tricky, though."

"What do you mean? Don't tell me Henry's car stalled out again."

"No, it's just that there was a ton of traffic, and then we got pulled over by a cop on the highway."

"Oh. That's scary."

"I didn't think it was that scary, but Henry sort of freaked out."

"Was the cop white?" Sandra had a way of getting right to the heart of the matter, and, for once, Rachel was glad.

"Yeah."

"What do you expect?"

"But that's just it. The cop was a little rude, maybe, but he wasn't that bad. Henry got all nervous. Then he got mad at me after."

"How come?"

"It turned out I knew the cop from my uncles. So I argued with him a little—all I said was that we weren't doing anything wrong. And we weren't. He wound up letting us go with a warning."

"So what's the problem?"

"It's just that Henry was convinced this had something to do with race, like he was pulled over because he's black and not because his car sounds like it might explode any second. I don't get it. Anybody could have been stopped in that car. And I've heard of white kids getting picked on by cops sometimes, too. Maybe this had nothing to do with race." Rachel was so intent on her words that she didn't realize how loud she had become. An African-American woman standing in line in front of them glanced back and raised her eyebrows.

Sandra took Rachel's arm, turning her until they angled the wall. "Maybe it didn't," she whispered. "But maybe it did. That's the thing—if a white kid gets stopped, right or wrong, he knows it isn't about race. But Henry can never know that for sure, can he? In his mind, there's always the possibility that it is."

"Oh. I never thought of it that way."

"Of course not. You never had to. Go." She pointed Rachel toward the open stall in front of them and that was the end of the conversation.

Rachel sat through the movie, a remake of a holiday fantasy, thinking about what Sandra had said. By the time the credits rolled, she thought she was beginning to understand.

"You guys want to do something?" Raphael asked when they exited the theater. Rachel remembered that only a few months ago his question would have set her spinning. The crush had evaporated now, and although she still thought that Raphael was breathtakingly good looking, she'd realized that she would never go out with someone like him, even if he were interested. Which he wasn't. She inched a fraction closer to Henry and looked at her watch.

"What do you think?"

"Whatever you want—I'm cool."

"I don't know, it's getting late. Maybe next time."

"Okay," Raphael shrugged. "Have a great Christmas."

"Yeah, hope Santa brings you something good," said Sandra, hugging Rachel and Henry both at once. "Call me," she said to Rachel, and walked off, arm in arm with her brother.

Rachel leaned back into the front seat of Henry's car, covering herself with the afghan. "What a day," she said. "I feel like I've been awake for a week."

"I know what you mean." Traffic had cleared and it was a cold, brisk night.

"Henry, I'm sorry about this afternoon. I talked to Sandra and she explained things to me. I think I understand how you felt now."

"You talked to Sandra? When did you have time to do that? You sat next to me during the movie. You didn't say a word to Sandra."

"In the bathroom."

Henry laughed. "Chicks are weird. When guys go to the bathroom, we pee. You go to the bathroom and discuss social issues."

"Anyway, I think I'm getting it about the race thing. I promise I'll be more careful next time."

"I'm sorry, too," Henry said. "I guess I overreacted. Anyway, hopefully there won't be a next time." He saw Rachel's expression and hurried to explain. "Not that we won't hang out again—I mean, hopefully we won't get pulled over again. I'm getting my car fixed right after Christmas. I might even get some heat." He reached over and tucked the afghan around Rachel's leg.

"And I'm going to talk to my family, and maybe invite you all over. I promise," she replied through a yawn. "You know what I feel really bad about?"

"What's that?"

"Your family was so accepting of me. It doesn't seem fair."

Henry hesitated for a second. "Actually, my grandfather had a talk with me after they met you at Damara's church fair—he got it in his head that I was going to marry a white girl or something."

"Would they think that was so bad?"

"They're old, and they worry a lot. They're afraid it would be hard, that's all. But I convinced them that we're just good friends and they were okay about that."

Rachel didn't know whether to feel insulted or relieved. She decided to settle for tired. She could barely keep her eyes open until they reached her neighborhood, which was ablaze with Christmas lights, and turned down her street. She saw from the cars in the driveway that everyone was home, but the house was dark.

"That's strange. They must have all gone to bed already," she said. "Bye, Henry. Merry Christmas."

"You, too. I'll talk to you later." They exchanged a quick kiss on the cheek and Rachel ran down the driveway, through the yard to the back door. She fumbled with her key for a minute because her hands were so cold, but finally managed to open the door, kick off her shoes and tiptoe through the kitchen. She breathed in the scent of cookies; Nana had been baking all day. When she entered the living room she jolted to a stop. There, seated in the dark, were Nana, Uncle Tommy and Uncle Johnny.

"Hello, Rachel," Uncle Tommy said. "You want to tell us where you've been all day?"

Chapter 15

Truth Telling

Rachel flicked on the light switch behind her, and they all squinted from the sudden brightness.

"Oh, hi. You scared me. What's everybody doing in the dark?" She tried to keep her voice as even as possible. Apparently Officer Grumpy had done his work more quickly than she'd expected.

"Sit down, Rachel," said Nana. She was in her night-gown and red bathrobe, and her hair was flat on one side. Rachel could tell that she'd been to bed and up again. Nana's face was drawn with worry. Rachel sat opposite of them in Grampy's armchair. It smelled of outside.

"Where's Grampy?" she asked.

"We thought it would be better to let him sleep," replied Nana. "He hasn't been feeling great, and this would make it worse." *This?* What, exactly, was *this?* Rachel asked herself, although she knew what was coming all too well.

Uncle Tommy continued. "Now answer my question. What have you been up to?"

Rachel had always wanted to have a family meeting, but she hadn't pictured it quite this way. She steeled herself to tell the truth. "I went to my friend's house to help decorate the tree, and then I went to the movies, just like I said. I haven't done anything wrong."

"You're lying," said Uncle Tommy coolly. Rachel flinched as if he had slapped her.

"Tommy, give her a chance," Uncle Johnny interjected.

"No, he's right, I have been lying, sort of." She wished she could erase the pain she saw in Nana's face. "But I meant it when I said I haven't done anything wrong. I did go to my friend's house and the movies today."

"You were seen, Rachel," said Uncle Tommy. "There's no point lying about it."

"I was with my friend, Henry. It's his house I went to. His parents were home. You can call them if you don't believe me."

"Henry. Who is this Henry?"

"I told you, he's my friend—my good friend." *My best friend*, she didn't say out loud.

"Where did you meet this Henry?" asked Nana. "Why don't we know anything about him? And where, exactly, have you been going? You haven't spent time with any of your regular friends for months."

Regular friends? What would that make Henry—irregular? She felt herself getting impatient. "How do you know that?"

"When Uncle Tommy came home tonight we made some calls. It seems none of your friends have seen you outside of school since Antonella left. Yet, according to your story, you've been out with them almost every weekend."

"Not every weekend. I told you when I went to Sandra's house that time."

"That was once, Rachel, and even then you didn't say who else you were with. I assumed it was the girls from school." Nana's voice rose. Rachel knew she shouldn't escalate the argument, but she couldn't help herself.

"I can't help what you assume. Did I actually say I was with them?"

Nana threw up her hands and groaned, while Uncle Tommy narrowed his eyes. Rachel realized instantly that she'd taken the wrong tactic; she wasn't very good at this. Only Uncle Johnny's expression remained placid.

"Come on, Rach," he said, "you can see why we're worried. This is not like you. What's really going on?"

"Okay, I'll tell you the whole story. But you have to believe me when I say I'm not doing anything wrong."

"Never mind what we have to do," said Nana. "I'm waiting for an explanation, although I don't know what you could possibly say to explain this behavior."

So much for sincerity. Rachel took a deep breath. "Okay. It all started at the beginning of the school year, when I met Sister Gloria."

"The nun from that program?" Nana asked.

"Yeah. She asked me if I wanted to join an after-school club. You remember I told you about that, right?"

"I remember—the cooking club."

"It wasn't a cooking club, Nana. I never said that. It was a club to get kids from different backgrounds together, just to get to know each other. So I joined. The thing is, the club meetings weren't held at school, they were downtown somewhere, at Sister Gloria's office."

"Her office?" asked Uncle Tommy. "Since when does a nun have an office?"

"She has this organization—*The Tolerance Project.* So I started going to these meetings every Thursday after school, and that's where I met Henry and Sandra and the others. We became friends and we've been doing stuff together. I told you, it's nothing bad."

"Back up," said Uncle Tommy. "How did you get to these meetings?" Rachel could tell he was heading toward the topic of Henry and his car.

"They sent a school bus for me."

"For you? Didn't any other kids from school go?"

"No. No one else wanted to join. I went by myself. But they drop me off right at the door. It's perfectly safe." Uncle Tommy sighed and rubbed his eyes.

"So what have you been doing with these new friends?" Uncle Johnny asked.

"I don't know—just stuff."

"What kind of stuff?" Uncle Johnny had taken over the questioning. Rachel began to relax a little. This was almost over.

"First we all met at Damara's church and helped out at this fall fair they had."

"Damara?"

"Yeah, Darrin and Damara are brother and sister. They go to the club, too."

"Go on."

"I don't know—we hung out at the mall a little, or we walked around the city. Sandra had a birthday party for Sister Gloria right before Thanksgiving. And last night we went to the Christmas program at Damara's church. And today we went to Henry's house, and then to the movies. That's basically it."

"That's it? You're sure?"

"Of course, there's the club meetings, but now those are over until after Christmas vacation. And we talk on the phone a lot."

"And what about this Henry you've been spending all this time with? What's going on there?" Uncle Tommy growled. Rachel wished he'd stop saying *this Henry*.

"I told you—we're just friends. He's not my boyfriend, if that's what you want to know. So you see? I told you I didn't do anything wrong."

Uncle Tommy shook his head. "No, I guess you didn't, unless you count sneaking around and lying for months." His voice was laced with quiet anger.

"And going to dangerous places without permission," added Nana.

"I was never in any danger, Nana. I can't stay in the house all the time." Nana pulled her robe tighter around her chest and looked away.

"But Rach, why did you have to lie to us?" asked Uncle Johnny.

Rachel sighed. With Uncle Johnny, sometimes you had to state the obvious. "I know that was wrong. But I guess I didn't think you'd like the idea of me hanging around with black kids." There—she'd said it. "Would you have let me go if I'd asked for permission?"

Nana pretended at indignation. "Rachel, we have nothing against colored people."

"People of color," Rachel corrected.

"What?"

"Not colored people—that's derogatory. It's people of color."

Nana looked confused. "What's the difference?"

"I'm not sure. But I know there is a difference."

"What do you think this is, cultural sensitivity training?" burst in Uncle Tommy. "Rachel, this is serious. Some of the black areas in the city are not safe for you. We should know—we used to work there every day."

"I wasn't hanging around on street corners with drug dealers, Uncle Tommy."

Uncle Tommy softened. "I know, honey. But you were riding around in a broken-down old jalopy with a kid barely old enough to drive. What if this Henry's car broke down and you were stranded somewhere in a questionable neighborhood? What then?"

Rachel had no answer because, although she hated to admit it, Uncle Tommy's scenario had been a distinct possibility. They sat in silence for a minute, until Rachel noticed Nana pull a tissue out of the sleeve of her robe and dab at her eyes.

"Anyway, it doesn't matter now. Henry's getting his car fixed this week."

"It doesn't matter?" asked Uncle Tommy. "It does matter, Rachel. We still don't want you hanging around in those neighborhoods."

"What do you mean, 'those neighborhoods'? You don't even know where I've been for sure."

"It's not safe."

Rachel stiffened. "So that's it? You're saying I can't hang out with my friends any more? That's not fair!"

"Maybe not," said Uncle Tommy, "but it's reality. There's reasons."

Where had she heard that before? "What reasons?" Rachel insisted. Nana continued to wipe her eyes without looking at Rachel. Uncle Tommy's face became hard as rock, and completely unreadable. She looked to Uncle Johnny for an answer.

"It's just that there's things you don't know, honey," he said.

"What kind of things?"

"Just things."

"Uncle Johnny, what kind of things?" Uncle Johnny looked at his brother, but Uncle Tommy was still glaring at Rachel.

"Things about your dad."

What did this have to do with her dad? "What are you talking about?" Rachel was determined to get to the bottom of this.

"It's just that ... you know your dad was killed on the job, right?"

"Yes. What does that have to do with anything?"

"Well, nothing, I guess." Uncle Johnny looked down at his bare feet. Nana sobbed and wiped her nose.

Rachel felt her heart rate speed up. "Is somebody going to tell me what's going on here?" she demanded.

"There's just things you don't know, that's all," Uncle Johnny said again.

"You said that. What things?"

Uncle Johnny looked at Nana. "Things we don't want to go into right now."

"Jeez, Johnny, don't start something you can't finish," Uncle Tommy almost shouted.

"Shh," said Nana. "Don't wake your father. That's all we need right now."

"Look, Rachel," said Uncle Tommy, "it's time you learned some details." His voice was gruff, as if every word caused him grief. "Your dad was shot during a routine traffic stop downtown, maybe in the same neighborhoods you've been driving through. It was late at night, but there was nothing overly suspicious—a kid had run a red light. He was a black kid, high on crack. He had a gun in his lap and he shot your dad before he even said a word. The next day he didn't even remember it. It was a long time ago, Rachel, but some things you never forget."

Rachel needed a minute to let this information sink in. Finally, after all these years, someone had seen fit to share the story of her father's death. She'd always pictured it differently, more heroically—maybe there'd been a shoot-out in a dark warehouse over a mountain of drugs, or maybe he'd given his life to save an innocent victim in a hostage situation. But this seemed almost mundane. She thought of her father, the forever-young man in the pictures, and she found in that moment she could not stir up even a drop of emotion for him. He was long gone and she'd never known him. Then she pictured Henry, and the idea of not seeing him any more caused an ache in her throat. Her eyes flooded.

"So are you saying that all black kids are crack addicts? Do you think Henry carries a gun? His grandfather is a minister and he spends most of his time in church!" She pushed away the tears and laughed bitterly.

"This is not funny, Rachel," said Nana.

"Of course it's not. I'm telling you, you have nothing to worry about. Henry is the furthest thing from a drug addict possible. He doesn't even drink beer. If he were white, I don't think we'd be having this conversation." She remembered Antonella and her cousins sneaking beer right under their parents' noses without so much as a second thought. Again, a foreign-sounding laugh escaped from her.

"This is only about your safety, Rachel. Can't you see that?" pleaded Uncle Johnny. "Let's not make this about race."

"It *is* about race," she answered in a low voice. She'd never been so sure of anything in her life. She looked Uncle Tommy right in the eye.

"It's about safety," Nana said, now calm and determined. "Why do you think we moved to the suburbs? We wanted you to grow up in a safe neighborhood, in good schools. Look, I've had enough. I'm going to bed. There's not going to be any more sneaking around, and that's the end of it."

"I'm going to see my friends," said Rachel.

Uncle Tommy's eyes flashed. "Excuse me?"

"I'm not doing anything wrong, and I'm going to see

my friends. But you're right, no more lying and sneaking around. I'm going to invite them over. When you meet them you'll see that there's nothing to worry about."

Nana thought for a minute. She looked so old, almost defeated. "Fine. Invite your friends over, Rachel," she said, standing. "I'm going to bed." She stopped on her way to the stairs and kissed Rachel on the cheek. "Don't ever worry me like that again," she said, voice shaking.

"I'm sorry, Nana." Rachel felt tears coming once more. She watched Nana walk up the stairs slowly, holding up her nightgown with one hand and gripping the banister with the other. The flood of remorse Rachel had been holding at bay now rushed over her. Nana was the last person in the world she'd wanted to hurt. Her eyes met Uncle Tommy's again, but this time she looked away quickly.

"She's not young any more, Rachel," he said. "She doesn't deserve this."

"I said I was sorry. I won't lie to her again." She stood and turned toward the stairs.

"One more thing," said Uncle Tommy. Rachel froze. What now? "You implied something before, and we need to clear the air. We're not racist. This is not about race."

Rachel did not answer. Apparently, something she'd said had hit home.

"Rachel," said Uncle Johnny, "we work with black cops every day. It's never been a problem."

"*Work* with and *friends* with are two different things," Rachel said.

"I'm friends with Fred," Uncle Johnny offered.

"Lucky Fred," Rachel murmured.

Uncle Johnny pretended not to hear. He walked over to Rachel and embraced her.

"Good night, honey," he whispered. "I love you—never forget that."

"Love you, too," she answered dully. "I'm tired. Good night." Uncle Johnny headed toward the kitchen, but Uncle Tommy didn't move. Rachel felt his eyes on her as she walked up the stairs to her room. She glanced at her watch, wondering if it was too late to call Henry.

———

Dear Dad,

So they finally decided to tell me how you died. It must have been horrible. I'm so sorry.

Rachel put down her pencil. She couldn't think of anything else to write.

Chapter 16

Dinner

True to her word, the day after Christmas Rachel approached Nana about inviting her friends over for dinner.

"I told you, Rachel, your friends are always welcome here. Invite them whenever you want."

"Uh—what about Grampy?"

"What about him?"

"He'll be here, too, right?"

"I can hardly ask him to leave, Rachel. This is his house."

"What I mean is, he's not going to act all weird or anything, is he?" Rachel pictured Grampy moving through the house in a silent, angry stomp. She didn't want to expose Henry and the others to that; it would be worse than never inviting them at all.

"Your grandfather will be fine. I'll talk to him."

"Thanks, Nana. And I'm really sorry about everything."

Nana acted as if everything were normal throughout the blur of holiday goings-on—exchanging gifts, greeting visitors, and of course the constant cooking and serving of delicacies. Behind the façade Rachel saw the strain, but she was determined to make things work. As for the uncles, Rachel supposed they would have seemed normal too, if she didn't know them so well. Uncle Johnny was overly talkative and festive, hugging Rachel every time she turned around. Uncle Tommy, on the other hand, was more quiet than usual, and Rachel caught him eyeing her more than once when he thought she wasn't looking. Late one afternoon when Nana had assigned Uncle Tommy an errand, Rachel followed him out to his car.

"What are you staring at?" she'd asked, wrapping her arms around her chest to shield herself from the wind.

"Rachel, go inside. You'll freeze out here."

"I will when you tell me what you're staring at."

"I don't know what you're talking about. I'm not staring at anything. Go inside." He turned to get into his car.

Rachel stood her ground. "Yes, you are. I feel like I'm being inspected for damage."

Uncle Tommy turned back toward her, a sour smile playing on his lips. "Maybe you are damaged ... how would I know?" he hissed. His words stung far worse than the cold. "I'm not sure I know who you are anymore."

"I guess I can say the same," Rachel mumbled.

Uncle Tommy's anger melted. He put his keys in his jacket pocket and walked to Rachel, encasing her in his arms. "I'm sorry, babe," he said. "I didn't mean that." He rubbed her shoulders and turned her back toward the house. "I'm just worried, that's all. You mean everything to us, you know that, right?"

"Uncle Tommy, please stop worrying," Rachel pleaded when they'd stepped inside the hallway. She wiped away a tear with her hand. "I told you, I'm not doing anything wrong."

"I know you're not. Okay, I'll try to do better, I promise. Do you forgive your stubborn old uncle?"

"You're not that old. But you are stubborn."

"Maybe that's where you get it from," he said. This time his smile was tender.

"Me?"

He released her and opened the door, ready to step back outside. "It seems you're stronger than I thought. It's gonna take some getting used to, but maybe it's a good thing. Now let me get out of here."

"Who's letting the cold air in?" Nana shouted from the kitchen. "Tommy, did you get the wine yet?"

"I'm on my way," he yelled back. He gave Rachel a final wink and was gone.

She called Henry that night.

"When can you come over?" she asked.

"Really? No more keeping it on the down low?"

"Nope. I'm inviting you all over for dinner. I hope you like Italian food," she added, knowing full well that Henry was not a picky eater. They chose a night later that week, and the next day she left messages with Sandra and Damara, inviting them and Darrin as well. Sandra returned her call, accepting immediately, but Damara didn't get back to her. Oh well, Rachel thought, maybe she's busy. She texted the invite instead of leaving another message.

She'd still heard nothing from Damara a few days later when she joined Nana on their annual gift-returning expedition at the mall. As they shopped Rachel kept watch on her cell phone.

"Shoot," she said, juggling the phone with her packages and the pretzel Nana had bought her. "My battery died."

"You'll just have to survive another hour without talking to your friends. How did we live without cell phones? Let's get a soda."

When they returned home Uncle Tommy greeted her with a message.

"Your friend called. She said your cell's not working."

"What friend?"

"What's her name again? Shaniqua?"

"Do you mean Damara?"

"Yeah, whatever. All those names sound the same to me."

"Uncle Tommy!"

"Okay, okay! Relax, I'm kidding. You gotta admit, it is a different name."

Rachel felt herself getting angry. "No different than Antonella. You never made fun of that name."

Uncle Tommy surrendered. "You're right. I'm sorry. I shouldn't have made fun of your friend's name. It won't happen again, okay?" He sounded truly sincere.

Rachel frowned and stalked away to her room, taking the cordless phone with her.

On the night of the dinner Rachel paced back and forth from the kitchen to the living room, looking out the window and listening for Henry's car.

"Rachel, for goodness sake, you act like the Queen of England is coming to dinner. If you need to walk, at least get some plates and set the table while you do it," Nana said. "What are you so nervous about? I've fed your friends before."

"Not these friends. Grampy will behave, right?"

"What do you think we are, monsters? Grampy will be fine. He hardly talks at dinner, anyway. You know that."

Rachel heard a loud knock at the door and jumped. She looked out the window again and there they were—Henry, Sandra, and Damara, standing on her doorstep.

"Hey. I didn't hear your car. Where did you park?"

"Right there," Henry answered, pointing to the end of the driveway. "Is that okay? Because I can move it if you want."

"It's fine. It's just that I didn't hear your car. Do you understand what I'm saying, Henry? I didn't hear your car!"

"Oh! Yup, it's all fixed. Now we're driving in style!"

"I wouldn't go that far," said Sandra. "It still rattles when you stop at a light, but at least it's a quiet rattle. So Rachel, aren't you going to invite us in?"

"Oh—sorry." Rachel hadn't realized they were still standing in the doorway. "Come on, I'll take your coats." She led them through the living room and into the kitchen, where Nana stood wiping her hands on her apron.

"Hello, everyone," Nana said. There was a formal ring to her voice, as if she were standing in front of a microphone, addressing the PTA about the results of the bake sale.

"Nana, this is Henry, Sandra and Damara."

"Nice to meet you, Mrs. Matrone," said Henry. He moved closer to shake her hand.

"My, aren't you polite," said Nana. Rachel felt a smidgen of discomfort; Nana sounded different, more prim and proper somehow.

"Rachel, go call your grandfather and your uncles. Won't you all sit down?"

Uncle Tommy, Grampy and Uncle Johnny converged on the dining area from three different directions. Henry shook their hands as Rachel introduced them.

"Rachel, hand me the plates," said Nana, standing at the counter. "I'll dish out the lasagna from here."

"So, tell us about yourselves," Uncle Tommy said. He spoke in the plural, but looked only at Henry. Sandra answered.

"Sure. What would you like to know?"

"Are you all juniors?"

"Yes, one more year in purgatory," said Sandra. Uncle Tommy laughed.

"Rachel loves school," Nana said. Rachel rolled her eyes.

"Any college plans yet?" It was becoming clear that Uncle Tommy was the designated speaker for the family.

"I'll probably wind up at the community college, at least to start. It's what we can afford, and besides, my SAT scores aren't that great yet," said Sandra, who had apparently assigned herself the same role for the younger side of the table.

Uncle Tommy looked at Henry. "And you?"

"I'm not sure yet. Maybe Morehouse, if I get in."

"I'm not sure, either," Damara said, speaking for the first time. "It depends on scholarships."

"Morehouse, huh?" Uncle Tommy remained focused on Henry. "That's an all boys' school, right?" His eyes lit up as if this were, for some reason, good news.

"Yes. It's where my grandfather went."

"Rachel tells us your grandfather is a minister."

"That's right."

Rachel glanced over at Grampy, who had just finished his last bite of lasagna. He handed his plate to Nana; she walked to the counter, refilled it, and handed it back to Grampy. Neither of them spoke a word.

"Mrs. Matrone, this lasagna is delicious," said Sandra. "My grandmother is a great cook, too. Maybe you could teach me how to make this someday."

"Thank you, dear. It's nice to meet some young people who aren't afraid to eat. Rachel's friend Antonella always picked at her food—I guess that's how she stayed so thin. That was Rachel's best friend—she used to live next door."

"Oh yes, we've heard all about Antonella," said Sandra.

"So where is his church?" Uncle Tommy continued his conversation with Henry as if they were alone in the room.

"It's over toward Germantown."

"And how long have you had your license?" Now we're finally getting to it, thought Rachel. The inquisition has officially begun.

"Maybe you could pull up Henry's driving record down at the station, Uncle Tommy." Rachel tried to infuse her voice with sarcasm, which Uncle Tommy ignored.

"Would you mind?" he asked innocently. "I'll be back in a few minutes." He held out his hand to Henry, whose eyes widened in surprise. Henry reached toward his back pocket.

"Henry, he's kidding," said Rachel. "Uncle Tommy, stop."

Uncle Tommy chuckled and went back to his lasagna, and Henry laughed, too.

"I gotta admit, that was good," he said to Uncle Tommy. "You had me for a second."

"So tell us what it's like to be the grandson of a minister," said Nana. "That must be an interesting way to grow up."

"I guess so. To me it just means I'm expected to be in church a lot, and we get to live in a parsonage."

"You should see Henry's house," said Rachel. "It's really big, and it has a tower, and it's painted different colors."

"One of those Victorians over in that part of town, I bet," said Uncle Johnny. "I love those big old houses."

"You would," said Uncle Tommy. Rachel threw him a warning look. He shrugged and reached for the bread.

"And do you have services often?" Nana asked.

"Well, Sunday morning, of course, and Sunday evening, and Wednesday night prayer service."

"My, how religious," Nana said, reverting back to her prim voice.

"Tell me about it," Henry sighed. He was so genuine, so open, that Rachel couldn't hide the warmth she felt for him. She smiled and leaned in to Henry's shoulder. Henry smiled back at her. Uncle Tommy stared.

"And that's not all. Sometimes there's special services, like the one coming up this week, on New Year's Eve."

"You're telling me that you spend New Year's Eve in church?" asked Uncle Tommy.

"Yup. They call it a Watch Night Service. Don't ask me where the name came from. It's actually pretty cool—choirs come in from all over the city. Damara's choir will be there. The music is great." He looked at Rachel. "I was thinking that you all might like to come."

"Maybe," said Sandra, "if I can drag Raphael with me."

"Raphael?" Uncle Tommy was instantly suspicious—another male name had entered the fray.

"He's my brother. Can I have some more lasagna?" Nana rose to dish out another round of pasta.

"Is that the brother that couldn't make it tonight?" asked Uncle Tommy.

"No, that's Darrin," said Rachel, talking rapidly. "He's Damara's brother. He's part of the club, remember, I told you? Raphael isn't."

"I see," said Uncle Tommy. Rachel wondered what, exactly, Uncle Tommy thought he saw. She imagined him mentally counting off the number of non-white boys she'd been hanging around with.

"Anyway, we never do anything much on New Year's Eve. I'd like to go," she said to Henry.

"I don't know, honey," said Nana. "People drink on New Year's Eve. It's not the safest night to be out driving around."

Rachel felt a flush of embarrassment. Grampy finished his second helping of lasagna and left the table, shaking his head imperceptibly.

"My parents say the same thing," offered Henry. Rachel glared at him—he was supposed to be on her side.

"I have an idea," said Sandra. "Maybe you could sleep over my house that night. Then at least you wouldn't have to be on the road too late."

"She'd still have to get there," Nana said.

"I could pick her up early, and she could hang at my house that afternoon before the service," said Henry. "My family will be home, I'm sure," he added.

"People start drinking early in the morning on New Year's Eve," countered Nana.

"I'll drive her," said Uncle Johnny. "We shouldn't have any problem. I'll borrow one of the cruisers if I have to," he joked, but he was the only adult in the room smiling. Uncle Tommy and Nana glared at him as if he'd just given over the combination to the family safe.

Rachel grinned. "Then it's all settled. Thanks, Uncle Johnny. You're the best!" Things had taken a definite turn toward the positive.

"Yeah, you're the best all right," Uncle Tommy said under his breath.

When dinner was over Rachel retrieved their coats and walked them to the door. "Thanks for coming," she said. "It wasn't too painful, was it?"

"It was great," said Henry. "Thanks for inviting us. It means a lot."

"Sorry about all the questions. It's just their way of getting to know you."

"I found the conversation stimulating," said Sandra. She stopped at the bookcase to admire a small elephant figurine that Nana had purchased at a yard sale. "This is cool," she said. "Come on, Damara, let's go warm up the car. Keys, Henry." Sandra held out her hand and Henry flipped his car keys to her. She linked her arm through Damara's and dragged her out into the cold.

Henry paused at the door. "So I guess I'll see you soon," said Rachel. Why did she feel awkward all of a sudden?

"Yeah, I'll see you on Tuesday." He pecked Rachel on the cheek just as Uncle Tommy entered the room, coat on and heading out himself.

"Goodbye, Henry," he said smoothly, "and don't forget I carry a gun."

"Uncle Tommy!"

"Kidding. Drive home safe." Henry managed a weak smile, but left without looking back.

"That wasn't funny."

"I thought it was hilarious. Listen, are you sure there's nothing going on between the two of you? I thought I sensed something there."

"We're friends, Uncle Tommy—why is that so hard for you to believe? And what if we were more than friends? Would that be the end of the world?"

Uncle Tommy peered at her. "It wouldn't be the end of the world, Rachel, but it would kill your grandfather."

"The world is changing, Uncle Tommy. Maybe it's time for Grampy to change, too."

"What are you saying? *Is* there something going on?"

"For the last time, there isn't. I'm just saying."

"And I'm just saying to watch yourself, that's all. Last I checked, boys were still boys, no matter what color they are. The world hasn't changed that much yet." Rachel thought about her conversation with Henry a few nights ago—if only Uncle Tommy knew, maybe he'd stop worrying. But then it wasn't her secret to tell. Besides, she still wasn't sure herself what Henry had been getting at.

Uncle Tommy put his arm around Rachel's shoulders. "Good night, honey. Your friends seem like nice kids."

Rachel closed the door behind Uncle Tommy and made sure it was locked. She brushed past Santa and the Nativity on her way to the stairs. "I'm not sure which one of you to thank," she whispered, "but thanks, somebody." She took the steps two at a time, bounded into the bathroom, and ran herself a steaming bubble bath.

Chapter 17

Plans

On the first day of school after the holidays Rachel woke feeling like she'd lost at least five pounds over the break. She stripped off her pajamas in the bathroom and stepped on the scale, but was disappointed to see the same number as usual popping up between her toes. Oh well, she thought, at least I didn't gain any weight this year. Maybe I lost inches—that's more important than pounds.

The bus ambled through the neighborhoods, and she thought she saw a robin on a front lawn as they passed. Spring must be coming early this year. Since the first day back to school was a Thursday, Rachel didn't have long to wait to see her friends again. That morning at breakfast she'd reminded Nana about the club meeting.

"Oh, so you're still going, then?" Nana had asked with a sharp edge. "Haven't you been out enough for one week? Maybe you need to slow down before you get sick."

"Of course I'm still going, Nana. Tell Grampy to pick me up at school at around six, like usual."

"What if he's not available?"

"He's always available."

Nana had looked like she might argue the point, but when Rachel glared up from her oatmeal, ready for a battle if necessary, Nana had acquiesced. "Just be careful," she'd said, turning back to the sink.

I really need to get my license, Rachel thought.

Although it had only been a little over twenty-four hours since she'd seen Henry, by the time the bus pulled up to Sister Gloria's office Rachel felt as if days had gone by. She hurried into the conference room, the last one to arrive, as usual. There he was, waiting for her, and there was the empty spot beside him on the red sofa. She slid in next to him, enjoying the easiness of the fit.

"I wish I lived closer," she said.

"It would sure save on gas," Henry agreed.

Sister Gloria pulled a chair over from the table to join them. "Now that we all know each other so well," she said, glancing at Rachel and Henry, "there's something I'd like to discuss with you." Sandra smirked, but Rachel was startled. Was Sister Gloria implying something about her relationship with Henry? She looked at Henry, trying to see if he'd noticed, but although his forehead was creased in a tiny frown, his eyes were fixed on Sister Gloria. "I've had an idea for a project, and I'd like to see what you think."

"A project?" Darrin groaned. Damara nudged him with her foot. "Stop kicking me," he hissed.

Sister Gloria continued. "I thought it might be interesting to visit each other's schools." Her suggestion was greeted with silence.

"Why?" Darrin asked finally. "School is school, what's the point?"

"Not all schools are as special as ours, Darrin," said Henry in mock seriousness. "We made the list."

"List?" asked Rachel. She knew that her school had made some top ten list because there was a large banner in the school office that said so. She wondered if that was the list that Henry was talking about.

"Yup, we're on the 'Worst 10 Pennsylvania High Schools' list—saw it just the other day on the Internet. Makes a young man proud." Henry and Darrin both laughed.

"Let's get back to the visits," Sister Gloria said. "I think it would be an educational experience for you all, and if you wanted to, you could even write a report about it, which I believe would count toward your senior projects."

"I'm only a sophomore," Darrin said. "I don't have to worry about my senior project yet." He slouched into the couch and folded his arms.

"Of course, this is strictly voluntary," Sister Gloria said. "If you're interested, I could make all the arrangements with the schools. You wouldn't be counted absent that day."

Darrin sat up. "You mean, if we do this, we'd get to miss classes? I'm in!"

"I guess we're all in," said Sandra.

"We wouldn't have to paint anything or pick up any trash, would we?" Darrin asked.

"No, nothing like that. This would purely be an observation. You'd take a tour of the buildings, and maybe visit a class or two."

"And we don't have to write a report if we don't want to?"

"Darrin, please," said Damara.

"I'm just checking for loopholes."

"No loopholes, Darrin," said Sister Gloria, clearly amused. "Just a visit to compare notes."

"But we don't have to take notes if we don't want to, right?"

Henry rolled his eyes. "It's an expression, you mongrel. Please stop speaking now before I come over there and sit on you."

Darrin glared at Henry. "Come on over, fat boy. I'll pop you like a balloon."

"So should I go ahead and make the arrangements, then?" asked Sister Gloria, standing and dragging her chair back to the table. Everyone except for Darrin, who was still mumbling threats under his breath, nodded in agreement. Smiling, Sister Gloria left the room.

"Come on, I'm starving," said Sandra. She stood and headed to the table for a snack. Rachel followed her to the chocolate fudge brownies, while the others gravitated toward the chips and dip. "Looks like even Sister Gloria knows about you and Henry," Sandra said in her stage whisper.

Rachel looked over to Henry, but if he'd heard he didn't let on. "There's nothing to know," she whispered back. "We're just friends, remember?"

"Please, Rachel. How stupid do you think we are? You like each other. It's obvious, at least to everyone else."

"What are you two whispering about?" said Henry, positioning himself between them.

"Nothing," Rachel answered quickly. She turned and walked back to the sofa and Henry followed. Out of the corner of her eye she saw Sandra shrug.

Thanks for rescuing me fm Sandra, she texted Henry on the way home.

yw

She was going on about us again.

I heard. Gotta go.

Rachel closed her eyes and tried to relax as the bus made its way to the highway, but she couldn't get Sandra's words out of her head. And why had Sister Gloria looked at them that way? Uncle Tommy had certainly been convinced that she and Henry were more than friends, but Rachel had chalked that up to his suspicious nature. Was Sandra right, was it obvious to everyone but them? Of course, none of them knew about Henry's secret. She tried to remember exactly what Henry had said to her that night. *I'm not sure about myself yet,* he'd said. Rachel knew she was completely inexperienced in these areas, but what, exactly, did that mean? She couldn't deny that she was drawn to Henry, that she felt happy and safe in a way that she'd never felt before when she was with him. Uncle Tommy was right about one thing—she *had* changed since she'd met him. Henry was her sparkling new mirror, reflecting a different Rachel, a new Rachel, a Rachel she liked much better. It wasn't that she'd suddenly begun to think of herself as pretty; it was more that pretty didn't matter so much when Henry was around. She also knew that, in some way, Henry was drawn to her. Was it really only as a friend? Was it possible he'd simply been trying to spare her feelings that night, letting her down easy because he sensed she was getting attached? Over the years she'd heard Antonella tell guys lots of strange things to put them off. Maybe he just didn't like her, and this was an easy way to get her off his back. No, she decided, that would be a very un-Henry thing to do. If Henry was anything, he was honest—that was one of the reasons she liked him so much. And in that moment Rachel realized that she did like Henry very, very much. Race might be the least of our problems, she thought with a sinking feeling.

Chapter 18

Changes

The date of the school visits was set for the following week, and Rachel explained the event to Nana as simply and directly as possible, handing her the permission slip, a pen, and her glasses.

"What's the point of this?" Nana asked. "School is school. Why can't you go to your own school?"

"It's just to compare notes, Nana. Just sign it, please."

Nana shook her head, put her glasses on, and signed. I can't wait until I'm eighteen and I never have to have a permission slip signed again, Rachel thought.

Henry had volunteered to do the driving, and Sister Gloria had accepted gratefully, glad to save a little money from her budget. "Of course, we'll reimburse Henry for gas," she'd said, "but that's much cheaper than sending the bus." The plan was set—they would visit Henry, Darrin and Damara's school in the morning, and Rachel's in the afternoon. There'd be no time for Sandra's school that day, but maybe they'd make it there another time. Sandra seemed just as happy—"It's not like there's much to see," she'd said.

The others were in the car already when Henry drove up in front of Rachel's house. Damara was seated in the front, but she abdicated her spot as Rachel approached the car, slipping into the back with Darrin and Sandra. Rachel protested, but it was too late—Damara had moved too quickly. Rachel took her usual seat next to Henry, wondering, does Damara think something is going on between us, too?

The kids standing at the school bus stop peered inside Henry's car as they drove past, looking more than a little surprised. Rachel smiled and waved. The sense of freedom she felt at that moment was almost intoxicating.

"This is fun, isn't it?" she asked, not trying to hide her excitement. She turned toward the back seat and saw Darrin sleeping under his New York Yankees baseball cap, headphones securely in place. Sandra was holding a lip gloss in one hand, digging through her purse with the other.

"I can't find my mirror," she complained.

Damara was already deep into an SAT prep book, studying vocabulary words.

Henry looked into his rear view mirror and laughed. "I guess not everyone is as up for this as you are, Rachel."

"I just thought it was cool to see all of you at this time of day," she answered, embarrassed that the others didn't share her enthusiasm.

"It is cool," said Henry, his voice gentle. He reached over and patted Rachel's hand, still smiling and shaking his head.

"What?" asked Rachel.

"Nothing. It's just that you're so low maintenance. It doesn't take much to make you happy, does it?"

"I never really thought about it before." Rachel was beginning to feel uncomfortable—did Henry think she was being silly?

"Don't get me wrong—it's good. It's one of the things I like about you."

"Why don't you two get a room?" Sandra asked. "I'm getting nauseous—but maybe that's Henry's driving. Do you think you could turn the heat down before I puke all over the back seat?"

Rachel sat back and thought about what Henry had said. He was right, it didn't take much to make her happy—she saw that now. In fact, she'd thought she'd been happy all those years tagging around with Antonella. But still, no matter how low maintenance she was, that couldn't account for how glad she felt right now. Here she was, in a broken down car (a car that Antonella would not have been caught dead in), driving into the city (which she had never liked), on a school assignment (sort of), with a group of kids she had met less than six months ago. She stole a glance at Henry, who was singing and hitting the dashboard in time with the music. Rachel could not deny the fact that it had something to do with him, but she couldn't quite figure out what, or how much. After a few minutes she realized that she'd been playacting—making believe that this was her morning routine, and that she went to school this way, with these friends, every day. She sobered a little when she pictured herself tomorrow, back at her old bus stop in her perfectly manicured neighborhood, surrounded by kids she'd known all her life.

Henry had decided to take the local streets to avoid the highway traffic. "We'll have to deal with the lights," he said, "but at least we'll be moving." Rachel watched the scenery change from suburban to ritzy urban. They jostled through cobblestone-lined streets under the cover of trolley wires, and Rachel wondered if it would be fun to ride a trolley. She'd asked Henry once, hoping he'd offer her the chance to find out, but he'd only shrugged and said, "It's no big deal." They drove through the mixture of elegant-looking homes and shabbier houses that made up Henry's neighborhood, and soon approached a large brick school building surrounded by a wrought iron fence.

"Here we are," Henry announced. He drove past the school and found a parking spot a few blocks away. "Lots of the kids we know go to a charter school," Henry told Rachel as they walked toward the entrance. "But not us. My grandmother's on the school board, and she believes in 'change from the inside out.' She convinced Damara's parents too, so I guess we're all stuck here."

"I'm sure it's not that bad," Rachel answered. As they approached the school building Rachel could see the concrete schoolyard behind it, barren except for two basketball hoops, one with a broken rim and both with backboards covered in graffiti.

"It's not as bad as it looks," Henry said. "There's some fields a few blocks away that the teams use."

Rachel surveyed the old four-story building. One of the windows on the first floor near the entrance was boarded up. The arched doorway was trimmed with stonework, and on the sides there were sculpted heads of what Rachel imagined once must have been stone cherubs, but most of their faces were chipped away now. They trudged up a set of cracked stone steps, pressed the doorbell and waited to be buzzed in. Once inside, they walked through a metal detector into the lobby, where they were greeted by the assistant principal, Ms. Burton-Grant. She was a tall African-American woman, dressed in a blue pants suit. She led them to the school office, where she instructed Rachel and Sandra to sign in. Rachel heard a loud clanging noise and jumped.

"Don't worry, it's not a gunshot," laughed Darrin. "It's just the heat coming up."

"I didn't think it was a gunshot," Rachel mumbled. "It just surprised me, that's all."

"Be sure these other three are marked present for today," Ms. Burton-Grant told the woman at the front desk.

"We're out of toner again," someone called from an inner office.

"It will have to wait until Monday," the woman at the desk called back without looking up.

"I'll be conducting your tour today," Ms. Burton-Grant said to Rachel and Sandra, but then turned to Henry, Darrin and Damara, adding, "although I'm not sure why you three can't go to class. You certainly don't need a tour of the school."

"Sister Gloria said for us to stick together," said Darrin.

"So I've been told. We'll start down here on the first floor." They followed Ms. Burton-Grant's clicking heels down a long hallway, and Rachel found herself staying close to Henry's side. Now that she was actually here her excitement had been replaced with a low-level anxiety. She tried to focus on the task at hand—Sister Gloria had said to take in as much as possible about the two schools. The lighting in the hallway was dim. Rachel looked up and noticed that about every third fluorescent light was out. The walls were covered by metal lockers, just like in her school, but these were a little rusted and dented in spots. They passed a ladies' room with a large "out of order" sign posted on the door.

"This is our library," Ms. Burton-Grant was saying. They stepped into a large room filled with books on metal shelves. Small wooden tables were scattered around, and a row of computers ran against the back wall. Rachel noticed more "out of order" signs covering several monitors.

"I'm sure this is nothing like your school," Ms. Burton-Grant said to Rachel. Her tone and expression were business-like, but Rachel felt her face get hot. She took off her coat and held it over her arm. Henry tried to catch her eye, but Rachel looked away.

"We're hoping for a grant to update our computers next year." Ms. Burton-Grant turned on her heel and walked briskly down the hallway. "Next is the auditorium.

We have a brief assembly in a few minutes, so we'll have to hurry to avoid the rush." Rachel adjusted her backpack on her shoulder and quickened her pace to keep up.

"God, it's so hot in here," Sandra whispered.

"Be glad we have heat at all," Darrin said. "Last year the teachers walked out because the temperature fell below fifty. We got the day off—actually, it was great."

"It's still cold on the third floor," Damara commented. "That's where the music rooms are."

They reached the auditorium and Ms. Burton-Grant held open the large wooden door. "You can go in and take a quick look," she said. "I'll wait here." Rachel and Sandra walked down the aisle and looked around.

"Seats and a stage," said Sandra. "I guess all auditoriums are the same."

Rachel didn't answer, although she could have pointed out several differences between this auditorium and the one at her school. First was the smell—it was musty in here. The floor, instead of being carpeted, was some kind of cement, painted black. The chairs were wooden, with no cushions, and a few of them had no seat portion at all. When she looked up at the high ceiling she noticed a few spots where the paint was peeling. Oh well, she thought, it's just old. That's how city buildings are.

As they walked back to the others the bell sounded, and streams of students flooded out into the hall. "This would be a good time to see the gym," said Ms. Burton-Grant, "since most of the students will be in here. Please follow me." Rachel noticed that hers was one of the only white faces in a sea of color, but she wasn't surprised since she'd known Henry's school was mostly black. I guess I'm getting used to this, she thought; it doesn't even feel weird any more. Henry turned to wait and she sped up to walk next to him. Darrin greeted a group of friends as they passed.

When they reached the gym Ms. Burton-Grant stopped. "You'll notice that our gymnasium is in need of repair. Unfortunately, the storms of the last several winters have taken their toll. The board just approved the funds last night, so this will be fixed over the summer break." She swung the doors open. Darrin yawned and stepped back, allowing Rachel and Sandra to enter first.

"Wow," said Sandra. "Even my school isn't as bad as this."

"Subtle, as always," Henry muttered under his breath.

The musty smell in this room was overpowering, and Rachel immediately spotted the source—the corner of the room to their left was roped off because of obvious water damage. Several ceiling tiles were missing, and the floorboards were warped in strong waves. Other than a few sections of wooden bleachers folded and pushed against the opposite wall, the gym was completely empty.

"Sucks, doesn't it?" asked Darrin. Ms. Burton-Grant silenced him with a stern look. They continued their tour, moving to the second and third floors of the building. Rachel walked through a science lab, the music room and the childcare center, which was a room with a shelf of picture books, a pile of toys, and a row of cots. Six or seven preschoolers sat at a square wooden table, eating Goldfish crackers off of paper napkins, while the same number of students, dressed in smocks, hovered over them. Every room was old and worn-out, and the entire school seemed weary, bending under generations of students walking its floors, opening and closing its doors, and sitting in its seats. The last stop was the cafeteria, where they were to eat an early lunch so they'd have time to get back to Rachel's school for an afternoon tour. Here Rachel experienced the only familiar sensation—just like her school cafeteria, it smelled like corn chips and canned green beans.

They piled back into Henry's car for the ride back to the suburbs. Darrin promptly fell asleep

Rachel stared out the window, quiet now.

"Are you still having fun?" Henry asked. Although his expression was kind, Rachel had the feeling he was laughing at her. She wasn't in the mood to be teased.

"Sure," she lied. "Are you?"

"It's fun hanging out with you. Walking around school with Ms. BG was a drag, though. I'd rather go to class. So what did you think?"

"About what?"

"About my school, of course."

"Oh. It was nice."

"Yeah, if you like dumps," said Sandra from the back seat. "It's even older and more decrepit than my school."

Henry and Damara laughed. "Oh well," Henry said, "it's just school, right? It's not like we really care."

"Yeah, it's not like we really care," repeated Damara absently, thumbing through her SAT prep book. "Sandra, can you ask me this list of words?"

"Okay, but if I get carsick it's not my fault."

Henry protested, rolling down his window, and a five-minute argument ensued. Normally, Rachel would have enjoyed listening to Henry and Sandra's barbs, but today she let their voices fade into the background. She couldn't quite figure out why she felt so low. Maybe she had some kind of disorder, like SAD—she'd heard of that on TV—people who got depressed in the winter months because there wasn't enough sunlight. She knew in her case, though, it wasn't about the weather, and besides, the day couldn't have been finer. She'd been so excited this morning—what was it about Henry's school that had deflated her so much? It was old—so what? Everything in the city was old. That's just the way it was, and Henry and the others didn't seem to care. Or maybe her mood swing had nothing to do with the school visit at all. She looked over at Henry. Life was getting complicated.

"Hey, are you okay?" Henry asked. "You look like you want to say something."

"Just thinking."

"What about?"

Rachel glanced toward the back seat. She wasn't sure what she wanted to say, but whatever it was, she knew she didn't want to be overheard. "I'll tell you later," she said.

"Deal. Can you come with me when I drive these guys home? Then we can hang out a while."

"Are you sure you want to drive back out here again?"

"Why not? I'm getting used to it." *The signs are there,* Rachel remembered Sandra saying, what seemed like ages ago. How had she not seen them before now, and how did they fit with Henry's mysterious confession?

Henry pulled into the spacious parking lot of her school, and Rachel examined the sprawling complex as if for the first time. Like the suburbs compared to the city, her school went *out* instead of *up*. The school complex was surrounded by fields used for several different sports, some with artificial turf and lights for night games.

"They're big into sports out here," Rachel said, feeling that some explanation was necessary. They were buzzed into the school office, where Rachel introduced the secretary, Mrs. Adams, who would be showing them around. Rachel had looked forward to this, but now she felt a strange sense of foreboding.

The first stop was the library media center, which was filled with students working on brand new computers. Of course, there were countless shelves of books, DVDs, and magazines. Posters on the wall outlined instructions on how to use the school's extensive collection of databases. Armchairs, sofas and coffee tables were clustered throughout the rectangular room, and in a far corner there was a fifty-inch, flat-screen plasma TV. A few students were watching something that looked like a documentary on the Civil War, taking copious notes.

"What the freak is this?" Darrin said.

"I'm afraid I'm going to have to ask you to watch your language while you're here," Mrs. Adams scolded.

"Oh—sorry," said Darrin sheepishly. Damara scowled at her brother, but Henry and Sandra were too shocked to have even heard the exchange. They stared at the media center with open-mouthed, dazed expressions.

"This is really ... nice," Sandra whispered.

"I'll say," said Henry. Rachel heard awe in his voice.

"The auditorium is just across here," said Mrs. Adams, pointing them toward a large doorway. "It's empty right now, but I don't suppose there's much to look at in there. We can just peek in before we move on." She held open one side of the double doors, allowing the visitors to step in. To Rachel, this room had been the location of many a boring hour, and she'd never seen anything particularly appealing about it. Now she saw it through different eyes. Like the media center, the auditorium was carpeted. The cushioned seats, covered in maroon twill fabric, had retractable wooden arms. Two large screens and two projectors hung from the front of the room.

"Nice," Sandra said again.

"Should we move on to the gym?" Mrs. Adams asked without expecting an answer. "We'll pass the TV studio on the way, but we're not allowed in there when they're taping."

"TV studio?" Darrin repeated. Mrs. Adams didn't hear. As they walked along the silent hallway, Rachel felt the sudden impulse to take Henry's hand to reassure him—or maybe she was the one who needed comforting. Henry looked straight ahead, and Rachel kept her hands at her sides.

"This is one of our gyms—we can look, but we'll have to stay out of the way." They stood in the doorway for a few minutes, watching a volleyball game. One side of the gym was roped off, but not because of a leaky ceiling; it held mats, parallel bars, and other equipment waiting to be used by the gymnastics team later in the day. From the bleachers to the floor, every ounce of wood in the room shone.

"Our new gym is down this way," said Mrs. Adams, leading them back out into the hallway.

"You have a newer gym than that one?" asked Henry.

"Yes, we're very proud of it—you'll see why in a minute." Mrs. Adams beamed at Rachel, but Rachel stared down at the floor as she walked. Her feelings were quickly morphing from embarrassment to shame.

Henry stopped in his tracks as they approached the "new" gym. They were able to see into the room before anyone opened a door, since it was separated from the hallway by a half-wall of Plexiglas. Rows of exercise bikes, ellipticals, rowers, and treadmills filled the room, all busily engaged by students. Directly across from where they stood was a door with a sign that read, "Pool Locker Rooms."

"You have a pool, too?" gasped Damara. Rachel nodded dully.

"I've always hated it," she murmured, "hated changing into a bathing suit in the middle of a school day."

"Is there anything else you'd like to see?" asked Mrs. Adams, looking at her watch.

"No, I think we've seen enough. We need to be getting back," Henry replied.

"Rachel, I've marked you present for today. Will you be joining your class now?"

"No, I have permission to leave early. Henry will drive me home." Technically, that was true, Rachel thought. She just hadn't said what time.

They left in silence, walked to the car in silence, and drove in silence, without even the noise of Henry's newly fixed car to distract them from their thoughts. Henry didn't fiddle with the radio, Darrin didn't touch his earphones, Damara didn't open a book, and Sandra didn't utter a word. At first Rachel thought Henry might forget their plans, but he got on the highway toward the city without taking her home first. She had expected more winking and teasing from Sandra, but Sandra wasn't paying attention. They sat, lifeless, looking in different directions as the car whipped along in an endless rotation of tires on pavement. Rachel's thoughts took the form of pictures— pictures of peeling walls, broken desks, glistening lockers and Olympic-sized swimming pools. She closed her eyes and tried to ignore the vise she felt clenching her chest.

When the others had been dropped off and they were finally alone in the car, Henry spoke. "Don't you have to call your Nana?" he asked.

"Yeah, I guess I'd better. What time should I tell her I'll be home?"

Henry shrugged. "Whenever you want."

Rachel was intentionally nebulous with Nana, saying, "Don't count on me for dinner, but I won't be too late." Finally, after several reassurances, Nana was convinced that Rachel's life was in no imminent danger.

"So where do you want to go?" Henry asked.

"I don't know. Wherever you want to go."

"I don't feel like being around people."

"Neither do I."

"We could just go back to my house—they won't be home until late tonight, and there's plenty of food."

"Okay, but I'm not really hungry."

"Me neither."

As they walked up the steps to Henry's house, Rachel imagined it looked less like a castle and more like a haunted mansion. She shook off the idea, knowing it was ridiculous. The only thing haunted this afternoon was her own dark mood. Maybe she should have gone home after all.

They settled into the living room sofa; Rachel sat at the end, while Henry took up the other three quarters of the couch. Rachel slid off her shoes and tucked her legs under her.

"So," Henry said, making eye contact with Rachel for first time since they'd left her school, "what did you want to talk about?"

Where should she begin? She'd wanted to bring up their relationship, to try to figure out these feelings she was having, and mostly to find out if Henry felt anything even close. But all of that had crumbled and been swept away by what she had seen at the schools. Now, all she could think about was her overwhelming guilt.

"Henry," she said, "I'm so sorry." She hoped he didn't notice that her voice cracked on the last syllable.

"About what?" Henry seemed honestly confused.

Was he really going to make her explain? "You know what." His expression remained puzzled. "About our schools," she said.

"Oh, you mean the fact that my school is a pit and yours looks like Club Med? You know, my school never seemed that bad until I compared it to yours. But hey, no problem. It's just school, right? It's not like I really care." He smiled as he spoke, but the edge to his voice betrayed him. Rachel didn't want to cry, but she couldn't stop herself. The tightness she'd felt in her chest expanded down to her stomach and the lump in her throat became a mound. She grabbed her bag and searched around for a tissue.

"I don't understand," she said. "It's so unfair. How can we have so much and you have so little? These are public schools, aren't they? Aren't they supposed to be equal?" The last sentence came out as a sob. Henry slid closer to her, frowning.

"It's okay, Rachel," he said, his voice filled with concern. "It's not your fault. Don't take it so hard."

"Then whose fault is it?" She was crying full force now, choking out the words between her tears. "All this time I've been going to school, not even appreciating what we have. I feel terrible—it's so unfair!" She turned away from Henry, wiping at her eyes and nose with her crinkled-up tissue. "I'm sorry," she said, "I don't mean to make this about me."

They were silent for a minute, except for the uncontrollable gasps of her crying, which she didn't think she'd be able to stop any time soon. Finally, she felt Henry slip his arm around her shoulders.

"Rachel, please," he pleaded. "I hate it when you cry." He turned her gently into his chest, at the same time reaching for a box of tissues on the table next to her and placing it on her lap.

"Thanks," she said between sobs, pressing her face into his shirt.

He held her firmly and rubbed her shoulders, waiting for her tears to subside. "Shh, it's okay," he whispered over and over again. "Don't cry, baby. It's okay." For the first time in her life Rachel didn't object to being called *baby*. Now and then Henry bent and kissed the top of her head, or wiped the tears from the side of her face with his hand.

Gradually, Rachel began to calm down. The warmth of Henry's body radiated through her like an electric blanket. Her sobs dwindled to small, quick gulps, and her tears slowed. She let go of the tissue box and put her arm around Henry's middle. He pulled her in closer, both arms around her now, and began to hum softly. Rachel thought she'd never been so comfortable in her entire life. She breathed in deeply and let the feel of Henry's body so near put her at ease. Although she had stopped crying, she made no move to sit up; Henry seemed in no hurry to change his position, either. They sat that way for what seemed like hours, Rachel listening to Henry's humming, her own breathing, and the sound of the grandfather clock ticking on the wall.

"I'm sorry I got your shirt all wet," she said finally. "You must think I'm an idiot."

"I do. I think you're the nicest, sweetest idiot I've ever met. Are you okay?"

"Better. But I still feel so sad."

"I know." He stroked the side of her face. "And you're right, it isn't fair. But it's not your fault, either. You're just a kid."

"I'm only a little younger than you."

"So we're both kids. There's nothing we can do about it."

"I wish there were," she said, looking up into his eyes. "Isn't there something we can do?"

He hesitated for a second, and then Rachel saw a different look come over him, as if he had made a decision. "I know something I want to do," he said. He held her face and leaned down until their lips met, and Rachel forgot all about the inequity of the public school system. She closed her eyes and tried to concentrate, all the while her insides screaming, *I can't believe this is happening to me!* The kiss only lasted a few seconds, but Rachel thought his lips were the smoothest, sweetest thing she had ever tasted. He stopped too soon; she wanted more.

"I'm sorry," Henry said. "I shouldn't have done that." He started to pull away, but Rachel didn't let him. She sat up straighter and reached behind his neck, trying to pull his head back down, level with hers. He was so much stronger than she that he easily resisted, looking at her questioningly.

"I want you to kiss me again, Henry." Her whisper was barely audible.

At first he blinked in surprise, but then he smiled and tilted his head. "You're sure?" he asked.

"Positive."

He leaned in again, pulling her up to his height so effortlessly that she felt small. He kissed her, still gently, but not as tentatively as before. She felt her lips respond, tingling in a series of mini-explosions. *So this is what it feels like*, she thought, moving her lips with Henry's. She felt a burst of pure elation. Just when she began to wonder how she would manage to breathe, Henry pulled back, brushing her cheek with his lips as he did.

"I'm sorry," he said again, but this time his eyes were glistening.

"I'm not," she replied, still whispering. "I think I've wanted you to do that for a long time." She tucked her head into his shoulder, afraid that any sudden movement might end the moment.

"Really? This doesn't surprise you?" He squeezed her arm lightly.

"Yes and no. I was feeling something, but I didn't know if you felt it, too."

Henry let that register. "I guess I was, but I didn't know it."

Rachel smiled. "I think everybody knew it before we did. Even Uncle Tommy."

Henry sighed. "Did you have to mention Uncle Tommy?"

"I'm sorry." She snuggled in closer, and he reached back and pulled out the elastic tie that had been holding her hair in a sloppy ponytail. Rachel felt a shiver at the nape of her neck. Antonella was right, she thought, and almost laughed out loud. Guys do like long hair.

That evening he held her hand almost the whole ride home, except when traffic demanded two hands on the wheel. She nestled close to him, her head against his arm. He glanced down at her and smiled.

"Are you happy?" he asked.

"Isn't it obvious? Yes, I'm very happy. Are you?"

"I'm happy when I'm with you."

Rachel liked that answer. Still, she couldn't shake a nagging thought—something she needed to clear up so that her happiness could be complete. "Henry, I didn't want to bring this up, but what about what you said that night, on the way home from Damara's church? I guess I'm confused."

A look of pain crossed Henry's face. "I know. I'm confused, too. Or I was. That was the night I started thinking about it—about us, I mean. I don't know, that's the truth." A wave of panic swept through Rachel. Was he going to take back what had happened today? They were passing a shopping center; Henry pulled into the far end of the parking lot, and turned off the ignition.

"Rachel," he said, turning to the side to face her fully, "I like you. I like you a lot. I meant everything that happened today." Was she that transparent, or could Henry read her mind?

"I'm not taking anything back, okay? I want you to know that." Rachel allowed herself a bit of relief, but she knew that Henry had more to say. "It's just that—well, I'm worried."

This was not what Rachel had expected. "Worried? About what?"

Henry hesitated. "It's just that … I could be dangerous to you."

Rachel would have burst out laughing if Henry hadn't looked so serious. Henry, dangerous? Boys like Raphael were dangerous, boys that got girls pregnant, boys that every other girl—every pretty girl—wanted, those kinds of boys were dangerous. Rachel knew plenty of dangerous boys from school, because Antonella had dated most of them, although she'd always turned out to be far more dangerous than they were. But no one had ever made Rachel feel safer than Henry.

"Henry, don't take this the wrong way, but you're too … well, you're too *good* to be dangerous."

"I don't want to hurt you, Rachel," he said. His expression was so earnest, so innocent, that her heart went out to him. She took his hand to reassure him again, but he stopped her. "No, hear me out. It's just that, I never really liked a girl before I met you. Here I am, seventeen, and never had a girlfriend, never even liked a girl from a distance. I don't know if you realize this Rachel, but that was my first kiss, too. I started to think there was something wrong with me. I'm still not a hundred percent sure that there isn't." He grimaced and looked away.

"Okay," she said, holding his hand between both of hers. She couldn't get over the softness of his skin, the feeling it gave her to touch him so freely. "So where does that leave us?" *Please don't end this before it begins*, she begged silently. *Please, Henry.* She steeled herself and waited.

Henry looked perplexed. "I told you, Rachel, I like you. I want to be with you. If you decide not to see me, I'll be sad, but I'll respect your decision."

If *she* decided not to see *him?* This time she did laugh out loud, out of relief more than anything. "There's not much chance of that happening, Henry. I guess we're stuck with each other, at least for now, anyway."

"Are you sure?"

She kissed the back of his hand, and then turned it over and pressed his palm into her cheek. "I'm sure."

Now he laughed, taking his hand away to turn the key in the ignition. When he had pulled out of the parking lot and turned onto the road again, he slid his hand back into hers, still chuckling softly.

"What?" she asked.

"It's just that, for a shy girl, Rachel, you're pretty good at this."

Chapter 19

Debrief

Isn't there something we can do?" Rachel asked at the club meeting the following week. Damara and Sandra sat on one sofa, facing Rachel and Henry on the other. Sister Gloria, who had joined them a few minutes into the session, was perched on a straight-backed chair. Only Darrin was missing.

"I'm hoping we'll talk about that soon, Rachel," Sister Gloria answered. Rachel hadn't said anything to anyone about her new status with Henry, but she saw Sister Gloria take note of it now. It would have been impossible to miss the way they sat, sides touching, holding hands. Sandra and Damara realized the change the instant Rachel had entered the room. Henry had stood to meet her, his grin unabashedly broad. Rachel had walked directly to him, her eyes only on him. He'd looked like he'd wanted to hug her, but instead he'd touched her hair (she was wearing it down) and slipped her backpack off her shoulder. Then he'd helped her off with her coat and led her to the sofa as if she were made of glass. As they sat he'd taken her hand and pulled her in close to him. Rachel hadn't been sure how Henry would act around other people, but she'd thought maybe he'd be reserved, too shy to touch her, and she would have been okay with that. Instead, he seemed completely uninhibited. More than that, he was clearly proud. Rachel could barely believe it—Henry was showing her off. She knew that she was glowing, and although she felt a little self-conscious, she couldn't turn down the beam.

"Well, well," Sandra had said. "It looks like there's love in the air—finally." Damara had simply smiled.

Before Sandra could interrogate them Sister Gloria had entered the room, turning the conversation to the school visits. At the end of that very long day Rachel's emotions had been soaring so high that she'd found it impossible to think about anything but Henry. Once she settled in back at school, though, the memory of what she'd seen returned, and her shame had turned to outrage. She'd put herself in Henry's place—this was personal now. At first Rachel had been amazed that Henry, Sandra and Damara did not seem to share her anger. The subject seemed harder for them; even Sandra was strangely reluctant.

"Before we begin discussing solutions, though," continued Sister Gloria, "it's important that we explore our feelings about what you saw last week. If it's okay, I think we should go around the circle and share. How did last week's school visits make you feel, personally?" No one volunteered an answer. Henry looked away; Rachel squeezed his hand gently.

Sister Gloria looked from person to person, stopping when she made eye contact with Rachel. "Since you've already shared some of your thoughts, Rachel, why don't you go first?"

"Oh … okay. Like I said before, I just think it's so unfair. Why should we have a beautiful school, with lighted fields and a media center and everything, and you have a shabby old building with a gym that you can't even use? It makes me mad to think about it."

"Why, exactly, does it make you mad?" asked Sister Gloria.

Rachel didn't need to think about her reason. "Because it's wrong," she blurted out.

"And?" Sister Gloria pressed.

"And … because it hurts my friends." Her voice was beginning to shake. Henry leaned closer.

"Thank you, Rachel. Henry, how about you?"

"Oh … yeah, okay. I guess I did feel bad about it."

"Bad in what way?"

Henry shrugged. "Well, I knew my school was nothing special, but I didn't know how nice a school could be until I saw Rachel's." He still looked away, aiming his words at the emptiness on the other side of the room. "Anyway, I only have one more year."

"Anything else?"

"Not really."

"Thank you, Henry. Damara?"

Rachel knew that this kind of discussion was hardest for Damara. She looked so uncomfortable that Rachel wished Sister Gloria would move on.

"I guess I agree with what everyone said so far," Damara said. Rachel waited for her to continue, but only silence followed.

"In what way?" asked Sister Gloria.

"I guess I did feel bad. And it is unfair." Her voice was so quiet that Rachel had to strain to hear her.

"Well, I'll tell you how I feel…" Sandra jumped in.

"Just a minute, Sandra," said Sister Gloria. "Damara, is there anything else?"

Damara looked grateful for Sandra's interruption. "Just that, I almost wish we hadn't gone," she replied, looking down at the coffee table.

"Thank you, Damara. Go ahead, Sandra."

Sandra sat up as if someone had just plugged her in and pushed the On button. "Okay, I'll tell you how I feel—the whole thing made me feel like total crap. I mean, I expected some differences, but I couldn't believe my eyes when we got to Rachel's school. Media center, TV studio, swimming pool … it made me feel like they think the white kids are better than us or something. Like they're worth more than us." She stopped to take a breath.

"Anything else?" Sister Gloria asked.

"Yeah. I feel like they just don't care enough about us to give us a decent school."

"So if you had to put your feelings into one word, Sandra, what would that word be?"

"I feel … left out … abandoned. That's it—I feel abandoned."

Henry shifted in his seat, and Damara nodded faintly. Rachel felt the stinging truth of Sandra's words.

Abandoned. Something about that word pierced her, changing her indignation back into injury, opening up some long-forgotten wound. She saw from the corner of her eye that Henry was studying her face; he let go of her hand and put his arm around her shoulders.

Henry wasn't the only one who'd noticed Rachel's reaction. "This is hard stuff," said Sister Gloria. "Thank you for your honesty. Now, the question is, what do we do with these feelings? How can we make a difference?" Rachel remembered why she'd joined the club in the first place—she'd wanted to make a difference. She'd thought she could donate a few hours a week, play with some little kids, maybe do some tutoring. She'd thought she could fix something. But it hadn't worked out that way.

"But what can I do?" she mumbled.

"Say again, Rachel?" said Sister Gloria.

"What can I *do* to make a difference? Besides sitting around here and talking?"

"You've already made a difference, Rachel, in others, but mostly in yourself. Are you the same person you were the first time you walked in here?"

Rachel shook her head. "No. I guess not." She felt Henry's arm around her. "Definitely not," she smiled.

"Change always begins on the inside. My goal in bringing you all together was simply to raise awareness, to get you to see and feel from each other's points of view. I think we've succeeded in that. Now we're ready to go a little deeper, maybe through the arts, or study, or some other activity. But time is almost up today, and we've done enough hard work for this week. Let's come back to this topic next time. How about you go get some cookies and relax for the next few minutes?" Sister Gloria dragged her chair back to the table and walked out to the reception area. Henry hugged Rachel's shoulders and put his lips to her ear.

"Are you okay?" he whispered. She nodded, fully aware that Sandra was staring.

"I thought she'd never stop talking!" Sandra exclaimed. "Let's get to the good stuff. So when did all this happen?" she asked, pointing at Rachel and Henry.

"I'll be right back." Henry stood and turned to Rachel. "She's all yours," he said, and headed off to the men's room.

"Well?" asked Sandra with a note of accusation. "Are you going to make us drag it out of you?"

Rachel had been longing to talk about this with someone for days, but now that she had the chance she was overwhelmed with timidity. Her face turned bright red. "I guess it all started last week, on the day we went to the schools, after we dropped you all off."

"It all started the first day Henry laid eyes on you, but you were both too stupid to see it. Go ahead," said Sandra.

"Well, we went back to Henry's house…"

"Were his parents home?"

"No."

"Uh-oh. Okay, then what?"

"Then … I don't know, it just happened."

"What happened?" Sandra was getting exasperated.

"I got upset, you know, about what we saw, and I started to cry. Henry was trying to make me feel better, and I guess one thing led to another."

"What led to what? How much better, exactly, did Henry make you feel?"

Rachel's mouth dropped open in absolute mortification. "It wasn't like that..." she stuttered, but Damara interrupted.

"Sandra, stop! You're embarrassing her, and that's none of our business."

"Okay, okay, you can't blame me for trying. It's just that when you walked in here today it was like an electric charge went through the room. Come on, Damara, you must have felt it too."

Damara smiled. "It's true," she said to Rachel. "I've known Henry for a long time, but I've never seen him like this. He's all about you."

"Can't you see how he looks at you?" asked Sandra.

Rachel had seen, very clearly, how Henry looked at her. But she couldn't help herself—she wanted to hear someone say it out loud. "Do you really think so?" she asked.

"Rachel, oh my God! It's like he's come alive! I hate to say 'I told you so,' but..."

"But we know you will," Damara finished. Henry came back into the room just in time to hear them laughing.

"I'm not even gonna ask what's funny," he said, walking to the table for a handful of cookies.

"Bring some for us," called Sandra. Henry filled a plate and sat back down next to Rachel.

"So," Sandra continued, "what does Uncle Tommy think?"

"We're not saying anything to our families yet," Henry said quickly. That had been his idea. "Let them think nothing's changed between us for now," he'd told Rachel. "I want to enjoy you without pressure from our families." Rachel knew this was Henry's way of protecting her, at least for a while. It had also not escaped her attention that Henry *enjoyed* her; this little phrase made her insides percolate like Nana's old stainless steel coffee pot. She knew that there would be difficult times ahead, but she was more than willing to put them off for now.

When it was time to go, Henry walked Rachel outside. He'd been carrying both their backpacks; he dropped them to the ground and stooped to kiss Rachel goodbye, tucking his hand under her hair and holding the side of her neck. He hooked Rachel's backpack over her shoulder, and kissed her cheek one more time.

"I'll call you later," he said.

Rachel slouched down into the seat, vaguely aware that the bus driver was watching her from the rearview mirror. She clutched her backpack and allowed her mind to wander. For the first half of the ride she thought about nothing but Henry—the look on his face when she'd walked into the room, the way his arm sheltered her shoulders. How did he always know how she felt, and why did he care so much? Her mind drifted to the conversations of the afternoon, savoring, especially, what Sandra and Damara had said. Henry had come alive, they'd said—she, too, felt like a part of her had risen from the dead. Then she remembered their discussion with Sister Gloria about their schools—Sandra's ire, Damara's hurt, Henry's resignation. There's got to be something we can do, something important, she thought for the hundredth time.

She broached the subject that night at dinner. Her newfound freedom had made her bold, and there was nothing she feared talking about now. Well, almost nothing. They didn't know the whole truth about Henry, of course, but she told herself that she needed time to adjust before she fought that battle. And in her heart, she knew it would be a battle. Right now she needed to pick her uncles' brains—after all, they were cops. They'd worked for the city for years. Maybe they could shed some light on how all this worked.

"Remember last week when I visited my friends' school, and they came to mine?" she asked as Nana scooped rigatoni into her plate.

"Yes. I remember. I asked you about it, and you said, 'It was okay.' That was it. You've been in a cloud lately, Rachel. Are you sure you're eating enough?"

"Pass the cheese," Uncle Tommy said.

"Is there any more diet soda?" Uncle Johnny asked, walking to the refrigerator.

"Look in the back—there's a brand new one," Nana answered.

"How can you drink that stuff?" Uncle Tommy looked revolted.

"Anyway," Rachel continued, "you wouldn't believe the difference between our schools."

"What school did you visit?" asked Uncle Tommy.

"Jefferson—that's where Henry and Damara go. Anyway, you wouldn't believe how run down it was.

The bathrooms didn't work, the ceilings leaked—even the chairs were broken. And the gym—what a mess. My school looked like a palace, in comparison."

"That's a shame," said Uncle Tommy, "that used to be a decent area. You know, Rachel, I'm still not crazy about you going to those parts of the city."

"Is that a bad neighborhood?" Nana asked, suddenly concerned. "Because I wouldn't have let her go…"

Here we go again, Rachel thought. She tried to keep the conversation on track. "It was the middle of the day, and I was perfectly safe. Anyway, the point is, it seems so unfair. Why should our school be so great, and theirs be so awful?"

Grampy looked up at Rachel. "Unfair?" he said, and Rachel was surprised at the hostility in his tone. "It has nothing to do with unfair. People need to take care of their property. That's all." He grabbed his glass so hard that the ice water inside shook and almost spilled over the top.

"Calm down before you have a stroke," said Nana, passing the salad.

Rachel had no idea what Grampy meant, and why he was so upset. "What? I'm not talking about anybody's property. This is a public school. Doesn't it belong to the city?" She looked to Uncle Tommy for an answer.

"Of course it's a public school," he said, "but it's more complicated than that."

"How?" Rachel persisted.

Uncle Tommy sighed. A piece of bread bobbed around in his mouth as he spoke. "The school gets funded mostly by people's property taxes. People who live out here, like us, pay more taxes than people who live in the city. So naturally, the schools get more money. That's just the way the system works."

"But that's not fair," Rachel said without thinking.

Grampy looked like he might erupt again, but Nana spoke first. "Rachel, I've told you before, people work their whole lives to be able to afford to live here," she said. "We earned that school you go to. No one handed us anything. We can't help it if other people don't work so hard. No one is stopping them from making a better life, the way we did for you."

If no one is stopping them, Rachel thought, then why did you freak out that day when I suggested Sandra move next door? She forced herself to keep to the subject of the schools. "So what are you saying—that it's Henry and Damara's *fault* that their school is a dump? That they don't deserve something better?"

Uncle Johnny tried to smooth things over. "Of course it's not their fault, honey. They're good kids, and they do deserve better. And it's great that you care so much about other people." He looked at Nana. They operate like a tag team, Rachel thought.

"That's true," said Nana. "Rachel is a wonderful girl," she announced, "it's important to care about others. Now, enough. Tommy, you haven't mentioned Joan lately. How are things going?"

"Wait a minute! I wasn't done talking about this yet. I wanted to know if there was anything we could do."

"*Do?*" asked Uncle Tommy. "What do you mean, *do?*"

"Yeah, *do,* to change things. To make things better."

Nana's voice was firm. "Rachel, that's enough. Things are fine the way they are. You're upsetting your grandfather." Grampy was scowling, rubbing at a bit of sauce that had spilled onto his shirt. Why was Nana suddenly so afraid of upsetting him? She was usually the one who was in his face.

Rachel carried her plate to the sink. "I have homework," she said, and left the room, defeated for now. But she couldn't give up the idea that there must be some way she could help, some way she could change things for the better. At least, she knew she had to try. For Henry.

Chapter 20

Boycott

The Civil Rights Movement—how ironic, Rachel thought, sitting through a video in history class the following Monday morning. Over the weekend she'd talked and talked with Henry, telling him what her family had said, and growing more frustrated every minute. He'd listened quietly for hours, until finally he'd pulled her in close and said, "Rachel, thank you for caring. But can we talk about something else for a while?"

On Saturday they'd caught a movie with Sandra, Damara and Darrin—Darrin's expression when he saw them together was worth the price of admission. He'd watched every move Henry made, astonished. Henry, of course, had played it up, keeping Rachel near, with his arm around her shoulders or waist every moment that they were together. While they were in line for popcorn, Rachel noticed Darrin staring at her. Henry noticed too; he held her chin and drew her up, bending forward until their lips met in a long, soft kiss that left Rachel feeling limp. "Sorry," he'd whispered when Darrin finally turned away, "I'm just trying to drive Darrin crazy."

"You're driving *me* crazy," Rachel said, but she laughed at the sight of Darrin shaking his head in disbelief.

That night, while Henry drove her home, Rachel felt a sudden unease. "Henry, we can probably trust Damara, but what if Darrin lets it slip about us around their parents? Aren't you afraid they'll say something to your family?"

Henry took a deep breath. "I thought about that, and you're right—Mrs. Thomas would be on the phone with my mom in a split second. So..." he paused and glanced at Rachel..."I told them."

"You did?"

"I didn't have a choice, Rachel. Word travels fast in our churches. I thought it would be better if they heard it from me."

Rachel didn't know how to feel. "I thought we were keeping it a secret," she muttered.

"I'm sorry."

"It's okay—I'm just surprised. Were they upset?"

"Not upset—maybe concerned. I told you, they just worry. My grandpa gave me all kinds of lectures about how to behave, being a man of God—the usual. It's not like we're the only interracial couple they know—there's several in our church."

"Oh. I haven't really thought of us as an 'interracial couple.' It sounds so weird."

"You did notice that I'm black, right?" Henry asked.

"Don't make fun of me, Henry."

"Sorry."

"What else did they say?"

"Not too much." Henry seemed to be intentionally tight-lipped.

"What did your mother say?" Rachel persisted.

"Well—she was probably a little disappointed. She's been trying to match me up with Damara since we were six." He stopped abruptly, but then added, "She likes you though—she said so."

They drove along quietly for a few minutes, Rachel staring ahead pensively.

"Are you okay?" Henry asked.

"Yeah—it's just that, I feel kind of bad that your family knows and mine doesn't. Maybe I should tell them." But even as she spoke the words Rachel knew she wasn't ready to do any such thing. She groaned inwardly when she pictured the confrontation that would surely take place. Henry pulled over.

"What's wrong?" Rachel asked.

"Nothing. I just can't give you my full attention while I'm driving. Listen, don't do anything you don't want to do for my sake. I'm fine with the way things are for now."

"But I don't want you to think I'm ashamed of you, because I'm not." She looked at Henry's gentle, honest face. "Maybe I'm the one who's dangerous to you, Henry, or at least my family is. I don't want to hurt you."

Henry reached under her hair and cupped the side of her face in his palm. "You're not hurting me, I promise. I don't care what your family thinks. I only care what you think."

"You know what I think."

"Okay, then." He kissed her cheek before turning back to the steering wheel and heading out to the road. "So what do you want to do tomorrow?"

"I don't know—Nana's making sauce. Do you want to come over for dinner?"

"I thought we just agreed that we weren't going to say anything yet."

"We did. But you could come over as my friend. The more they get to know you, the easier it will be later, when I tell them."

"I don't know, Rachel. I don't think I could do that."

"Do what?"

"Pretend that we're just friends. I don't think I could trust myself to be that close to you and not touch you. It would be torture."

Rachel hugged Henry's arm. "Thanks."

"How 'bout if we just walk around—maybe go to a museum?"

Rachel had to admit that she was beginning to enjoy the anonymity of urban life. "But I hate to keep making you drive back and forth. Maybe I can take the train in."

"Is Nana gonna be okay with that?"

"I think so, as long as she knows I'm getting a ride home later, when it starts getting dark. I'll ask Uncle Johnny to drive me to the train station."

After a dream-like Sunday alone with Henry (not counting the other millions of people brushing past them in Center City), here she was, back in school, watching this video on the Civil Rights Movement, and thinking, how many years ago did all this take place? Forty? More than two of my lifetimes ago. The narrator went through a timeline of events, beginning with the Montgomery Bus Boycott and ending in the late sixties. So, if all this happened so long ago, why are the schools still so unequal? It didn't make sense to Rachel. She thought of asking the teacher, but when the lights came on she saw that none of the other kids looked even mildly interested. Besides, the bell rang and class was over.

She gathered up her books and headed to the gym for her least favorite period of the day, finding her spot next to Tina Marie in the locker room.

"Hey," said Tina Marie, "let's get a pass to use the machines today. I'm sure Ms. Kerby will let us."

"Okay," answered Rachel. "Anything is better than volleyball." Ms. Kerby, a short-haired young woman who loved volleyball, gave them the passes and they left the gym, making their way through the hall to the exercise room. Rachel tugged at her shorts self-consciously.

"I hate walking around like this," she complained.

"It's only down the hall. Besides, you're looking good. Are you losing weight?"

"I don't know—I haven't weighed myself lately."

"Well, something looks different. Maybe it's your hair. Did you get it cut?"

"I just had Nana trim the ends. But I, um, wear it down now." Henry likes it that way, she thought, remembering how it felt when Henry touched her hair.

"Rach, we're here!" Tina Marie exclaimed. She'd walked right past the door to the exercise room. Tina Marie pulled her back. "God, you're more of an airhead than usual today. Come on."

Rachel chose an exercise bike on the end of the row, lowered the seat, and got on. She pushed the pedals, adjusting the tension so that it wasn't too taxing. She needed to think, but being in this room brought back the painful memory of Henry, Sandra, Damara, and Darrin standing outside looking in, and all she could think about was the disbelief on their faces. Was that what they were—outsiders, looking in? What are they doing at their schools right now, she wondered, while I'm here on this expensive equipment? It didn't even seem right to use it any more. It's so unfair . . . the words echoed in her head in rhythm with her feet on the pedals . . . it's so unfair . . . The difference between their schools was just as unfair as the segregation she'd just learned about in history class. Both were part of a larger—what was the word Uncle Tommy had used? *System. That's just the way the system works,* he'd said— probably the same thing people said forty years ago. Maybe someone had said it to Rosa Parks when she sat down at the front of that bus . . . *that's just the way the system works . . .*

The idea came to Rachel like a bolt of lightening. She jumped off the bike so suddenly that it startled Tina Marie.

"Where are you going?" she asked.

232

"I'm done," Rachel replied, storming out of the room. She headed down the hallway, walked right past the girl's locker room, and stomped into the principal's office, still wearing her gym shorts.

"Dr. Shank," she said in the firmest voice she could manage, "My name is Rachel Matrone. And I'm declaring a boycott."

Chapter 21

The Truth Hurts

Rachel's boycott lasted exactly two hours. Her suspension lasted three days.

At first, Dr. Shank had smiled, thinking Rachel was joking. "Sit down, Rachel," she said. "Tell me what this is about."

Rachel had not smiled back.

"I'm doing what Rosa Parks did—I'm boycotting the gym, the exercise room, the media center—anything that we have and other schools don't. I guess the TV studio too, except I've never been in there anyway. I don't think we should use them until things become more equal." Rachel knew she was making very little sense. Her voice shook.

Dr. Shank's smile faded. "Rachel, please sit down. I have no idea what you're talking about, and why you're out here in your gym uniform." Rachel looked down at her thighs, barely covered by thin, gray cotton shorts; she felt exposed in more ways than one. "Why don't you start from the beginning?"

She sat down and tried to explain more coherently. "You know Sister Gloria, right? Well, I'm in her group—we have this club, after school. And she arranged these school visits a few weeks ago."

"Yes, I remember. I approved it—I thought it was an interesting idea."

"That's when it all started. You wouldn't believe what their school looks like…" Rachel did her best to describe the images that she hadn't been able to shake since that day. She talked on and on, faltering, uncertain of her words, but strong in her intent. Dr. Shank listened patiently until Rachel was finished, leaning forward at her desk and holding her glasses in her hand.

"Rachel," she said, "I'm not unsympathetic. If I were, you would not have visited Jefferson, and, in fact, we would not have instituted the multicultural education program here at all. It took quite a bit of persuading to get the school board to approve it. Sister Gloria is a personal friend of mine." The notion that nuns and high school principals had friends distracted Rachel for a moment. "And I'm glad that you're paying attention in history class. But just what form do you envision this boycott taking?"

Rachel had not thought that far ahead. "Oh. I'm not sure."

Dr. Shank smiled. "Might I suggest that first you go change your clothing?" Rachel sensed that she was being dismissed. She suddenly felt very foolish. What could one person do, anyway? And it's not like anyone would listen to her—no one even knew who she was. What she needed were student leaders…she pictured the student council, and she knew that they would never get behind something like this. Right now they were busy planning the prom—Tina Marie had told her that. They would have no idea what she was talking about, and she doubted they would care to find out. Rachel realized that she was on her own. She stood.

"I will go get changed, Dr. Shank, but I'm serious about the boycott, even if I'm the only one. Starting right now, I refuse to use anything at this school that my friends don't have at their school."

"Rachel, I respect what you're trying to do. Be aware, though, that your actions, however well meant, will have personal consequences. Are you prepared for that?" No, thought Rachel, I'm not. But I'm going ahead anyway.

She left Dr. Shank's office and went to the empty locker room to change, trying to formulate a plan. How, exactly, would one go about boycotting school activities? Should she just stand out in the hall and refuse to move? A lot of good that would do—no one would even notice. No, she needed some way to draw attention to herself. Rachel shuddered—up until now, she'd spent most of her time shying away from attention. This did not come naturally to her. How can I make people notice what I'm doing? Maybe a sign would help—it seemed stupid, but it was the only idea she could come up with at the moment.

Tina Marie and the others were still at gym, but the period was about to end so she'd have to hurry. Her first stop was the art room, where Mr. Spinozzi was conducting class. She slipped into the room as quietly as she could.

"Hello, Rachel. What can I do for you?" Mr. Spinozzi was one of her favorite teachers. He was young, and good looking in a homey, casual sort of way. His sandy-brown hair fell into his eyes, and his clothes were always covered in paint, or clay, or some other globby material.

"I need to make some signs," Rachel said truthfully. "Can I borrow some paper and markers? Oh, and do you have any tape?" She didn't say what the signs were for; she knew Mr. Spinozzi would assume she was working on a school project.

"Sure—help yourself. You know where everything is." He waved toward the wall of supply shelves, and turned back to the class.

Rachel gathered several sheets of newsprint, a thick black marker and tape.

"Be careful with that marker," Mr. Spinozzi called as she left the classroom, "Don't get it on your clothes—it's permanent."

"Thanks," Rachel called back. Now, where should she begin? She approached the media center—this was as good a place as any. Wishing she had a table to work on, she spread the newsprint out on the floor. The bell rang, and the hall quickly filled with students. A tall boy walked out of the media center and almost tripped over her.

"Watch out," he said, annoyed.

"Sorry." She scooped up the paper before anyone could step on it. She took one sheet of newsprint and taped the edges to the wall next to the media center door. Then she wrote in the biggest letters that would fit on the paper, SCHOOLS SHOULD BE EQUAL! BOYCOTT!

She went over the letters several times to be sure they were dark enough. A few people stopped to watch, but then shrugged and walked away. Rachel followed the same process outside of the gym and the TV studio. By this time the halls were empty again. Now what? She sat down on the floor to wait. Maybe the editors of the school newspaper would come by and see her—in fact, she probably should have gone to them first, and told them what she was doing. Oh well, too late now. She felt obligated to stay put.

The longer Rachel sat, the more ridiculous she felt. The moments ticked on until half the class period was over. Finally, Mrs. Morton happened by.

"Miss Matrone, would you like to tell me what you're doing out here? Why aren't you in class?" Rachel stood, her heart beating up to her ears.

"I'm boycotting," she answered in an unsteady voice. She pointed to the sign.

"I see that. Is this related to a class assignment? Where is your hall pass?"

"No, it's not an assignment. I don't have a pass."

"Then I suggest you get to class. You're already very late. And please take down that sign."

"No, I can't do that. It's a boycott, I told you. I'm boycotting school activities until things get made more equal. You know, like Rosa Parks." Rachel knew she sounded preposterous. "I'm not moving from this spot."

Mrs. Morton stared at Rachel as if she couldn't believe her ears. "Are you defying me?" An incredulous smile played on the corners of her mouth.

Rachel tried to swallow, but her mouth was too dry. "Yes," she answered. "I guess I am."

"Oh, for goodness sakes! For the last time, take down that sign and go to class!" Mrs. Morton reached past Rachel and ripped the sign from the wall. Unfortunately, the words remained, clear as day—the writing from the permanent marker had bled through the thin paper to the pristine white surface of the wall.

Events after that were a blur. Mrs. Morton began screeching something about defacing school property, Dr. Shank and the assistant principals were called, and when Rachel still refused to move, school security arrived. Class let out, and word of the disturbance spread quickly, as students welcomed any diversion from their usual boring day. They pressed in around her, smirking, laughing, and trying to get a better look at the mousy girl who was at the center of the ruckus. More teachers arrived, assigned to disburse the crowd. Rachel was terrified, but held her ground. Dr. Shank informed Rachel that they'd called her grandmother; Rachel knew exactly what that would mean.

Sure enough, before long Rachel heard a familiar voice. "What's going on here?" Uncle Tommy pushed through the school security. His eyes moved from the guards, to the administrators, to the marred wall, to Rachel, where they settled in a cool, calculating stare. Rachel pictured Uncle Tommy working a crime scene, and she realized with horror that she was the criminal. Somehow her lifelong protector had just become her prosecutor. She pressed her back against the wall.

By this time the students had been ushered back to class; a few teachers in nearby classrooms stood in open doorways, straining to hear what was going on.

"And you are?" asked Dr. Shank.

"I'm Detective Tom Matrone, Rachel's uncle. I share guardianship with her grandparents."

One of the security guards took Rachel by the arm. "We need to move out of the hallway," he said, trying to lead her toward the office. Rachel did not budge and he pulled a little harder. She wasn't sure why the guard chose this moment to get tough—maybe he was showing off for Uncle Tommy.

"Please take your hands off my niece," Uncle Tommy said in a low growl. The guard moved away, shaking his head. "Now, Rachel, do you want to tell me what this is all about?"

Rachel tried her best to explain her actions to Uncle Tommy. He listened impassively as she tried to make him understand what she'd done and why she'd done it. When she was finished, Uncle Tommy turned to Dr. Shank.

"I apologize for my niece's actions. We will, of course, pay for any damage to the school." Then he turned back to Rachel. "I think you have made your point, whatever it was. You will come with me now to Dr. Shank's office, or I will pick you up and carry you." His voice remained stolid.

Rachel caved. She followed Uncle Tommy to the office, where the two of them waited in silence while Rachel's sentence was determined in the next room. After a few minutes Dr. Shank returned with the verdict: a three-day suspension and a fine of $300, plus the cost of the paint to cover the marker on the wall. Uncle Tommy apologized again and led Rachel out of the building, through the parking lot, and into his car. Rachel expected an explosion, but Uncle Tommy said nothing. She cried a little, quietly.

When they reached home she went directly to her room and closed the door, but that did not keep out the muffled sounds of Uncle Tommy explaining what had happened to Nana. Although she couldn't make out their exact words, she could hear the tenor of their voices; Uncle Tommy, still calm and even, while Nana became increasingly shrill. She waited for a knock at her door, but it didn't come. Apparently they'd decided to leave her alone for a while. She couldn't imagine whose idea that was—it certainly wasn't like either of them. And why was Uncle Tommy so calm? He must be so angry that he doesn't trust himself. She knew this was the quiet before the storm. She stirred around in her room, checking the clock every few minutes—only 1:30. Henry would still be in school. She realized she hadn't eaten lunch, but thankfully, for once Nana wasn't trying to force feed her. She turned on her TV and watched the afternoon soaps, waiting for the time to pass. At exactly 3:15 Henry called her cell.

He knew she'd been crying immediately. "What's wrong?" he asked. It took several minutes to make Henry understand the situation. He interrupted her story with questions, trying to get the sequence of events straight. When she finished he sighed, "Rachel."

"The worst part was everybody staring at me. I felt like a zoo animal."

"I wish I could come over," he said. "I can't stand to think of you all alone there." She heard footsteps in the background—Henry was pacing.

"I wish you could, too. But I don't think that would be a very good idea. Anyway, I'm not alone. They're all downstairs, waiting to pounce."

"You know what I mean. I wish I'd been there with you at school, too."

"I'm glad you weren't. At least you're not in trouble."

"Maybe I could have stopped you."

"I didn't want to be stopped. I'm glad I did it." Rachel felt calmer after she'd said that. It wasn't the end of the world, and at least she'd tried to make a statement.

"Maybe I could have held the paper—you could have gotten marker all over my chest instead of the wall."

She laughed in spite of herself. "That part was an accident. But it did make things much worse." If it hadn't been for the *defacing school property* charge, they probably would have left her alone until the end of the day. Her only crime would have been cutting class, and her punishment would have been an afternoon detention.

"So what do you think they'll do to you?"

"You mean other than the suspension and the fine?"

"No, I mean your family. They'll probably ground you, at least."

Rachel's calm was short-lived. She hadn't thought of that. Grounding would mean no after-school meetings, no weekend activities, and most importantly, no Henry. The idea slapped her hard. "Oh my gosh," she said. She started to cry again.

"Calm down, Rachel. Don't cry—please. Let's see what they say, okay?" Henry sounded so worried that Rachel covered the phone with her hand and tried to compose herself for his sake.

"Rachel, are you okay?" The words were becoming Henry's mantra.

"I'm fine," she lied. "Don't worry. Henry, I'd better go. They'll be up here any minute."

"Promise you'll call me later, okay?"

"Of course I'll call you. That is, if they don't take my cell phone away."

"Maybe they won't think of it."

When Rachel hung up, she turned her off her phone and hid it in her sock drawer. Out of sight, out of mind, she hoped. A few minutes later she heard the long-awaited knock on her door. Nana, Uncle Tommy, and Uncle Johnny lined up next to her bed like a firing squad.

"I want to know who put you up to this, Rachel," Nana said.

"What?"

"It's not fair that you should take the punishment alone. Whose idea was this stunt?"

"Nana, it was no one's idea but my own." Rachel looked at Uncle Tommy. "I told you, I thought of it after history today. Uncle Tommy, didn't you tell her?" The idea of going through the whole story again with Nana was unbearable. She suddenly felt exhausted.

"He told me," said Nana, "I just didn't believe him."

"This is not like you, Rachel," said Uncle Johnny, more gently. He sat at the edge of her bed. "Was it these new friends of yours? You can tell us. It couldn't have been the nun, could it?"

Rachel sprang up to her feet. "Uncle Johnny, please! They had nothing to do with this. It was a spur of the moment decision—no one was in on it. It just sort of happened. Please don't blame anyone else!" Rachel felt close to panic.

"Okay, okay!" Uncle Johnny said. "Take it easy, Rach. Sit down."

Still in dread, she sat.

"I guess I don't have to say how disappointed I am in your behavior," Nana said. "I simply do not understand."

"I'm sorry. I didn't mean to disappoint you. I was trying to do something good. I guess it didn't turn out so well." No one answered. The silence made her misery worse— why were they keeping her in suspense? Were they going to ground her or not? Finally, Nana spoke.

"And just so you know, you'll be earning that $300 by working for me, starting with cleaning the house tomorrow. Now, I'm going to go start dinner. We've decided not to mention this to your grandfather—it would kill him. I hope you've learned a lesson, young lady." With that, Nana left the room, and Uncle Johnny followed, looking almost as miserable as Rachel felt.

Rachel waited for Uncle Tommy to say something. Perhaps they'd left it to him to dish out her punishment; that wouldn't have been a surprise. Nana was too softhearted, at least when it came to Rachel, and Uncle

Johnny was too much of a kid himself to do any serious disciplining. Uncle Tommy pulled out her desk chair and sat quietly; he picked up the ruler on her desk and felt its edges absently. He still seemed to be stewing.

When she could stand it no longer, Rachel asked, "Are you going to tell me my punishment now?"

Uncle Tommy seemed surprised. "I think you've been punished enough for one day," he said.

Compassion was the one thing Rachel had not expected. "Really? So that's it—cleaning the house for Nana?" They're not very good at this punishment stuff, she realized. But then, since she'd never been in any real trouble before, they hadn't had much practice.

"Rach, when I saw you standing in that crowd of people, humiliated like that..." Uncle Tommy shook his head, and she heard an ache in his voice. "You looked scared to death."

"I was," she admitted. "But you seemed so...I don't know...cold. And the way you talked to me—I was really afraid you were going to carry me out of the school."

"Someone had to save you from yourself, Rachel." He paused for a moment, and then his expression grew kind. "No, I'm not going to punish you, babe. I stayed behind to tell you something." Rachel waited. Uncle Tommy cleared his throat. "It's just this—I get what you were trying to do today. I may not agree with you, but I respect you for standing up for what you believe in. Not a lot of kids your age would do that. In a crazy way, I'm proud of you. But don't tell Nana I said that." He put the ruler down and picked up a paper clip, tossing it from one hand to the other. "It's good to have convictions. Your dad was like that—once he got an idea in his head, nobody could tell him different. And he was always going on about helping people, too."

"Really?"

"Absolutely. He had some pretty good fights with your grandfather sometimes." He paused, but then continued, resolved. "Yeah, your dad was always in it for the underdog. In fact, I always thought that was what drew him to your mom—he thought he could help her. And he did for a while, too. Then he died, and she fell apart."

"What do you mean?"

"She loved you, Rachel, but she struggled … drugs."

"Oh." Rachel let this information wash over her. She loved me, but she loved heroin, or crack, or whatever it was, more. It was too much to absorb at once. She tucked it away for a later time, a time when Henry was near. "Why didn't you ever tell me this?" she asked.

"You know how Nana is. She gets all worked up, and it seemed easier to leave the past alone. Maybe she was afraid you'd turn out like her, like your mother, I mean. I see now that we were wrong—we should have been honest with you from the start. I see him when I look at you, Rachel—you're so much like him. I don't know how I didn't see it before. Sweet, and kind, but solid as a rock. And brave—you did a very brave thing today, even if it was pretty stupid." Uncle Tommy smiled. "Anyway, you keep standing up for what you believe in. Don't let anybody tell you different."

"I might hold you to that someday, Uncle Tommy."

Uncle Tommy nodded, his eyes thoughtful. "I know you might, babe," he said. A moment of understanding flickered between them, and then was gone. "One more thing," he added, standing to leave. "You can vacuum my car after dinner."

Chapter 22

The Letter

𝔗𝔥𝔢 𝔗𝔬𝔴𝔫𝔰𝔥𝔦𝔭 ℭ𝔯𝔦𝔢𝔯
Coventry Township High School's Voice of the Students

Several students witnessed a disturbance on the first floor last week, as heretofore unknown junior Rachel Matrone vandalized the hallways in an attempt to call attention to herself. Matrone used permanent marker to write on the walls in a misguided effort to mimic the Montgomery Bus Boycott—an event that triggered the Civil Rights Movement.

Economics teacher Mrs. Morton was the first to discover Matrone's antics. "This kind of behavior can never be condoned," she stated. "It goes against everything we believe in, and everything the leaders of the Civil Rights Movement stood for, I might add."

Matrone was suspended from classes and received a fine. She couldn't be reached for comment.

Again Henry sighed, "Rachel." He handed the newspaper to Sandra and tightened his arm around Rachel as much as he dared with Sister Gloria in the room.

"At least you got your name in the paper," said Sandra. Henry glowered at her.

"Just looking at the bright side," she said. "What do they mean, 'couldn't be reached for comment'?"

"No idea," answered Rachel. "No one asked me anything."

"May I see that, please?" asked Sister Gloria. They sat in their usual places in the familiar multicolored conference room. Sister Gloria read through the article quickly. "Rachel, I'm so sorry this happened. I wish you had come to me first."

"It was a snap decision. I thought I could make a statement." Rachel resisted the urge to turn and bury her face in Henry's shoulder, wishing she could hide herself there forever—or at the very least, until high school was over. But in the present company she'd have to content herself with sitting here, pressed into his side, which was far better than sitting alone in her room as she had been for almost two weeks. She'd missed last week's meeting because of her suspension, and when the weekend came, Henry had suggested they lay low.

"I want to see you, too," he'd said, "but we don't want to push our luck. Even though they didn't ground you, we need to give your family a chance to chill out. We gotta think long term. Next week, things will be back to normal, you'll see." Rachel had agreed, reluctantly, wondering two things: first, what did Henry mean by *long term*, and second, how could things ever be normal again? She'd waited until she'd hung up to cry.

"You must be so embarrassed," said Damara. Embarrassed was only the introduction to this experience, Rachel thought. Abashed, mortified, dismayed, disgraced—her life at school now read like a thesaurus of humiliation. And the newspaper article had closed the book on any chance of normal. She was now, officially, a pariah. Henry nudged her a centimeter closer.

Darrin was reading the article now—he looked up at Rachel and laughed. "Way to go, Rachel," he said. "The wild child strikes again! And the marker on the wall— great touch! Although spray paint would have been better..."

Henry loosened his arm around Rachel and pushed toward the edge of the couch. "Would you excuse me, please," he said to her politely, "while I take Darrin outside and beat the crap out of him?" Rachel saw that he wasn't kidding. She tried to pull him back.

"Come on, fat boy, I'm ready," answered Darrin, trying to stand. Damara held on to the back of his shirt.

"I think that's enough, boys," said Sister Gloria sternly. "This is not helpful to Rachel."

Henry smoldered for a minute, but eventually sat back and pulled Rachel close again. "Sorry," he whispered to her.

Darrin snatched his shirt away from Damara, but also sat down. He scowled at Henry, but softened when he turned to Rachel. "Seriously, I think what you tried to do was cool."

"Yeah," said Sandra, "So do I. Thanks."

"I don't see why you're thanking me. I didn't accomplish anything." Rachel pointed to the newspaper. "They didn't even get what I was trying to say. I just made a mess of the whole thing."

Sister Gloria leaned forward and looked directly into Rachel's eyes. "Don't be so hard on yourself," she said. "Not everyone has the capacity, or the compassion, to feel things as deeply as you do. You tried to make a difference, and that's all any of us can do. We learn from our mistakes—next time, you'll think things through more carefully."

"Next time?" asked Henry. "I don't want Rachel getting into any more trouble."

"Of course not—no one wants that. But there are other avenues one can take to make a statement."

"Like what?" Rachel asked. She felt, rather than heard, a low rumble coming from Henry, but she ignored it. "Do you think we could do something more organized—like a real boycott?"

Henry sat up straight and took Rachel by the shoulders. "Have you lost your mind? If your family gets wind of something like that I will never see you again. Maybe I'm being selfish, but it's not worth it to me." He loosened her hair where it was tucked behind her ear and combed it through with his fingers.

"I'm going to puke," said Darrin.

"Actually, I was thinking of something a little less ambitious," said Sister Gloria, "like perhaps, a letter to that school newspaper, or maybe to the school board."

"What good would that do?" asked Darrin.

"It might help to raise awareness. At least it would give you an opportunity to explain what you did, Rachel. And if I'm correct, the school board meetings are broadcast on local TV. A letter might have more impact than you think. And you may find you have allies that you didn't know about."

"So you're saying if we write a letter they might read it on TV?" asked Rachel.

"It would only be on your local cable station, but possibly, yes."

"Would we have to sign this letter?" asked Darrin. Damara rolled her eyes.

"Yes, that would be important. But no one is asking any of you to do anything that you're not comfortable with. It's just something to think about."

A letter. Rachel knew she was a decent writer—a letter was something she could handle easily. Why hadn't she thought of that? She felt hope returning.

"We don't have much more time left today," said Sister Gloria, looking at her watch. She stood to leave. "Rachel, keep the faith. Things are going to get better."

"Thanks." Rachel returned her smile. "I guess they can't get worse." Sister Gloria glided from the room. Henry started to say something, but stopped, frowning. Rachel sensed he was annoyed—was he finally losing patience with her? Maybe he thought the letter was another bad idea—it would certainly be easier to forget the whole thing. Suddenly, she felt unsure.

"Let's wait outside for the bus," Henry said. "I need some fresh air."

"Good idea," Darrin agreed. "It's stuffy in here."

"I was talking to Rachel," said Henry. Sandra and Damara laughed.

"We'll wait for you here, Henry" said Damara. "Call us when you're ready to leave."

Henry took Rachel's hand and led her out of the office, pulling her down the dim hallway. He seemed determined about something. When they stepped out of the building he closed the heavy steel door behind them, turned Rachel into the shadow of the doorway and took her in his arms, pressing her close against his chest.

"I missed you so much," he whispered. He leaned down and kissed the top of her head, burying his face in her hair. "I needed to be alone with you, just for a few minutes."

Rachel could barely breathe, Henry was holding her so tight, but the thought of complaining did not occur to her. "I missed you, too," she managed to squeak out.

He laughed and relaxed his grip a little. "Sorry," he said. "It's just the last few weeks seemed like years."

"I'm the one who's sorry. It's my fault we couldn't see each other."

"Shut up," Henry said. He entwined his hand in her hair and kissed her, and Rachel thought, yes, things are getting better already.

Chapter 23

Birthday Present

Henry had been right, and things did go back to normal, at least at home. Nana cooked and cleaned and Grampy worked outside, getting his garden ready for the change of seasons. They both seemed to move a little slower than before, as if the winter had left a layer of heavy snow that the spring sun couldn't melt away. Sometimes Rachel had to tell Nana things more than once. She asked Uncle Tommy if he'd noticed the change.

"They're getting older, Rach," was all he'd said, as if that were explanation enough. Rachel continued to keep her secret from them. She'd told Nana there'd be no more lies; now she'd have to learn to live with the guilt of that broken promise. It seemed, somehow, more for their sake than hers.

She tried to settle back into anonymity at school, ignoring the icy stares or the sly laughter, until eventually a new scandal erupted; some seniors were caught with their parents' prescription medications in their lockers. Thankful for the fickle nature of planet high school, Rachel kept her head down and trudged through, biding her time each day until school let out and she could talk to Henry, or on really good days, be with him. They wrote the letter to the school board over the course of a few weeks, changing and adding to it to include each one's personal feelings and perspectives. To Rachel's surprise, even Darrin got involved, taking pictures of his school with his cell phone. When she felt satisfied that they'd done their best, they put the letter and the pictures into a packet and gave it to Sister Gloria, who promised to see that it got into the right hands. That's that, she thought—at least we tried.

In late March Henry had his seventeenth birthday, which happened to fall on Easter Sunday. A few days before, Rachel chatted on the phone with Sandra.

"So," Sandra asked, "have you thought about what to give Henry for his birthday?" The question seemed innocent enough, but there was an insinuation in Sandra's voice that Rachel had come to know all too well. She played dumb.

"I'm thinking of getting him some CDs, and maybe a gift certificate for clothes. Oh, and I guess I'll take him out to dinner, but not until after Easter."

"I can think of something else you could give him that he'd probably like much better."

Rachel took a deep breath. "And what would that be, Sandra?"

"Yourself, of course. Unless you've given him that gift already." Sandra had tried to steer the conversation in this direction before, but Damara had always been there to stop her. This time Rachel was on her own.

"Not that it's any of your business, Sandra, but no, I have not. Can we talk about something else now?"

"Okay, okay. It's just that, the way you two can't keep your hands off each other, I was sure something had happened by now."

Rachel had to admit that she, too, had feared something would happen by now, and was very relieved that it hadn't. As much as she craved Henry's touch, as much as she relived every soft kiss when they were apart, she knew she wasn't ready to go further. She'd been worried, at first, that Henry would want more, but he seemed as content as she was, and very much in control. When they were together Rachel sensed an imaginary line, their own personal equator, that Henry would not cross.

On the night of his birthday she'd announced to Nana that she was going to church with Henry's family, which was the absolute truth.

"Rachel, it's Easter," Nana had complained. "Why can't you go to your own church?"

"I went to our church this morning, remember? It's Henry's birthday, and his parents invited us. We're going back to his house for cake after. And I have off from school tomorrow." Nana couldn't think of any more objections, so after stuffing Rachel with ravioli, she reluctantly gave in.

"Do you need a ride?" asked Uncle Tommy.

"No—Henry's picking me up." Rachel sensed Uncle Tommy straining to control himself, but he said nothing.

It was late that evening when Henry took her home; he hummed dreamily as he drove. Rachel decided to approach the subject of her talk with Sandra.

"I had a funny conversation with Sandra the other day," she began.

"Do tell."

"Well, not really funny, but, well, you know Sandra. She wanted to know, um ... I guess she asked me ... well, she didn't really ask me ..."

"Spit it out, Rachel."

"She implied that I should give you something different for your birthday."

"I love the stuff you got me! Don't listen to Sandra."

"No—actually, she meant something more in the way of an experience." Rachel felt herself blushing; she hoped it was too dark for Henry to notice.

"An experience? You mean like tickets to a show or something?" Henry's voice lilted—he liked that idea.

"No, not a show. Remember, this was Sandra talking. She meant a different kind of experience." Henry waited for her to continue. "Between you and me," Rachel explained.

"Oh—ohhh. Good old Sandra. And what did you tell her?"

"That it was none of her business."

"Good, because it isn't."

"Right, I know. It isn't."

"Okay, then."

The silence that followed was so awkward that Rachel was sorry she'd said anything. She breathed a ragged sigh.

"You want to talk about this, don't you?" asked Henry.

"Only if you do."

"You started it. Go ahead."

"It's nothing, really. I just wondered if you'd thought about it at all. Not that I'm saying I want to…" Rachel added quickly, "…well, not that I don't want to, either, it's just, maybe not yet…"

Henry pulled over and turned off the ignition, which Rachel knew meant he had something important to say. "You want to know if I've thought about it at all?" he asked.

"Well, yeah."

Henry squinted, trying to concentrate. "Let me think. Since we started going out—that was, what, two months ago?"

"Two months, two weeks, three days," Rachel replied.

Henry grinned. "Okay. In that two months, two weeks, and three days I might have thought about it once or twice…a day. An hour. A minute. Is that what you wanted to know?"

Rachel was flustered. "I guess. I just wondered, that's all. You've just been so careful…I'm glad, though, really. Don't get the wrong idea."

Henry shook his head. "Rachel, you're so funny. But I'm glad you brought this up—we probably should talk about it." His hand lay absently on Rachel's shoulder. "You remember all the 'man of God' stuff I told you my grandfather goes on about sometimes?"

"Yeah?"

"Here's the thing. He's kind of right. What I mean is, I am thinking of following in that direction." Of course, Rachel knew Henry's family was religious in a way that was different from her family. She wasn't sure what that had to do with anything, though. She waited for him to continue.

"So, what I'm trying to say is, underneath all the crazy services, and the music, and the thee's and thou's, I guess, I really do believe. I wasn't sure for a while, but God answered a big prayer for me. And I guess I owe him something."

"Okay … ?" Rachel still wasn't following Henry's logic. "What does that have to do with what we were talking about?"

"Well, I'm not a saint or anything, but it's just that things are supposed to go in a certain order. I guess I don't think we should rush into sex." Rachel cringed; every ounce of shyness in her soul rose to the surface. "What I'm saying, Rachel, is that I want to do things right. I know it sounds crazy, but that's the way I was raised."

"Oh. Well. That's fine. That's great. Good." The conversation had taken such an unexpected turn that Rachel began to giggle.

"Do you think that's funny?" Henry asked.

"No, Henry, I'm sorry. You just took me by surprise, that's all." She put her arms around his neck and pulled his head down toward her. "But you're wrong about one thing—you are a saint. How did I get so lucky?" She reached for his lips in a series of short, quick kisses. He rubbed the back of her neck.

"One thing, Henry," she asked, resting her head on his shoulder. "When you said God answered your prayer—was that anything you can tell me about?"

"I thought that was obvious, Rachel," he said. "It was you, of course. God gave me you. I promised him I'd take care of you, and that's what I plan to do." Rachel couldn't answer—she'd started to cry. "Shh, don't cry," Henry whispered, holding her, stroking her hair. "Of course it was you. Shh, baby, don't cry."

Chapter 24

Long Night

They want me to do *what?*" Rachel felt her stomach lurch.

"The school board has invited you to attend their next meeting to read your letter to them. It's a wonderful opportunity, Rachel, and I suspect it was Dr. Shank's idea." Sister Gloria was beaming.

"Can't you read it?" Rachel asked. They sat on a bench at the park, facing a winding garden of perennials in full bloom. She and Henry had spent a few peaceful afternoons here over the last month, and this spot among the tulips was Rachel's favorite. But right now she might as well have been sitting inside a cardboard box.

"It's important that you read it, Rachel," Sister Gloria explained. "I'll be there, of course, but what makes this special is that it came from you, from a young person in the district."

"We all wrote the letter together—why do I have to be the one to read it?" Rachel looked at Henry pleadingly. He squeezed her hand.

"I'll read it," Sandra volunteered.

"It's Rachel's school district," Sister Gloria said again. "She should read the letter." Rachel had never known Sister Gloria to be so firm—what happened to "you don't have to do anything you're not comfortable with," she wondered? Her stomach tied itself into a tight knot. She stared at a little boy chasing his sister around a blanket a few yards away.

"But people are just starting to forget about me again." Rachel tried not to beg, but it was hard to keep the desperation out of her voice.

Henry came to her rescue, echoing the words Sister Gloria had said so often. "Rachel doesn't have to do anything she doesn't want to do."

"Of course she doesn't," Sister Gloria agreed. "But I hope you'll reconsider, Rachel. You would simply be reading the letter. I really think you could handle this. You may find you're stronger than you think." Sister Gloria stood. "I'm off, now. I'll see you all on Thursday." She walked down the pathway, narrowly avoiding a collision with the little boy. His mother apologized and sat him down on the blanket with a box of Cheez-Its.

"What's the big deal, Rachel?" Sandra asked. "One minute, you're staging a boycott, and the next, you're afraid to read a letter to a few people sitting around a table. I don't get it."

"Yeah, well, you wouldn't," said Henry, leaving the rest of the insult to Sandra's imagination. "Don't you have to be somewhere, Sandra?"

"Henry, don't," said Rachel. "She's right. I started this, and I should finish it. I'm just being a baby."

Henry kissed the top of her head. "You're not a baby."

"Actually, I do have to be somewhere," Sandra said abruptly. "I'm gonna catch that bus. I'll call you later, Rachel." She grabbed her watermelon-sized purse, which had been sitting on the ground between her feet, and ran.

"Bye," Rachel called after her. Sandra made it to the bus just in time, and Rachel saw her digging around for her wallet as the bus pulled away. "That wasn't very nice," she said to Henry.

"I know. I'll call her and apologize later."

"I know I should do this, Henry. I'm just so nervous in front of people. But I guess it doesn't matter what anybody thinks of me at this point." Rachel pictured the jeers at school starting all over again. Without realizing it, she grimaced.

"It does matter," Henry answered. "You still have another year left at that school. I don't want you to be miserable. You should have friends there, too."

"I think I stopped having friends there the day Antonella left." When she'd said the name, Rachel realized how long it had been since she'd even thought of Antonella. "I'm not sure what happened."

"Come on Rachel, there's gotta be some nice kids at that school."

"There are. There're plenty of nice kids. I guess none of them were friends with Antonella and her crowd, though."

"I can't picture you hanging out with the mean girls."

"I didn't realize it, but I guess they were the mean girls, in a way—kind of stuck-up, like a clique. I know, it seems crazy now. I guess I was sort of a mascot—Antonella's little friend from next door."

"You're nobody's mascot," Henry said. "You're worth five hundred Antonella's. Five thousand. Five million."

"Okay, Henry, I get the point. Thanks."

"If you really want to do this, though, I can help you."

"How? It would look weird if you stood there at the microphone with me."

"That's not what I meant. I could help you practice. You could read the letter to me over and over again until you get it down. That's what I do when I have to speak at church."

"When do you speak at church?" Rachel asked. There were still so many things she didn't know about Henry. Now she pictured him behind the big wooden pulpit in the sanctuary of his grandfather's church. Henry's church, too, she realized.

"Every now and then, whenever my grandpa makes me. Nothing big—I read Scripture, or make an announcement, or maybe take the offering. It's no big deal."

"You're amazing," Rachel said.

"There's nothing amazing about it. You get used to it after a while. It helps if you feel prepared."

Henry always managed to make her feel better. "Okay, I guess I can try. I'll call Sister Gloria tonight."

By the evening of the meeting a few weeks later, Rachel did feel prepared. She'd practiced reading the letter in front of Henry a hundred times, until she could have recited it from memory. This won't be so hard, she told herself. Just read the letter and sit down. Rachel sat in the first row, Henry on one side, Sister Gloria on the other, Sandra, Damara, and Darrin in the row directly behind them. They waited through an hour of school board business, which gave Rachel plenty of time to study the adults sitting behind microphones at the long table up on the stage. There was a tall, white-haired man on the end— Rachel knew he was Dr. Boyd, the district superintendent. The rest, she figured, must be the members of the board— four men and two women that she had never seen before. They varied in age, although most of them looked to be somewhere in their forties. They were all white—funny, I never would have noticed that before, Rachel thought. The meeting droned on and on in what, as far as Rachel was concerned, could have been an unknown tongue. If only she'd been allowed to go first; the longer she waited, the more she felt like hiding under her seat. She heard Darrin yawn.

"Try to stay awake," Sandra whispered to him. Rachel looked around the middle school auditorium—it was smaller than the one she was used to now, but still newly renovated. The last time she'd been in this room was the night of her eighth grade graduation, almost three years ago. It had been packed that night; she remembered spotting Nana in the crowd, looking so proud, with a bouquet of roses in her lap. It was much less crowded tonight, thank goodness. Rachel counted fifty or so people scattered around the room. She noticed Dr. Shank sitting a few rows behind them, and she craned her neck to see if Nana or the uncles might have come. Rachel had mentioned it casually at dinner, not sure if she really wanted them there.

"Tonight? You're reading something at the school board meeting tonight? Rachel, why didn't you say something sooner?" Nana had asked.

"I didn't want to make a big deal out of it."

"What, exactly, are you reading?" asked Uncle Tommy between mouthfuls.

"A letter about the schools, about how they're unequal."

"I thought you'd forgotten about that," Nana said. "You're not going to get into any trouble, are you?" She glanced at Grampy, but he was looking down at his plate.

"Nana, I'm just reading a letter. I'm not crashing the meeting—the school board invited me. Like I said, it's not a big deal. You don't really have to come. You can watch it on cable later, if you want."

Grampy stood. He'd hardly touched his food. "I don't feel so good," he said. "I'm gonna go lay down." He pushed in his chair and left the room.

"What's wrong with Grampy?" Rachel asked. She wondered if she'd upset him. As far as she knew, he was still in the dark about her previous experience.

"His stomach has been bothering him lately. It's probably indigestion."

"We'll try to be there tonight, babe," Uncle Tommy said.

"Do you need a ride?" asked Uncle Johnny.

"No, thanks. Henry's picking me up." Again, Rachel noticed a strange look cross Uncle Tommy's face. He knows, she thought, but he's not saying anything yet.

Now she sat and sat, waiting for her turn. Finally, after a heated discussion over the school boiler, Rachel heard her name being called. Henry, who had been careful to keep his hands in his lap until now, nudged her hand quickly with his. "You'll do fine," he whispered. "Just read the thing and sit down." He seemed almost as jumpy as she was. She clutched the folded letter and approached the microphone, which was angled at the side of the room in full view of everyone there, including the man behind the TV camera. Sister Gloria walked to the other side of the table and handed Dr. Boyd the pictures. Rachel opened the letter and began to read. Her hands were trembling.

"Dr. Boyd and Coventry Township Area School Board, thank you for the opportunity to speak before you this evening."

"Speak up, please," instructed a bald man to Dr. Boyd's left. His face was beat red. Rachel cleared her throat and tried to project her voice.

"A few months ago we participated in an activity arranged by Sister Gloria Beverly, coordinator of *The Tolerance Project*." Rachel told herself to pause and look up, but the adrenaline pumping through her body wouldn't permit it. "We visited each other's schools to compare the quality of education being offered at each one. The visits took place here at our own Coventry Township High, and at Jefferson High School, in the city district. What we discovered shocked and appalled us." Rachel needed to swallow—would she remember how? She wished for a glass of water. "As you can see from the enclosed pictures, the conditions at Jefferson are far below those here at Coventry. The plumbing doesn't work, the ceilings leak, and in some cases, the furniture is broken. Even the heat doesn't work properly. The computers are outdated or not working. There are no athletic fields, no media center, and no exercise equipment, and the gym is barely usable. Teachers are paid an average of ten thousand dollars a year less. Standardized text scores at Jefferson are far below those at Coventry." Rachel had found the last two bits of information on the Internet. "Coventry High, on the other hand, has the latest and most updated equipment, from its fields to its computer technology. In comparison, we are rich. We believe this is not fair, and something should be done about it. Students at schools like Jefferson feel abandoned by our society. Don't they deserve an equal opportunity? We respectfully ask that the school board consider this issue carefully." Rachel read the names at the bottom of the letter—her own and those of her friends. "Thank you," she said, finally looking up. She'd done it—now she could go sit down.

A murmur went through the board members, as some of them covered their microphones and whispered to each other. "Just a minute, Miss Matrone," said a large woman on the end closest to Rachel. "We'd like to ask you a few questions." Rachel froze. No one had mentioned anything about questions. She glanced at Sister Gloria, who nodded in encouragement.

"Aren't you the girl who vandalized the high school a few months back?" asked the bald man. Rachel's heart, which had been beating so wildly, now seemed to stop dead in her chest. She tried to formulate an answer, but thankfully, Dr. Shank interceded.

"That incident is in the past, and it's not relevant to our discussion tonight. Let's remember that Rachel is our invited guest." She smiled reassuringly at Rachel.

"Who, exactly, invited her?" Rachel heard the man whisper.

"Thank you, Dr. Shank, and thank you Rachel, for being here tonight," said Dr. Boyd. "We appreciate your concern. I'm not sure, however, what you expect us to do about it. What do you suggest?"

Rachel stared at him blankly. She was dimly aware of the TV camera—if I cry now the whole town will see it, she realized. People will record it and play it over and over again. It will probably be up on YouTube before I even sit down. She looked over at Henry, who was tensed at the edge of his seat; he looked ready to jump up and carry her out of the room at any second. She tried to compose herself.

"To tell the truth, I don't really have any suggestions. It just seems like there should be something we can do. Maybe we could give their school more money."

"Rachel," Dr. Boyd said kindly, "we don't control how much money each school district receives. That's a matter for the state to decide. We only decide how to spend the money we receive."

"Oh—yes, I guess I knew that. Well, maybe some of those kids could come to our school." Several of the school board members laughed.

"You're describing something called *busing*," Dr. Boyd explained. "And that was tried many years ago. No one was happy with the result—people want their children to attend school in their own community."

"Oh," Rachel said again.

"If it pleases the board, I have a proposal," said Dr. Shank.

"I thought you might," Dr. Boyd replied. "Thank you, Rachel, you may sit down now. Dr. Shank, we have five minutes before we must move on to the next issue. Go ahead."

"Good job," Dr. Shank whispered as she passed Rachel on her way to the microphone. Rachel sank into her seat, filled with relief. Sister Gloria patted her hand and smiled her approval. Henry leaned toward her so that his arm just barely touched her shoulder.

Dr. Shank put on her glasses and read, "I propose we form a committee to study the issue of educational inequity within our surrounding area. The committee would be charged with several tasks: first, a continuation of the multicultural education program which was piloted at the high school last fall; second, the creation of an exchange program between the suburban and city districts; and third, formulation of a plan to begin work at the state level to raise awareness and push for change. With the help of *The Tolerance Project* and other organizations like it, the committee would work to secure a grant toward these ends." Rachel noticed a look pass between Sister Gloria and Dr. Shank. They'd planned this, she realized with amazement—Sister Gloria, you sneaky devil! "There would be no added financial expenditure to the district." Dr. Shank emphasized the last sentence. "It would be my privilege to set this process in motion, beginning next fall. Do I have the permission of the school board?"

"Are there any questions?" asked Dr. Boyd. The board members looked too stunned to speak. A few smiled, but others frowned and glanced over at the camera—maybe they're worried about being on TV, too, Rachel thought. "Well, then, I suggest we vote." Dr. Shank's proposal was approved by a vote of four to three.

"Thank you," said Dr. Shank. Again her eyes met Sister Gloria's as she returned to her seat.

"We can sneak out now," Sister Gloria whispered. They followed her into the lobby, where she carefully closed the auditorium door behind them.

"Rachel, that was wonderful," she said, smiling broadly. "You should all be very proud."

"Huh?" said Darrin. "What just happened?"

"Yeah—I didn't really get it, either, and I was awake," Sandra said.

"The school board just approved a program that Dr. Shank and I have been talking about for a long time. It means schools like Rachel's will be able to partner with the city schools to improve conditions. It means better educational opportunity for kids from the city, and greater awareness for kids in the suburbs. It means people like you will become friends more often."

"They said all that?" Damara asked.

"In a manner of speaking, yes. They approved the formation of the committee; now we need to get to work."

"Are they going to fix the gym?" Darrin asked.

"I can't make any promises, but that's the kind of thing we hope this committee will address. I think this calls for a celebration! Rachel, is there a place nearby where we can get some ice cream?"

Damara looked at her watch. "Um, actually, Sister Gloria, we need to get going. My mom wants us home by nine—somebody still has homework." Darrin gave her a dirty look. "Sorry," Damara said.

"No problem, we'll postpone the celebration for another time. I'll be glad to take you home."

"Could you give me a lift, too?" asked Sandra. She looked meaningfully at Rachel.

"Of course," Sister Gloria said. "Henry, I assume you'll see Rachel arrives home safely." That's a strange way to put it, Rachel thought. Henry only nodded.

"You owe me one ... again," Sandra whispered as she brushed by Rachel. Rachel rolled her eyes, but smiled.

It was a warm night, and ice cream sounded good. Henry drove to the ice cream stand at the town center and they ordered two double chocolate cones.

"So I guess that's that," Rachel said. They leaned against Henry's car, diligently licking their cones. "It seems sort of anticlimactic, doesn't it?"

"I don't know—what did you expect?" Henry asked.

"I guess I expected more drama. But it's good—Sister Gloria was happy, anyway. Maybe we did help, a little. At least I didn't make a total idiot out of myself."

"You did great." Henry went to take Rachel's hand, but then remembered where they were and stopped. "I like it better when we hang out in my neighborhood," he said.

"Me, too. Much better."

Rachel's cell phone buzzed again and again, until finally she turned it off. "I'm not in the mood," she said.

Cars sped through the busy intersection, trying to make the light before it turned red. A few times someone yelled out Rachel's name.

"It looks like you're a celebrity," Henry commented.

"It must be a slow news day. Let's get out of here, Henry. This place makes me nervous."

"Okay—just let me finish this." He shoved what was left of his cone into his mouth in two large bites. "I'll get some napkins," he said. Just as he turned and walked back to the ice cream stand, a green Mustang flew into the parking lot toward Rachel. It pulled up alongside her, and the back window opened. She peered in to see who it was.

"Hey Rachel," a boy's voice yelled, "why don't you tell your friend to go home?" Something flew out of the window toward Rachel—it was a mega plastic cup filled with soda. Before Rachel understood fully what was happening, the soda hit her in the chest, splashing cola down her shirt and onto her jeans. The occupants of the car laughed wildly and took off.

"Oh my God," she gasped, dropping the remains of her cone.

Henry ran to her. "Rachel, are you okay? What happened?"

"Someone in that car threw a soda at me!" Rachel was covered in the sticky substance. She held her arms out at her side, shaking out her sleeves. "I can't believe he did that!"

"That car, right there, at the light?" Henry asked. Sure enough, the car had raced out of the parking lot only to get stuck at the light. Henry was fuming. He handed Rachel the napkins and headed into the street. "Stay here," he ordered.

"Henry, don't," Rachel called. "Just get the license plate. I'll call my uncle."

"I'll handle this," said Henry. "We don't need your uncle." He ran into the street more quickly than Rachel had ever seen him move.

"Hey, he's coming," Rachel heard someone yell from inside the Mustang. When Henry was a few feet away from the car, the light changed and the car jolted ahead. He made a last ditch effort to hang on to the door handle, but the motion threw him off balance and he fell backwards, dangerously close to the path of an SUV that was making a right turn toward him.

"Henry, watch out!" Rachel screamed, but it was too late. She saw Henry go down—was he hit, or had he just fallen? The SUV screeched to a halt, and the driver, a woman in a nurse's uniform, jumped out.

"Someone call 911!" she shouted. "He's been hit!"

Chapter 25

Not Over Yet

Although she was sitting still, Rachel felt herself spinning, reliving the flashing lights, sirens, and the barrage of questions of the last few hours. She heard the echo of her own unfamiliar voice replaying involuntarily in her head in progressive stages—at first shrill and panicked, then small and quivering, and finally, hoarse and exhausted. She had told her story over and over again to what seemed like an unending parade of people carrying clipboards until she'd had no idea who she was talking to any more. She'd called home, but no one answered. Where could they be? Nana and Grampy hardly ever went out at night. And where were the uncles? Why hadn't they gotten the message that she needed them? Why wouldn't anyone tell her what was going on? When would she be able to see Henry?

The young resident at the hospital asked her for the second time, "Are you sure you're okay? Does anything hurt?" How could she answer that question? Nothing hurt on the outside, but how could she describe the pain she felt? It wasn't a sharp pain, or a burn, either, or a break. It was more like a throb—a huge, dull, pounding bruise that pulsated at her center. Is that what this doctor wanted to know?

"I'm fine," she'd said. "I told you, I was up on the sidewalk when it happened."

"What's that on your shirt?"

Did she think Rachel was bleeding? "It's just soda, see? When can I see Henry?"

"Who's Henry?"

"Henry, the boy that got hit by the car." The boy who would be comforting me right now, if he could. The boy that was trying to protect me. The boy that I love. "How is he? When can I see him?"

"I'm not sure. Do you want to call someone?"

"I did. No one answered. I'll just wait here for now. Can you find out about Henry for me?"

"I'll try my best," the resident said. She wrote something on her clipboard and walked away. After that, Rachel sat for a long time, waiting, watching people pass her by, some rushing with an air of determination, others strolling languidly, probably like her, with nothing to do but wait. When would someone tell her about Henry? She walked down the hall to the public phone—there was no service on her cell—and tried to call home again. Still no answer. Maybe they were sleeping by now. Why hadn't they heard the phone?

Finally, Henry's family arrived, minus his dad. He must be on an overnight trip, Rachel realized. They only nodded and walked past her, ushered in quickly by an emergency room nurse. "Sorry, family only," the nurse said. She wasn't family. What was she, then? Again, she waited, alone.

A while later she thought she heard a familiar voice headed toward her. It was Uncle Tommy, at last. He was walking with someone she didn't know—a man not dressed like a doctor, but with an ID badge clipped to his pocket indicating he worked for the hospital. Rachel jumped up and ran to Uncle Tommy, throwing herself into his arms.

"Rachel, there you are! Thank God!" Uncle Tommy said. "Here she is. Thanks" he said to the man, who nodded and hurried away. "Where's Uncle Johnny? What happened to your shirt?" He held her a little away to have a better look.

"It's soda—didn't they tell you what happened? What took you so long to get here?" Finally, the faucet that Rachel had been squeezing shut burst open, and her body began to shake in great, noisy sobs.

Uncle Tommy held her tightly. "What do you mean, Rach? I've been here all night. We've been looking all over for you. Thank God Uncle Johnny found you. Where is he?"

"What? I've been here all night, too, waiting for you. I haven't seen Uncle Johnny. Don't you know about Henry?"

"Henry? Rach, what are you talking about? Calm down, and tell me what happened." He led her to a seating area and sat her down, his arm around her shoulders.

Rachel did her best to describe what had happened, choking out the words. "So you're saying Henry is here, at this hospital?" Rachel nodded.

"Yes. Why else would you be here?" Uncle Tommy hugged her again, but didn't answer. She sat up and looked at him closely for the first time. His hair was disheveled, his eyes were red, and his expression was grim. Something else was very wrong. "Uncle Tommy, what happened?" she asked. Her tears stopped immediately; she gathered all her strength to brace herself for his answer.

"It's Grampy," Uncle Tommy said quietly. "He had a heart attack, Rachel. He's gone." And then Uncle Tommy started to cry. He covered his eyes with his hand and made little choking noises in his throat. Rachel checked to see if she might be dreaming, but no, she was definitely awake. Everything inside her, every tear, every feeling, every thought, dried up and stopped—she held on to Uncle Tommy and waited. She had never seen him cry before. "Come on, we need to find Nana," he said finally, struggling to collect his emotions. They walked through the corridor hand in hand, Rachel dully aware that every step took her further away from Henry. Uncle Tommy led her to a small room where Nana sat with a young woman. The woman was talking quietly, and Nana was signing papers. When she saw Rachel she stood so quickly that she almost lost her balance; the woman reached out and grabbed her by the arm.

"Rachel, thank God," Nana said, holding out her arms. Rachel rushed to her, but as they held each other, she felt surprisingly calm. Nana, too, was quiet. Uncle Tommy coughed and covered his eyes again.

"Just a little bit longer, Mrs. Matrone, and then we can let you get home. Does anyone want anything?"

Although she felt too guilty to admit it, Rachel still wanted to find out about Henry. "Can I get a drink? I'll just walk down to the soda machine."

"Sure honey, go ahead," Nana said. "Are you hungry? Tommy, give her some money."

"I have money. I'll be right back." She kissed Nana and walked into the hallway, looking for someone who might know about Henry. Grampy's dead, Rachel told herself every few seconds. Why can't I feel anything?

Coming toward her were a man and a woman; the man had a duffle bag slung across his shoulder and carried a video camera down at his hip. They looked official, but not like they worked at the hospital. Rachel moved aside to let them pass. To her surprise, the woman approached her.

"Are you Rachel Matrone?" she asked.

"Yes?"

"I'm Miriam Solace, from *Channel Eight News*. We've heard you were involved in a racial incident at the town center this evening. Was the boy that was hurt a friend of yours?"

Is that what it was, a racial incident? "What? Yes, but I don't think I should say anything else..."

"This is going to be on the morning news, Miss Matrone. Don't you want to tell your side of the story?"

Before Rachel could answer, Uncle Johnny burst through the double doors to her left. If Uncle Tommy had looked disheveled, Uncle Johnny looked like he had just been spewed out of a volcano. He grabbed Rachel by the shoulders, crying, "He's dead, Rach, he's dead!" and hugged her. "Where's Nana?" he asked, turning her away from the reporters without even noticing they were there.

Miriam Solace turned to her cameraman, eyes wide. "This is going to be a bigger story than we thought," she said.

Chapter 26

Ending

Uncle Tommy had helped Rachel get a little information before she left the hospital that night. Henry was in stable condition, and had been admitted to a room.

"He's gonna be okay, Rachel," Uncle Tommy had said. "Stable is good, it means he's fine. Now we need to get Nana home." Rachel knew that Uncle Tommy was right. Although she hadn't been allowed to see Henry, the nurse said she could come back during visiting hours tomorrow. So she held on to Nana and helped her to the car. She tried to feel sad for Grampy, and she tried to feel relieved about Henry, but the truth was she still couldn't feel anything.

"Why can't I cry?" she whispered to Uncle Johnny on the way home.

"You're just in shock, honey," Uncle Johnny answered. "It's normal. Don't worry, it will come."

Before she went to bed she walked downstairs in the dark to the living room and sat in Grampy's chair, resting her head on the arm and breathing in deeply. This is what he smelled like, she thought. I don't want to forget this smell.

Uncle Tommy insisted she turn her cell phone off before she went to sleep, and he turned off the ringer on the home phone, too. Rachel slept fitfully, aware in her dreams that something bad had happened, but not remembering what it was until she woke up early the next morning. Uncle Tommy and Nana were in the kitchen, drinking coffee, discussing the funeral arrangements. The local morning news was playing in the background on the little kitchen TV. Not wanting to disturb them, Rachel took a bowl from the cabinet and reached for the cereal as quietly as she could. That's when she heard Miriam Solace say her name.

"Rachel Matrone, who had appeared before the school board this evening to discuss the issue of racial inequity, was involved in a racial incident which reportedly took the life of a young African-American male in the central suburbs last night. The male's name has not yet been released. We hope to bring you more of this story as new information becomes available." The report must have been taped during the night—it was still dark, and Ms. Solace stood outside of the emergency room entrance. Rachel's bowl fell to the floor and smashed into a million tiny shards, and for a few horrible minutes she waited in limbo while Uncle Tommy called the hospital.

"I'm calling to ask the status of one of your patients ... Henry Sayers. Yes. Yes. Are you sure? Okay—thank you." Uncle Tommy hung up and turned to Rachel. "He's fine,

Rach—his condition has been upgraded to good. I don't know what happened, but that report wasn't true."

Rachel, pale and shaking, closed her eyes and held on to the counter, letting the cold of the granite seep into her hands. "Oh my God," she whispered over and over again.

"Tommy, get her some water and take her in the living room before she faints—that's all we need right now," Nana said. "And be careful where you step. Let me sweep up this mess."

Uncle Tommy obeyed, sitting Rachel on the sofa next to him. "Take it easy, babe," he said. "It's gonna be okay." He propped a pillow behind her and sat up straight, muscles tensed to catch her if she fell over.

Rachel sipped the water. Who else might have heard the broadcast? she wondered. Henry's family was probably at the hospital with him, and Sandra, Damara and Darrin were in school by now. How strange, she thought, it's a school day. "Thanks, Uncle Tommy," she said. "I'll be all right. That stupid reporter—I just got so scared."

"I'll call the station and set them straight. I bet that will be her last broadcast," Uncle Tommy said. "Well, you got what you wanted, in a way. She put attention on your issue, even if her information was wrong."

"I didn't think of that."

"I'm sure the phone will be ringing off the hook in a while. But you don't have to talk to anybody if you don't want to."

"Okay. Uncle Tommy, I know it seems horrible to ask, but can I go to the hospital to see Henry today? Just for a few minutes?"

283

She'd expected him to be angry, but Uncle Tommy only looked worried. He stared into Rachel's face, trying to gauge her mental state.

"I'm fine, Uncle Tommy, really," she said.

"Okay. It might be a good distraction. Uncle Johnny will take you this afternoon."

"Thanks." They sat, listening to the sound of Nana's broom scrape the kitchen tiles.

"Rach," Uncle Tommy said, "I'm going to ask you something, and I want you to know you can trust me. I need you to tell me the truth, okay?"

Rachel took a longer sip and nodded. She knew what was coming.

"You and Henry, Rach—there's more going on there than just friends, right?"

Rachel nodded again.

"Do you want to tell me about it?" he asked.

What was there to tell? That her relationship with Henry was the most important thing in her life? That she would do anything to be with him? That as much as she loved her family, it didn't matter what they thought anymore? The phone rang in the kitchen. She heard Nana answer, and heard her voice break as she spoke to Antonella's mom.

"I didn't lie to you," Rachel said. "When I told you we were just friends, that was true. But then things changed. I didn't plan it, Uncle Tommy, it just happened. I hope you understand." Rachel heard her own resolve, and she knew Uncle Tommy heard it, too.

"How serious is this, Rachel?"

"I don't know—we're still in high school. But it's serious enough, at least as far as I'm concerned. And I think Henry feels the same."

"Rach, as nice a kid as Henry seems to be, you know you're setting yourself up for problems, right? Like last night, at the ice cream stand. Are you ready for more of the same?"

"It was a prank—they were just stupid kids. Most people aren't like that."

Uncle Tommy tilted his head toward the kitchen and listened to be sure that Nana was still on the phone. "Okay, Rach," he sighed, "this is not the time to discuss it. We won't say anything to Nana, yet. She's got enough on her mind right now."

"Okay." Rachel put her glass down on the coffee table and walked over to Grampy's recliner. She stroked the worn, brown upholstery. "I don't understand, Uncle Tommy. How can he not be here? I was just talking to him yesterday—he was right here, in this chair. How can he be gone?" She sat down, touching the items on the end table next to her. "See? These are his glasses, and here's the paper he was reading, just yesterday. I have to keep reminding myself—keep telling myself that I'll never see him again. It can't be real."

"I know, Rach, I feel the same way. It can't be real, but it is. It's gonna take a while to sink in, for all of us."

"Uncle Tommy, he didn't know about me and Henry, right? I mean, he didn't suspect anything, did he?"

Uncle Tommy leaned toward her. "Rachel, don't you for a minute think this was your fault. No, he didn't suspect. His heart was bad, and you know how he was about doctors. This had nothing to do with you, Rach. Okay?"

Rachel sighed. "Okay. But I'm worried about Nana."

"Nana will be fine. She has us. And we have each other, right?"

Rachel felt too numb to do anything but nod again. There were still no tears. She wondered if she'd used them all up for Henry; surely Grampy deserved some, too.

She heard Nana hang up and move around the kitchen. "Rachel, come in here," she called. "Have something to eat."

"I'm not hungry," Rachel told Uncle Tommy.

"Eat anyway," he answered. "She needs to take care of you right now."

"Okay." She went into the kitchen, took a new bowl of cereal from Nana, and returned to Grampy's chair, where she sat for the rest of the morning.

One month later…

Dear Dad,

   I'm sorry I haven't written for so long—I guess I've been kind of busy. But the most wonderful thing happened tonight. Henry came over for dinner. That's it. I know it doesn't sound like much, but you see, he came over as my boyfriend. Everyone knew he was my boyfriend! No more hiding. It was the most glorious night of my newly grown-up life.

Love,
Rachel

P.S. Say hi to Grampy for me.

Epilogue: Beginning

"Are you okay?" Henry asked. He shifted the cardboard box he was carrying to the side, resting it on his hip.

"Yes, Henry, I'm okay. I'm just thinking."

"Can you think in the car? We really need to get going."

Rachel sat on her bed holding the white bear, which was still dressed in its soccer uniform. "I know," she said, "I'm coming." She stroked the bear, but didn't move to get up. Henry placed the box on the empty desk and sat down beside Rachel.

"What is it?" he asked. "Are you sure you still want to do this?"

She laid the bear next to her and slid closer to Henry. "Of course, I'm sure," she said, putting her arms around his middle.

"Rachel, I'm all sweaty," he warned.

"I don't care. You always smell good to me." She tucked her head under his chin.

"So why the long face?"

"I'm sorry—did I look sad? I'm not, really. I was just thinking about life."

"Is that all? I thought it was something serious."

Rachel laughed. "No, I was just thinking about my plans with Antonella—we always said we were going to be college roommates. If you would have told me back then that I'd be going off to college in Atlanta with my boyfriend, who, by the way, happens to be black, I would have said you were crazy."

"And if you would have told me that I'd fall in love with a white girl with two cops for uncles, I would have said you were crazy, too." He ran his hand gently down her ponytail, which now fell to the middle of her back. "Are you sure that's all it is?"

"Well, I guess I am a little sad—about leaving Nana, you know."

"I do know. She'll miss you, that's for sure. But she still has Uncle Johnny, and Uncle Tommy and Joan will be right next door. I'm sure she'll keep herself busy supervising Joan's cooking."

"Poor Joan," Rachel laughed again. "She really is such a nice person."

"She's gonna have to be, living next door to her mother-in-law. And before you know it, the baby will be here, and Nana will start all over again. She'll be in grandma heaven."

"You're right." Rachel sighed. She still made no move to get up.

"Baby, listen, right now we're just going to college. I know we made plans for the future, but plans can always change. We're not married yet. We're not even officially engaged."

"But we will be at Christmas, right?"

"If you still want to be."

Rachel sat up and gave Henry the meanest look she could fake. "Are you insane? Of course I still want to be. We agreed, Henry—you're going to Morehouse, I'm going to Georgia State—two years as single students, two years married. Don't you dare change your mind on me."

Henry pulled her back close to him. "I would never change my mind. I just don't want you to feel trapped."

"For the last time, Henry, this is what I want. Don't ever bring it up again. Okay?"

"Okay." He looked up to be sure no one was standing in the doorway, then held on to her ponytail and kissed her. It still made Rachel's lips tingle.

"You taste salty today," she said.

"Wonderful. Can we go now? Your uncles are waiting to argue over where to put the last box." Henry stood and picked up the carton. "Are you taking that with you?" He nodded toward the bear. "There's a little more room in here, if you want."

"What? This? No. I was just putting it away." She picked up the bear, tossed it into the closet, and shut the closet door. "Okay," she said, turning off the light, "I'm ready. Let's go."

Discussion

1. In the opening scene of the novel, Rachel saves an ant that is trapped in a spider's web. Why do you think she feels sorry for the ant? How is Rachel's action related to one of the themes of the novel?

2. Many of the characters in the novel are keeping secrets. What secrets does Rachel's family keep from her? What secrets does Rachel keep from her family? What secrets does Henry keep from his family? Why do you think close family members keep things secret from one another?

3. Which character in the novel do you most closely identify with, and why? Would you change that character's actions if you could, and if so, how? Why?

4. Why do you think Rachel remained close friends with Antonella for so many years? How did Rachel's new friendships with Henry and the others differ

from her friendship with Antonella? How would you describe your friendships? What things would you change about them if you could?

5. Why was Grampy against Rachel's involvement in the multicultural education program at her school? Why was Nana against the idea of Sandra's family buying the house next door? Do you think their feelings were fair?

6. At the end of chapter 2, Rachel writes for a school assignment that she lives in a "regular" neighborhood. What does she mean by that, and what does it show about Rachel's assumptions concerning race?

7. In chapter 10, during Sister Gloria's birthday party, Henry suggests to Rachel that her family is racist. Why does Henry think that? What feelings does Henry have about it? Do you think Henry's suggestion is fair? How does Henry's suggestion make Rachel feel?

8. After their conversation at Sister Gloria's party, Rachel continues to keep her friendship with Henry a secret from her family. Why? What would you have done if you were Rachel?

9. The theme of safety and danger is important throughout *The R Word*. Why does Rachel think that Raphael is a dangerous boy to like? In chapter 18, Henry worries that he might be dangerous to

Rachel. What does he mean? Still later, in chapter 20, Rachel worries that she and her family might be dangerous to Henry. Why does she think this? Have you ever had a friendship or relationship that was emotionally dangerous?

10. When Rachel, Henry, and the others visit each other's schools they are surprised by what they discover. How do the school visits make them feel? How does each character deal with his or her feelings?

11. Through her new friendships, Rachel begins to view racial issues differently. What does she learn, and how do her ideas change? Why do you think Rachel had never thought much about race before?

12. Have your ideas about race changed through your reading of *The R Word*? Why or why not?

13. In addition to her ideas about race, how does Rachel grow as a person throughout *The R Word*? How does Rachel's conversation with Uncle Tommy at the end of the novel prove her growth? In what way(s) would you like to grow as a person?

Afterword
The Story on the Story

Perhaps I'm a lot like Rachel, who felt it was less painful to point out her own physical flaws before anyone else had the chance. With that in mind, I'm forced to admit that *The R Word* is a novel that some people won't like, for a variety of reasons. Here are some of those reasons, and my explanations for why I offer the novel in its present form anyway.

Some people will think that the racism Rachel discovers throughout the story is seriously out of date. They hold the belief that we are a "post racial" society, in other words, that racism isn't a problem any more, or is far less of a problem than *The R Word* depicts. They will note the election of President Obama in 2008 as evidence that the situations Rachel faces and the way her family behaves are unrealistic. In a way, I understand their point. It is true that overt racism is so politically incorrect that the use of ugly racial slurs is no longer tolerated in most environments, which is why even the most intolerant characters in my story (like Grampy, for example) do not act in overtly racist ways. Unfortunately, political correctness has done little to change the continuing structural inequities and underlying, often hidden, intolerant attitudes that I tried to explore through Rachel's eyes in *The R Word*.

Take, for example, the differences between the suburban and city schools that Rachel and her friends discover. Surely, some might think, the problem of educational inequity was solved with the famous Supreme Court decision, *Brown v. Board of Education*, way back in the 1950s, and with the desegregation policies that followed. All this happened decades ago, everybody knows that. What everybody might not know, however, is that during the 1980s the courts lifted sanctions against racial segregation in the schools, and since many neighborhoods were still segregated, many schools went back to being segregated, too. Although Rachel and Henry's schools are fictional, they represent a combination of real schools that do exist in urban/suburban school districts around our country. A quick browse via the Internet will reveal suburban schools that are up to 96% white, and city schools with the same percentage of students of color less than an hour apart. Some suburban school districts spend thousands of dollars more *per student* than nearby urban districts spend. Perhaps most importantly, standardized test scores and graduation rates in urban schools are often far below those of suburban schools. These facts were recently highlighted in Davis Guggenheim's documentary, *Waiting for "Superman."* While Guggenheim critiques suburban schools too, his depiction of failing urban schools, and of hopeful young students whose only chance at a decent education depends on winning a lottery is especially heartbreaking. People who study urban education know that our nation still struggles to provide equal educational opportunity for all its students.

Another outdated concept, some might think, is Nana's reluctance to see "the neighborhood change." Come on, some might say, in this day and age people of all racial backgrounds are free to live wherever they choose, aren't they? Yet the fact is that many neighborhoods around the country remain largely segregated, and research shows that property values are still lower, and the value of homes increases at a slower rate in neighborhoods that are racially and ethnically mixed than in mostly white neighborhoods. So, although unfair and intolerant, Nana's concerns are based on reality.

People might also think that Rachel is not a believable character; she's simply too naïve. How can it be possible that a modern teenager has never thought deeply about racism? Students study the Civil Rights Movement in school (as Rachel did). Even very young children learn about Dr. Martin Luther King's "I Have a Dream" speech, don't they? Again, this is true. However, it's also true that most students learn only the skeleton version of the Civil Rights Movement, and are not taught how unjust policies of the past, policies created and sanctioned by our own government, continue to have an effect on people today. Sadly, this adds to the notion that racism is no longer a problem. For more information on this topic, check out the excellent PBS video, *Race: The Power of an Illusion.* I especially recommend chapter three, "The House We Live In."

What about the scenes in the novel where Henry, Damara, and Darrin are followed around a department store, or where Henry is stopped by a white police officer after his car skids in the snow? This is called racial profiling, and according to Amnesty International, it still exists today. African Americans are not the only victims of racial profiling; people from many other racial, ethnic, and religious groups experience it, too.

A famous author named James Baldwin once said, "Not everything that is faced can be changed; but nothing can be changed until it is faced." I know that our country has made great progress along the bumpy road to racial equity since the days of the Civil Rights Movement. That progress would not have been possible if people hadn't been willing to face the ugly reality of racism head-on. But, as I've tried to show, we're not there yet. As Rachel discovered, the effects of past racist attitudes and policies live on in a variety of ways. Because many of us think we're not supposed to talk about race any more, racism is much harder to see now than it used to be, and things that are hard to see are even harder to change.

REFERENCES:

Adelman, Larry, executive producer. *Race: The Power of an Illusion.* VHS and DVD. San Francisco: California Newsreel, 2003.

Anacker, Katrin B. "Still Paying the Race Tax? Analyzing Property Values in Homogeneous and Mixed-Race Suburbs." *Journal of Urban Affairs*, Volume 32, Number 1 (February 2010): 55–77.

Baldwin, James. "As Much Truth As One Can Bear." *The New York Times Book Review*, (January 14, 1962).

Gollnick, Donna M., and Philip C. Chinn. *Multicultural Education in a Pluralistic Society.* 8th ed. Upper Saddle River, NJ: Prentice Hall, 2006.

Guggenheim, Davis, and Billy Kimball. *Waiting for "Superman",* directed by Davis Guggenheim. Hollywood: Paramount Pictures, 2010.

To check out school district statistics—http://www.publicschool-review.com.

On racial profiling—http://www.amnestyusa.org/racial_profiling/sevenfacts.html.

CPSIA information can be obtained at www.ICGtesting.com
Printed in the USA
BVOW11s0235200814

363461BV00004B/11/P